WESTERN VENGEANCE!

It was Allan, running like a deer, and shouting like a madman, for the spirit of the fight was in him. Yonder were enemies no more to be protected or respected...

Behind him came Lefty and Tom Morris, gasping and blowing, their teeth set for the work which now lay at their hands. As for Allan, he leaped high above the circling rocks. That leap saved him. The bullet which had been aimed for his heart whirred past his leg, and he descended on him who had fired the shot. One blow of the rifle butt; and when he looked up, Morris had finished the second man.

Here, at last, was some revenge...

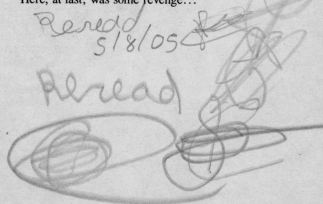

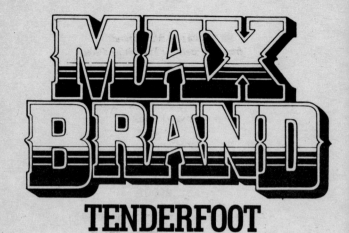

MAX BRAND

TENDERFOOT

(FORMERLY TITLED OUTLAW'S GOLD)

B

BERKLEY BOOKS, NEW YORK

This Berkley book contains the complete
text of the original hardcover edition.

TENDERFOOT

A Berkley Book / published by arrangement with
Dodd, Mead and Company, Inc.

PRINTING HISTORY
Warner edition / October 1976
Berkley edition / February 1988

ISBN: 0-425-10636-5

Berkley Books are published by The Berkley Publishing Group,
200 Madison Avenue, New York, N.Y. 10016.
The name "Berkley" and the "B" logo
are trademarks belonging to Berkley Publishing Corporation.

PRINTED IN THE UNITED STATES OF AMERICA

10   9   8   7   6   5   4   3   2   1

The characters, places, incidents and situations in this book are imaginary and have no relation to any person, place or actual happening.

CONTENTS

TENDERFOOT

CHAPTER 1

A WEAKLING?

He was a sleek young man, not flabby, but with that same smooth-surfaced effect which a seal gives as it swishes around in a pool. He had a round neck which filled out a sixteen-inch collar with perfect plumpness, a round chest, and a pair of long arms. He had pale, mild blue eyes, and a little smile of diffidence played about the corners of his mouth. Yet that gentle smile brought to him only troubles, for sometimes when men saw it they thought that Vincent Allan was deriding them with quietly controlled contempt. The president was one who made that mistake.

He was not the president of the little uptown branch bank where Vincent Allan for five years had inscribed swift, delicately made figures in big ledgers or worked an adding machine with patient deftness. That branch bank was only a tiny little link in the chain of financial institutions of which the great man was the chief, but nothing in his organization was too small for the personal attention of the president. His favorite maxim—and he was a man of many maxims—was: There is plenty of time for everything that one really wishes to do! He not only applied his maxims to himself, but to every one else, and because he could get along with four hours of sleep per day, he felt that all other men should be able to do the same. He even begrudged the four hours of unconsciousness. He considered sleep a habit, and a most pernicious one.

On this day he had time to attend a luncheon at which the people of his little branch bank were present. After lunch, he made them a speech. He had several speeches which he could use. He had one on honesty, and where it leads! He had another on he who saves. He had another on faithfulness, the golden virtue. He could talk also on the topic: Conscience, the master of us all! But to-day he chose quite a different topic. Usually he was moral, but he liked to surprise people, and on this occasion he chose to speak of the body.

"We are given by God two great things," said he. "We have a mind which we cannot help using if we wish to survive. We are given a body also, almost equally divine. But how many of you young ladies and young gentlemen use your bodies as they should be used?"

He stabbed a rapid forefinger at them all, one by one, driving home the bitter point of his remark so that the weak knees of those city dwellers quaked; and the president himself quivered with his intensity—every bit of his hundred and twelve pounds trembled.

"Find a gymnasium," he said. "In this machine-driven age, there are few practical uses for bodily strength. But find a gymnasium. Be brave to admit your weaknesses. Out of such admissions comes strength. It is the strength of the weak—humility! Humility of body, humility of mind, and a devout resolution to make the best of what we have by the careful culture of it——"

He broke off suddenly, flaring red.

"You, young man, may smile. But the scoffers be damned, and the reverent spirits go on to great victories!"

This blast was delivered against poor young Vincent Allan. It wiped the fluttering smile completely off his lips.

Seeing that one among them was being martyred, the other clerks grinned behind their hands. Only the manager of the branch bank grew a little hot of face. He knew the true worth, the shrinking modesty of young Vincent

Allan; however, he did not quite dare to speak up to the great man before all these people. He might draw a counter blast upon his own head and be shamed before those whom he employed.

"Stand up!" went on the president. "Stand up that we may see what manner of man dares to mock me when I speak of the culture of the body!"

Vincent Allan rose. His face was flame. Any other would have looked miserably down at the table, but Vincent Allan had this peculiarity—that when he was most shamed and most afraid, he always looked straight into the eyes of that which shamed or that which frightened him.

"How old are you?" asked the president.

"Twenty-three, sir," murmured Vincent Allan.

It was the meekest, softest voice that ever issued from the throat of a man. The president knew instantly that he had made a mistake and that instead of a hardy cynic there stood before him only a lamb. However, he could not break off so suddenly from the purpose on which he had started. He had prepared the fire, and now he must complete the sacrifice.

"Twenty-three," sneered the president, frowning at that answer as though it were an admission of the greatest guilt. "Twenty-three years old. And how tall are you, young man?"

"Five feet nine inches, sir."

"Five feet nine inches? And what do you weigh?"

"A hundred and seventy-five pounds, sir."

"Fat!" thundered the president. "You are fat. You have twenty-five pounds of fat on you, at least. Perhaps you have forty pounds of fat upon you. Do you know what fat is? It is a sin. It is to the body what idle hours are to the day, what sin is to the soul! You must strip that fat off. You must show your true self. Be yourself. Don't sit back and scoff. That earnest young man sitting beside you who seems to listen to my words, may very well outstrip you in the race. He may very well do it!"

The earnest young man grew crimson with joy. It was the greatest moment of his young life. It was the greatest moment that he was ever to have in all the long vista of future years.

"Leave idleness and mockery to fools!" thundered the president. "Go to the gymnasium. Learn to know your bodies as you know your brains! You, young man—how many games can you play?"

"None, sir," murmured the miserable Vincent Allan.

"None! What? Have you never played catch?"

"No, sir."

"Were you an invalid in your boyhood?" asked the president, relenting a little.

"I—I was working my way through school," said Vincent Allen faintly. "I—I didn't have much time, sir, to play."

"No time to play! No time! Young man, young man, there is time enough for everything that men really want to do. What were you doing at recesses? Why couldn't you play then?"

"I stayed in the schoolroom, sir."

"In the schoolroom. The teacher was pretty, I suppose?"

At this feeble jest there was a great uproar of laughter.

"No, sir," said Vincent Allan, blinking. "But my lessons were always very hard for me. I was slow, sir."

The president bit his lip. Here was a young man whom he would much rather have held up as an example than as a failure. But he had gone so far that to retreat would be difficult and awkward.

"For the sake of shame, my young friend," he concluded, "strip the fat off your body and the sleep out of your mind. Be awake. Be alive. Be humble but never stop endeavoring. There is a great goal ahead. A great goal for endeavor! Find a goal. Cleave to it. Now sit!"

He passed on to his main topic, but Vincent Allan heard only a blur of words. He felt that he had been found out in the commission of the cardinal sin. Just where his great guilt lay he could not be sure, but guilt there was. He felt the burning shame of it hot upon his face and like fire in his heart. He wanted to shrink away from the table, but, as always, he could do nothing but sit and look steadily, expressionlessly, into the face of the president across the long table.

After the luncheon ended he went back to his high stool

in the bank. He tried to work, but only an automatic part of his brain was fixed upon his labor. The rest of his consciousness was filled with the certainty that, in some mysterious manner, his existence was for nothing, his life had been thrown away.

Even the back of his neck was still pink with his shame. The other clerks, passing back and forth, saw that color and pointed it out to one another with subtle chucklings. He knew that they were laughing at him. Perhaps they had wanted to laugh all the time. They had seen that he was flabby and fat. No doubt he was a weakling, but if God gave him life, he would make himself as strong as his frame permitted. He would, as the president said, strip the fat from him and leave the reality. So, looking down at his rather small, compact hand and at the feminine roundness of his wrist, he sighed. It seemed plain that there were small possibilities in his physique.

For that matter, there were small possibilities in his brain, either. He was a dull fellow; he had been dull from his birth. His memory of school was a long nightmare. Hardly had one difficulty been overcome before another was to be mastered, and from the brutal struggle with short division he had passed into the intricate mysteries of long—of numerators, denominators, divisors; grammar school had been bad enough, but high school was a long four years of slavery. The very name of algebra still made him shudder. Chemistry was a haunting demon. He always was at the foot of the class until examinations. But when examinations came he did very well. For, slavery though it was, he never shrank from a labor until it was overcome. What he learned was his forever. So it had been in the bank. For the first six months the manager had been on the verge of dismissing him every pay day, but somehow he could not look into the gentle blue eyes of Vincent Allan and speak unkindly. Against his conscience he retained poor Vincent. But at the end of the sixth month he found that Vincent was doing better—astonishingly better. To use a forced simile, he was like a rock, which grew. He was only a pebble at first, but that pebble could be built upon. Little by little it became more important. Others might make mistakes, but after Vincent Allan had mastered the intricacies of a job, it seemed almost *impossible* for him to make a mistake.

Of these things the manager thought when he returned to the bank after lunch.

"I was a little hard on that young man," said the president on parting.

"You were," said the manager. Then he added:"As a matter of fact, he is the surest, soundest person in the bank!"

He was astonished at himself when he said this, but emotion had forced him to discover the truth even to his own mind. On the way to the bank, he thought it over, but his reflection simply made him more certain. Vincent Allan was the best man on his staff!

So he paused behind the lofty stool of the young clerk in the middle of the afternoon.

To-morrow, he told himself as he went on, he would give that youth a promotion which would astonish him, and dumfound some of the sleek-haired college boys who were in the institution. But his kindly message brought no cheer to Allan. The latter only said to himself: "He pities me. It's almost better to be tongue lashed than to be pitied!"

And as soon as he had finished his work, he headed straight for the gymnasium.

CHAPTER 2

NATURAL MUSCLE

Allan had known the gymnasium for years. It was only two blocks from the room which he had kept ever since he began to work in the bank. It was on the second floor over a series of shops, and on the windows was painted in great letters: "Casey, the man maker." Smaller inscriptions begged the passersby to enter and become a man—the real man—the man in himself which he had never known before. There was a huge picture, too. It showed "the man before" and "the man after." The "man before" had stooped shoulders, hollow chest, and his weight slumped down about his hips in folds. The "man after" was the same face, but how different a body! The breast thrust out like the breast of a pouter pigeon; the waist pinched in; and the upper lip of this magnificent gentleman was adorned with a little tuft of black mustache. From beneath, Allan, on this evening, looked up at that picture and wondered if such miracles were possible. It might be to the childlike mind of Vincent Allan, anything might be.

He saw a pair of youths walk into the entrance; he

heard them bound up the stairs toward the gymnasium. Oh, to be winged with strength like them!

He climbed in turn, slowly, heavily, as he did everything. He rarely ran, even for a street car. As a matter of fact, there was little in life for which he really cared; for he accepted the facts which confronted him, things to be overcome with weary mental exertion, and when he had accomplished what lay just before him, he had very little enthusiasm left for the minor details of existence. He accepted himself, and had always accepted himself, as a person so mentally deficient that he could do nothing but hammer away at the nearest goal with unfailing energy and devotion; otherwise he would perish.

So, quietly, his gentle blue eyes rounded with curiosity, he entered the gymnasium. Instantly the stale odor of perspiration was in his nostrils. A burly Negro lounged in the chair near the door.

"What'll you have, boss?" he asked, surveying Vincent Allan with reddened little eyes.

"I wish to have permission," said Allan, "to work in this gymnasium. Do you think it could be arranged?"

He said it appealingly. Even an office boy was a human being to Vincent Allan, and had a place in the world worthy of respect. But the Negro, being an office boy, had of course learned to despise all who did not despise him. His fat lip curled as he slouched from his chair.

"Ah, dunno," he said. "You'll see Mistah Casey."

He knocked open a door at one side and leaned to peer inside.

"Ain't in," he said tersely. "Sit down in here a minute. Ah'll give him a call."

Vincent Allan stepped into the office, selected a chair in the corner, and sat down, with his hat on his knees. Then he began to observe things one by one while the husky voice in the distance was bellowing: "Casey! O-o-oh Casey!"

What Allan saw was a series of pictures of stalwart young men dressed in trunks only, some with flags tied around their waists, in various attitudes of striking terrible blows. Their faces exhibited scowling ferocity; their muscles seemed to quiver with life even in the photo-

18

graphs. They were variously signed: "To my pal, Paddy Casey;" "To the king of 'em all, Paddy Casey;" "To him that taught me, Paddy Casey;" "To the best that ever wore the green, Paddy Casey." Even to these formidable fellows Paddy Casey was apparently a man of men.

There now entered the room a little chap not more than three or four inches above five feet in height, but so broad, so solid, so heavily muscled that he rolled in his walk like the gait of a sailor along a pitching deck. He wore white trousers and a gymnasium shirt over which his coat had been huddled and was still wrinkled with the haste with which it had been donned. Mr. Casey entered with a broad smile of cheerful and respectful greeting which a doctor might have envied. Some of the respect disappeared as he encountered the mild eye and the shrinking form of Vincent Allan. The latter, discovering that this was the great Mr. Casey himself, declared that he had read the stimulating offer which was written in such large letters upon the windows of the Casey gymnasium and that he desired with all his heart to become such a man as Mr. Casey could make of him.

By this time Mr. Casey had proceeded so far in his analysis of his visitor that he discarded all unnecessary forms.

"If you come here, kid," he barked at Allan, "you come here to work. This ain't no rest resort, and I ain't no magician."

He had definitely placed Allan as an undesirable. Paddy Casey wanted two classes only. First came the rich who were wealthy enough to pay for their follies and to whom whole gymnasiums might be sold, eventually. Second were the youngsters who had in them the making of distinguished athletes—heavy young men with ropy muscles who might do as wrestlers one of these days—light-footed young gentlemen with heft in their shoulders who might become famous in the ring if Paddy Casey could give them that mysterious little touch of divine fire. Such being the interests of Paddy, he considered time spent upon such as Vincent Allan as time wasted. And, of course, he was right. As for the sign which spoke from his windows, that had been painted for him when he began his gymnasium career, and though the purposes of the gymnasium had changed greatly since those early days, Paddy, for the sake of luck, would not have altered his sign. When young men came to Paddy's gymnasium he regarded them carefully, and if he observed either that they were rough and tough or that they possessed the spark of that divine fire of conquest which is sometimes inborn and which is sometimes passed from hand to hand, he would keep them with him and try to make them, as he boasted, "men." But he saw in Vincent Allan one who was not rough and tough and who had no fire at all. Certainly not a likely candidate.

"What's wrong with you?" he asked Allan sharply.

"I'm fat," said the latter, growing brightest red. "I want to get down to my right weight."

The stubby fingers of Mr. Casey sank into the shoulder of his visitor. There they worked deep and deeper into the flesh, while he felt for those rubbery cords which are muscle. He found nothing. The whole mass seemed without a central core. It was of one consistency—thick, almost sticky. And Paddy Casey dropped his hand with an exclamation of disgust.

"There ain't no chance!" he said. "*I* can't help you!"

Then, as the dismay in the face of poor Vincent touched even his hard heart a little he added: "I'll tell you what you're up against kid. You ain't took no exercise. You got *no* muscle. You just got meat with the fat grained right in through it. I dunno how you could ever get it out. Look how soft you are! The devil, kid, I could drive my fist clean through you. It'd bust your heart tryin' to get into shape. You go home and forget it. You've waited too long!"

The whole body of Vincent Allan was quivering a little. Like a jellyfish, thought Casey.

"I could work very steadily," Allan was saying. "I have great patience, Mr. Casey. And—I shall not mind physical exhaustion, you know."

"Huh!" said Casey, and hesitated in the act of turning finally away. What held him there, unwilling, was the steady glance of the youth. Casey had never before seen any one so young who persisted in looking him straight in the eye in spite of personal embarrassment.

"I'll tell you what I'll do. I'll put you through a try-out.

I got a standard. If you come up to that, all right. If you can chin yourself five times and dip three times and do some other things, you'll be good enough to get in. Tumble into that room, yonder. Yank off your clothes. Put on that pair of trunks and them gym shoes. Then the first door on the right."

Young Allan undressed in a dream through which the terrible judgment kept ringing: "You ain't got no chance!" That was exactly it, and he had often felt it about himself. He was handicapped both physically and mentally compared to the adroitness of others. And on this day, two men had seen through him with a single fiery glance.

When he was togged out at last in the trunks and the gym shoes, he went obediently through the prescribed door and found himself in a long chamber with a lofty ceiling at one end of which a strong-bodied young man was whirling around and around a bar, making himself into a pin wheel. He ceased with a violence which threatened to tear the arms from their sockets, gave himself a violent wrench, and came into a sitting posture on the bar around which he had been spinning. It was a miracle, to Vincent Allan, that one's balance could be maintained with such an exquisite nicety, and withal so carelessly.

In the meantime, Mr. Casey hurried in accompanied by a beetle-browed gentleman who carried the signs of his profession with him—a pair of boxing gloves swinging from one hand.

"Here you are," said Casey. "He don't look so bad. He ain't got no belly, y'see? Feel his arm, Bud!"

Bud took the round arm of Vincent Allan in his immense grasp. Under the pressure of his digging finger tips the thin satin of the skin turned white, then glowed red.

"There ain't nothin' there," said Bud, almost whispering the awful intelligence to his companion. "Nothin' but that fat stuff—and then the bone!"

"That's it," said Casey.

"All right," Bud said sharply to Allan. "Take hold of that bar. Turn your hand in to your face—palm in. Catch tight hold, and chin yourself."

"What does that mean?" asked Vincent Allan.

"The devil!" said the instructor. "It means pull yourself up till your chin is on top of the bar. Go ahead—five times, kid!"

Vincent Allan looked up to the bar with a sigh. Then he fastened his left hand about it and began to draw himself up. There was a shout of laughter and something about two hands—he was not quite sure of what he had heard, so he relaxed.

"Go on," cried Paddy Casey, his face working with amusement. "Go on and pull yourself up with one arm."

There were others interested. He could hear the youth who sat on top of the horizontal bar at the farther end of the room shouting, and at his call half a dozen others ran into the doorway. All began to laugh the instant they saw. And Vincent Allan wished himself in the center of the earth to cover his shame.

However, he resolutely laid hold of the bar above him and tightened his arm muscles. That one small arm could lift all the weight of his body seemed absurd, but the more he tested its power the more he found to respond. Something began to live and quiver and then writhe up and down his arm and through the flesh of the shoulder; it sent a tremor through all his body—and then he felt himself come clear off the floor!

There was a sharp yell—like so many dogs barking in unison. They all rushed closer to him so that he almost felt they were about to attack him, and then he saw that they had come near only to wonder. In the background of his mind he heard the voice of Paddy Casey saying over and over: "My heaven, am I seein' straight?"

"Look!" cried Bud. "What you and me called fat, was muscle. Natural muscle, Paddy. Will you look at it come to life. How did he get it?"

The whole group had gathered on the left side of Vincent Allan, and there they gazed with open mouths, clutching one another, elbowing each other's ribs while Allan raised himself slowly and surely above them. His chin came above the top of the bar.

"Is this high enough?" asked Allan quietly.

"Yes!" gasped out Paddy. "Come down now."

Down came Allan, smoothly and without a jar, while all the mysterious twists and worms of muscle disappeared from his arm and left it as round and as smooth and as soft as the arm of a woman. But there he hung with his knees twisted to one side so that they might not touch the floor. One could realize, suddenly, the great length of his arm; he reminded those startled watchers of an ape in the zoo, hanging with equal ease.

Then again the arm began to flex, the bulges and the swift rivulets of strength leaped into being; there was life in his arm like the life which tangles and recrosses in a river flowing down a rapids—a thousand currents leaping toward an end. But these things were seen by glimpses under the delicate skin of Vincent Allan. His whole arm swelled to what seemed twice its former size, and under the surface there were ridges, shadowings, and rippling bulges to suggest the presence of the individual muscles. Five times he hung the full length of his arm; five times he raised himself without a swing or a jerk, but with a fluent smoothness, until his chin was above the height of the bar. Then he dropped lightly to the floor.

"Is five times enough?" asked Vincent Allan.

CHAPTER 3

THUNDER IN BOTH FISTS

He was amazed to hear peals of laughter while they patted one another on the back.

"This is on you, Paddy!" they said.

"I been made a fool of," said Paddy courageously, though he grew a deep crimson. "But," he said to Allan, "you had me beat, pal. How could I know that you was a professional? And where you been showin' your stuff? On the other side of the pond?"

"What stuff?" asked Vincent Allan. "And I haven't the slightest idea of what you mean, Mr. Casey."

He said it so earnestly that even the bystanders did not laugh.

"S' help me," gasped out Casey, "it's real. It ain't no fake!"

The spectators nodded.

"Look here," said Casey, "what d'you do with yourself?"

"I work ir a bank, Mr. Casey," said Vincent Allan.

Then the red joy of prophecy descended upon Paddy

Casey. His eyes bulged and his throat was so full of emotion that his voice was small.

"You ain't no bank clerk!" he said in that whispering passion of the seer. "You ain't no bank clerk. Know what you are, kid? You're the champeen of the world. The champeen heavyweight of the world! The champeen heavyweight of all time of the whole world. Or call me a walleyed fool!"

So solemn was this utterance that the others were shaken and awed to quiet by it. As for Vincent Allan, so much had happened in so few seconds that he only knew those who had come to mock had remained to admire, though why they admired he could not quite make out. He had done or said something remarkable. That was all he knew.

"Don't fill the kid's head full of the bunk," said Bud.

"Why bunk?"

"Suppose he ain't got no speed?"

"Is he muscle bound? Ain't he loose and soft all over? Why, Bud, he's as fast as a cat! Did you ever box, kid?"

"Never," said Allan.

"Get the gloves on, Bud. You got twenty pounds and three inches reach on the kid, but I'll bet on him."

"He ain't never boxed," said Bud, scowling. "Did you hear him say that?"

"He ain't never chinned himself, either," said Mr. Casey, and there was much laughter, while a little quiver ran through the body of big Bud.

So the gloves were tied upon the hands of Bud and of Allan and they were brought to an eighteen-foot ring whose rosined canvas was smeared and spattered with innumerable dark stains whose nature Allan shuddered when he guessed.

"We're going to make this real," said Casey.

"He ain't never held up his hands!" protested Bud, very red. "Am I one to make a choppin' block out of—"

"Shut up and do what I tell you. We got to see if he can take it, don't we, before we can start in campaignin'? Shut up and do what I tell you. You fight four regular three-minute rounds, and I bet on the kid!"

The "kid" was placed upon a stool which swung into the

right from one corner of it. There Mr. Casey knelt behind him and placed a hand upon his shoulders.

"Look at Bud," commanded Casey.

"Yes," said Vincent Allan, and his mild blue eyes looked steadily across the ring toward Bud, who sat on a similar stool with his elbows on his knees, glaring at Allan and meantime kneading the toe of each glove into the palm of the other as though he wished to pack them on more firmly.

"How does he look to you?"

"He seems very angry," said Allan. "What have I done to him?"

"It ain't what you're going to do to him that makes him angry; it's what he's going to do to you, kid! Lemme tell you! He's going to try to smear you over this ring so darned loose that I'll have to scrape you together after he's through with you."

"Ah?" said Allan.

"Are you scared?"

Allan looked inward upon his secret soul. "My stomach feels a little empty," he said thoughtfully, at the last. "And—and I'm a little chilly, all at once."

There was a slow growl of disapprobation from Casey.

"Look here," said Casey. "You can't box none. If Bud wants to hit you, he'll hit you. The only thing for you to do is to get in at him and hit him right back. You understand?"

"Ah?" said Allan.

"That's it. Plough in and before he can hit you the second time, belt him. You won't be able to get at his jaw. He's too smart for that. But sink a fist into his ribs. That's all you got to do. Hit him as hard as you can in the ribs, and that'll be the end of the fight."

"But," said Allan, amazed, "he's much larger than I am."

"Size ain't nothin', kid," said Casey. His thick, muscular hand began to pat the shoulder of Vincent Allan—whose sticky softness now had so much meaning. "Look at the old yarn about David and Golier. Look at old Bob Fitzsimmons. That baby didn't weigh no more'n a hundred and sixty-five and they didn't come too big for him. You got five pounds on old Bob, and—lemme whisper to you

26

—you're twise as strong as old Bob ever was. If only you can learn to hit, kid!"

Half a hundred people had collected by magic. Someone struck a gong.

"All right, kid," said Casey, "Sop that big bum in the ribs and we'll call it a day's work."

Having been shoved off his chair and seeing Bud rushing toward him, Allan walked with measured steps toward the center of the ring—with his hands hanging idly at his sides!

"He don't know nothin'!" screamed Casey. "Put up your mitts, you fool, you—"

"What did you say?" said Vincent Allan, and turned his head toward Casey.

At the same instant Bud struck with all the energy of a hundred and ninety pounds. He had to finish this contest in short order if he wished to get any glory out of it, and into that first blow he put all of his might. He did not need to feel out his antagonist with any artistic sparring for an opening. He had only to drop his head, lunge with all his weight behind the point of his shoulder, and drive his right fist with a straight piston movement into the chin of the greenhorn. And straight and true sped that terrific right-hand drive. The head of the kid was turned toward Casey. Therefore the "button" was exposed and upon the button landed the punch. That is to say, it struck an inch from the point of the jaw and the thud of that impact was as audible as a hammer blow throughout the big gymnasium.

The audience rose upon its knees with an indrawn breath and then emitted a wild "wow!" of fury and joy. It is the same cry which rises from the crowd during the ninth inning rally; or when the touchdown which will win the game is in the making. The whole half-hundred of the onlookers tilted to one side as though in sympathy with the coming fall of the kid.

He did not fall.

Instead, the blow seemed to pick him up, put wings beneath his feet, and float him back across the ring until his shoulders pressed against the padded ropes. There he stood, looking with the same mild blue eyes toward his foe, a little surprised, rubbing with the tip of his glove the place which had just been struck.

If there had been a shout before, there was furious babel now. "He can take it! Oh, how that kid can take it!" they yelled. And Casey turned a handspring! As for Bud, he looked down in amazement upon the good right hand which had failed him.

"He's got sawdust in his jaw!" he grunted at last and moved onward, daunted but still ferocious, to the attack.

He washed young Vincent Allan before him with a shower of blows. He stood at long distance and smashed across tremendous facers and body punches which sounded on the ribs of Allan like beating on a drum. So Allan leaned through the hurtling gloves and clutched his opponent. He felt that stalwart body give in his clutch. There was a frightened gasp from Bud and then: "Take that bear off of me! Is this a wrestling bout?"

"I'm sorry," said Allan, stepped back.

"Soak him, kid!" screamed Casey.

Allan, obediently, tapped the other upon the cheek.

"No! All your might!" shouted Casey through his cupped hands. But the other shook his head. "He's no good after all," groaned Casey. "The stiff ain't got no fightin' heart!"

In the meantime, Bud had recovered a little from the effects of that tremendous hug. He pushed out an automatic straight left, that keystone upon which all good boxing should be built; he stepped in, rising on his toes, and as he descended to his heels, his right fist darted out, stooped over the shoulder of Allan, and landed solidly upon his jaw. It was a right-cross, delicately executed, with nearly two hundred pounds of brawn to give it significance, and it rocked Vincent Allan like a ship in a gale.

"Fight! Fight! Fight!" yelled Casey, seeing his protégé driven into retreat.

Instinct and imitation were teaching Allan. He put up his hands as his opponent did; he began to strike out with a straight left arm; but there was no spirit in his blows, and Bud shook them off and slid in for further execution. He came to half-arm distance, dropped a fist almost to his knee, and whipped it to the head. It landed on the point of Allan's jaw and tilted his head back on his shoulders. He was not stunned. These heavy blows in a shower had not affected his brain. But the scraping glove had flicked off a bit of skin. He touched the stinging place with his glove and, lowering it, he saw a dark little round spot. In that instant one self died and another self was born, for the gentle lessons of pity, of mercy, of human kindliness were shed from his mind into a deep oblivion. He had been aware, before this, of driving fists, of the perspiring, shining body of Bud, of the yelling voices around the ring, of the snarling, lashing voice of Paddy Casey, but now all of this was forgotten. He stood in the midst of a thick silence and there existed before him only the bright, battle-eager eyes of Bud; there existed within his heart only a ravening desire to make those gleaming eyes dark as night, helpless, blank.

Bud came in, with both fists whipping to the mark, but Allan put a hand against his breast and pushed him away. He seemed to float off like a feather. Before he was settled. Allan was at him. He came as the tiger comes, with every nerve tingling, with every muscle working. He was inside the reach of those milling gloves. His feet gripped the floor as though glued there, his toes digging for a hold, and then he struck. His fist struck; something cracked. The fist sank in, in to the very vitals, and Bud sank in a writhing heap on the floor.

He became aware of the shouting through its cessation, then. Half a dozen men swarmed through the ropes and lifted Bud while Vincent Allan stepped closer and looked down into dull, dead eyes which gazed up to him without recognition. It would be pleasant, now, to say that Vincent Allan felt pity and remorse, but if the cruel truth must be told, he tasted only an incomparable sweetness of victory. He wanted only one thing from the bottom of the animal heart which had awakened in him, and that was to fight again.

They carried Bud from the ring; they stretched him on a couch; a doctor hurried in with a satchel in his hand and kneeled by the motionless figure.

"Two ribs gone," he said. "A lucky thing he was not hit on the left side or you would have a dead man here, Casey."

Then they carried Bud out.

No one came near to Allan during all of this time. He knew their eyes were feeling him over from head to foot, watching the easy rise and fall of his breast, studying the smooth rippling of those mysterious muscles which clothed his arms and padded his chest, and lay thick and dimpling across his shoulder blades. But no one came to him with a friendly word or a hostile one, and their eyes reminded him of the eyes of children watching the black panther of the zoo asleep in a shadow of his cage, himself deeper black than the shadow.

Then Casey, without a word, grappled his arm and dragged him back to his private office. There he searched Allan from head to foot, white faced, tight lipped. He kept mumbling to himself: "I dunno how it it—I dunno where it comes from. How d'you feel here? And here?"

With a hard forefinger he prodded the jaw and the body of Allan where the crashing blows of Bud had landed.

"Don't you feel nothin'?" he asked almost savagely.

"Oh yes," said Allan. "My chin stings a great deal."

"Your chin stings a great deal!" mocked Casey with a snarl. "Oh, the devil! And don't you feel nothing here on the jaw—or where he soaked you in the stomach?"

"No, I'm afraid not."

"You're afraid, are you? So's a buzz saw afraid of wood! What you thinkin' about now?"

"I was only wondering when the next man boxed me," said Allan.

"You'd like to start ag'in?"

Allan sighed. The whole picture of that boxing contest was flashing again and again through his mind. He was seeing all the intimate little details without missing one, just as his practiced eye could run up a column of figures with dazzling speed and then put down the total without an error. There was the time when Bud had struck so heavily at him the very first time. Suppose that he had ducked under that driving punch and then hit up sharply at the lunging body? Or when Bud dropped the right cross upon his jaw, what if he himself had flicked his left hand straight into the face of his foe, with a shoulder twitch behind it?

"I'd like to do that over again," said Allan. "I see so many places, now, where I could have struck him."

There intervened a long moment of silence.

"Do you know who Bud is?" asked Casey.

"No."

"He's a crackerjack heavyweight. He's a comer. Fought eighteen times. Four decisions, two draws—and twelve knock-outs! He ain't never been beaten—never! And then this—this! One round!"

"It wasn't a minute," said Allan anxiously. "I was just beginning, you know. And if—"

Paddy Casey groaned.

"You go home," he said. "To-morer you trot down to that bank and tell 'em that stayin' behind a counter ain't your line. Look, kid! I been waitin' for five years for this to happen. I been waitin' for a *right* one to come along. And you're it. Not too big to be chain lightnin' with feet and hands. Nothin' hurts you. And thunder in both fists. In six months d'you know what? The Garden for yours and the championship of the world. Go home. Be a good kid. Tomorrow you and me start!"

CHAPTER 4

ALLAN WINS MUSTARD

Allan went home and sat by the window, in his little room. He had not turned on the light, though the darkness was thick as ink in the chamber, for he wanted to look out on the night world. It was the first time in his life that he had such a desire. As a rule, there was supper to eat, and then a certain necessary chapter in a book to read, for he must not cease pushing his dull brain ahead. After the reading ended, he must undress and go to bed, according to that maxim of his dead father: "Early to bed and early to rise, makes a man healthy and wealthy and wise!" But his father used to add with a bitter significance: "Except fools—except fools!"

"Hush, father," Vincent's mother used to say, "how can you talk so—of your own boy—your own dear son!"

"Truth is like murder," his father would answer. "It will out!"

Neither of them had ever loved him. He had had an elder brother, graceful in body, quick in mind. On him all their hopes and their affections centered until scarlet fever carried him off. "If he had had Vincent's constitution, he would have laughed at the fever," the doctor had said. And from that moment they had rather held it against their younger son. They could not help letting him guess that, in their estimation, a whole gross of Vincents would not have been worth a single Ralph. So his home life had been a curse to him. Indeed, how little joy there had been in his life, either before or after the death of his parents? In fact, he could remember nothing so important as this day of days. He was revealed to himself as a new man. There was power tingling in his hands great enough to have struck down a professional pugilist so much larger than he. There was power in his heart, too, as untapped as the power in his hands had ever been. Romances of others had often appealed to him; suddenly he wakened to the belief that there might be romantic possibilities in himself, and the thought was stunning.

A block away the Third Avenue elevated roared and whined and rattled. It was hurrying throngs of men and women and children—alas!—back to their homes from the work of their day. To each of them the night had some meaning. There was a family to see for which they provided; there was a brother or a sister to greet; there was a table around which faces of dear ones smiled upon them. Oh, to Vincent Allan how dear was that picture! He had yearned to be a part of it all his life, but instead he had never been more than tolerated to his face and despised in secret.

On this magic day, however, a new avenue of escape was opened to him. Something might be done. There was strength in his hands—how much strength he himself could not so much as guess, but it haunted him. It was a domain which he would explore. Its distant borders he would examine and define. For what he had done against Bud was nothing. That final blow, he felt, could have been thrice as hard. Up his arm the muscles flexed and leaped at the thought, and fire came into his heart.

He could not stay in his room after that. Yonder in the street men were stirring, talking, laughing. He had a place among them now. They might supply the friction out of which he would be able to discover all the power that was in these hands of his. So he tugged his hat upon

33

his head and went down the stairs to the street, now that his course was decided.

He began to wander idly, letting the streets lead him. He reached the Bowery where the congested traffic thickened from Fourth Avenue and Third and where the people swarmed like flies on the sidewalk. Three ruffians came before him, arms locked together, sweeping before them a wide swath. He braced himself—he dug for a foothold with gripping toes—the trio cracked open, and he was through. Vincent Allan stopped and turned and laughed. It was an invitation, but the three suddenly dropped their heads and hurried on.

He went on.

Out of all these hurrying thousands surely there was some one, or some two, who would stand against him, and let him vent the newly found power of his arms, so long wasted. He turned a corner and wandered down a dim alley.

There came a chorus of shrill cries behind him; he turned and saw a child down and an automobile speeding on. Allan was off the curb in an instant. He raced at full speed in the direction of the speeding car. As it shot up beside him, he leaped onto the running board and caught at the wheel.

The driver crouched lower, barking at his companion. The companion whipped from a pocket a gleaming bit of steel, and Allan had no chance to see that it was a revolver. He struck as his eye caught the first flash, and the other crumpled in his seat. Then he seized the driver and the latter jammed on the brakes. They came to a halt bumping on the cobbles. He dragged the man from his seat onto the pavement. Behind them a hundred furious men and women were rushing, but they were still far away when the crisis came, for though the man whom he held twisted and writhed ineffectually in the grasp of Allan, like a child held by a man, his companion had now recovered and lurched from the automobile with the gun held stiffly before him. What was to be done? For the fastest hand could not outspeed a bullet. He thought of one thing only, and, lifting the man with whom he had grappled, he heaved the body around his head and flung it at the assailant. The flying mass struck home. Down they went in a heap, with the muffled roar of the gun booming at the ear of Allan.

Then the van of the approaching crowd swept up on them, engulfed them. He saw the two fallen men picked apart. The foremost of the crowd washed back. Some one gasped: "He's dead!" And Vincent Allan slipped back into the throng which had piled up even in this breathing space of interruption.

A man was dead; he had been the cause of that death; and for one killing the law exacted another. Such was the working of his mind as he hurried down the alley. He felt, vaguely, that he had been justified, and that he had only striven to bring punishment upon these brutes who had knocked down a child with their car and yet had driven recklessly on. But no matter what his intentions might have been, the fact remained that a man had died because of his intervention and because of that death he himself might be sent to the chair.

He thought of only one thing, and that was to flee as fast as he could. He had in his pocket all his cash which was not deposited to his bank account. That cash was woefully little, and yet it might carry him to a distance. He went straight to the Grand Central as fast as a taxi-cab would carry him. There he bought a ticket to Boston; in an hour the wheels were roaring under him upon the steel rails, and Manhattan had become a ghost of danger behind him.

The next morning he left Boston for New Orleans; and he reached New Orleans without a cent in his pocket. The tip to the porter had exhausted his exchequer. But still he had not placed a sufficient distance behind him. For it was in a New Orleans paper that he read the first account of the killing. It struck him like a blow—a headline on the third page.

"Man Used As Club" ran the headline. And beneath it: "Speeding Bandits Knock Down Child. Man Stops Pair Single-handed. Disappears."

The article beneath it ran: "When Steve Martin, twenty-seven of 92 West Charlesworth Street, New York City, and Mike Hanery, twenty-five, alias, 'Dan, the Mug,' of the same address, held up the paying teller of the Wheat Exchange Bank, Seventh Avenue Branch,

35

Manhattan, they were given the cash which was on hand, amounting to seventeen hundred and forty-eight dollars. They did not stay to congratulate one another on their haul, but ran out of the bank before the alarm could be given and jumped into a stolen car which was waiting at the curb with the motor running.

"They sped down Seventh Avenue, soon eluding pursuit in the first traffic jam. Then they turned east, passed down Fourth Avenue to the Bowery, and left that famous street for a side alley running to Second Avenue. As they swung into the alley little Rose Kochansky, 192 Little Hanover Street, ran out on the cobble stones to escape a playmate who was attempting to tag her, and the machine struck her a glancing blow which knocked her down, inflicting severe bruises and perhaps dangerous internal injuries on account of which she now lies seriously ill in a hospital.

"The robbers, however, did not pause. They had other things to think about and gave their car the gas in spite of the shout of rage which arose from the pedestrians up and down the block. They would have escaped beyond doubt had not an unknown decided to take the affair into his own hands. He jumped on the running board of the automobile, stopped the car, and when the two attacked him, he picked up Martin and threw him at Hanery. The bullet from Hanery's gun passed through Martin's heart. The police are now searching for the man who used Martin as a club."

There was the significant sentence left to the very end like the snap and cut of the whiplash. The police were looking for him!

Let them reach far, then! That same day a freight train rattled West through the embowering green of Louisiana plantations and carried Vincent Allan on its rods. At the end of the first division, a brakeman discovered him, pulled him forth, and swung his heavy lantern to knock the hobo down the steep bank. So, before the lantern landed—weighted and reinforced with iron as it was— Vincent Allan stabbed his left fist into the shack's stomach and drove him into space. There was a roll down the lower bank, a half-stifled shout of fear and surprise,

36

and then the splash as the green waters of the marsh received him.

Vincent Allan did not stay to observe further. He wandered on down the track, walking lightly and happily, for he knew that the magic had not yet left him—that it would never leave him and that he could make his way by the might of his hands wherever he might be. With this wealth of strength in his hands, however, how could he spend it? What could he do next?

He hardly knew. He hardly cared. Every day would take care of itself in its own turn, and he refused to worry over such nonessentials as clothes or food or a sleeping place. He had only to stretch out his hand and take what he would. He was in a farming district where his strength had a value. He spent a week pitching hay. He broke the handles of three forks and blistered his hands raw until he mastered that peculiar little knack of getting under a large load of hay with the most ease. But Vincent Allan had learned to acquire information swiftly. All his life he had ever believed that there was a mystery behind everything, from the dexterous fashion in which a woman used a broom to bring the dust out of a thick carpet to the exquisite dexterity of a smith welding steel or tempering it; but he had always accepted his own stupidity so completely that he had not dared to attempt to imitate.

That bout with Bud had changed his mind. He had seen that his hands could do what other hands could do, and perhaps a little better than most of them! He kept on for a month. He learned, in that time, not only how to pitch hay but how to handle the bales, which is a very great mystery indeed! He learned how to ride a horse, how to drill fence holes with a hand auger, how to swing an ax, how to run a great cross-cut saw. Of course he did not become proficient in so many things at once, but he learned prodigiously every day. He learned with his body; he learned with his mind. He was in a new field, sinking roots into a new soil, and with the passage of every moment he felt his body coming into its own. The natural might with which he had been born was now being multiplied by exercise. For two weeks he went to bed with a thousand wearinesses in his flesh and wakened the next morning with a thousand aches. These pains began to disappear. By the end of the month his face was lean, his skin healthily flushed and tanned, and in his very finger tips the tingling certainty of his power.

What was in his spirit, however, hardly showed in his face. The mild, kindly blue eyes had not changed their light; his voice remained soft with a note of confiding and of appeal still in it. The habits of a life could not be changed so suddenly. He could not even ask for direction without adopting the attitude of one who begged for bread. Such was Vincent Allan as he found himself in this new land, save that now he called himself Allan Vincent, feeling that even this small inversion might help to keep him from the knowledge of the police. For a few weeks of safety had not made him feel immune. An old saying rang in his brain day and night. Murder would out, and having been the cause of the killing of a man, his guilt must be eventually discovered.

So he pressed steadily West and West. At the end of the second week he considerably improved his position, for a farmer made a certain foolish wager concerning a three-hundred-pound bale of hay and the height to which it could be lifted, whereat Allan took the monster in his hands and heaved it to arm's length above his head. He could have put fifty dollars in his pocket, but instead the farmer offered a horse, a stoutly made and even rather beautifully finished animal with a strong Roman nose and long, mulish ears. That horse was offered in payment of the debt, together with an old saddle of which most of the leather had been worn from the wooden frame, and Allan, thinking that the farmer must have lost his mind, saddled and bridled the mare.

"What's her name?" he asked.

"Mustard!" said the farmer.

Allan had no sooner settled into the saddle than he was unsettled, sailed high into the air, and landed on his back. He sat up to find that Mustard was regarding him with a genial and whimsical eye while the laughter of the farmer and his men was a jovial thunder.

After that, when Allan journeyed West—a day of travel and then a day of work, here and there—he was accompanied by the roan mare. Not that he rode her, but that she strolled, contented, beside him. Every morning he attempted to stay in the saddle; every morning the battle was more and more desperate, more and more prolonged; but every morning Mustard pitched him upon his head and stood by panting to enjoy the picture of his fall. He was covered with bruises which were her handiwork, but he stuck by his guns. He was receiving a condensed, postgraduate course in the riding of a bucking horse. In the meantime, he passed from the district of farms. He came into open country. Bald, brown mountains lay before him in the day, and turned blue with the coming of evening, and it was now that he found a companion.

CHAPTER 5

THE COMPANION

It was on the shoulder of a hill that he had camped, with plenty of dead shrubs near by to supply him with firewood and with a not over-clean brook near by for water. Squatting by the fire with the sooty frying pan and the equally blackened coffeepot upon it, who could have recognized in young "Allan Vincent" the white-faced bank clerk? It is upon the tenderest skins that the sun paints most quickly. And tenderfeet always are sure to expose themselves to the sun more than others. Allan, instead of the wide-brimmed sombreros of the natives of that district, had upon his head a rag of felt which had once been black and which sheltered him only at high noon, for whenever the sun shone at a slant its rays were certain to scorch his neck or his face. His color was now a rich mahogany. Hard labor had flattened the line of his cheeks and squared his chin. And for clothes he had a cast-off coat, ragged at the elbows, an old blue-flannel shirt, a pair of overalls with the dye rubbed pale at the knees, and heavy cowhide boots. A very rough diamond was Allan now, but in spite of exteriors he felt happier than ever, for every day the maturity of his full strength had been growing upon him. It was the wealth of Croesus, quite incalculable.

Allan had fried his bacon and warmed up his pone and the coffee was steaming when Mustard lifted her head and neighed. At the same time he himself heard the regular click of the armed hoofs of a horse trotting over the rocks up the hillside, and presently the rider came into view, a small figure on a beautiful little pinto, which was weaving deftly among the boulders. The flat red face of the westering sun was in the eyes of Allan; he did not see until the stranger was very close that it was a girl. Indeed, she rode with all the careless vigor of a man, and when she came closer she loosed the reins and twisted about sideways in the saddle.

"Hello, stranger," she said.

"How do you do," said Allen, and shaded his eyes to look at her. Her face was as brown as an Indian's except that when she pushed her sombrero back he saw a pale streak where the band had rested, and a fuzz of blonde hair, not overabundant. But her eyes alone would have proclaimed her a white woman. They were very big, very blue, very feminine in everything except their expression, and that was bold past the boldness of a man—bold as the eyes of a ten-year-old boy compared with which all other things are tame. She did not wear gloves. Now she rested her elbow on the pommel of her saddle and dropped her chin on a sun-blackened fist. In the meantime she was considering him gravely and in detail.

"You're a tenderfoot, ain't you?" said she.

He glanced down at himself. In his opinion he was

rough enough in appearance to have passed as a veteran of the West.

"I suppose I am," said Allan. "I didn't know that it showed. Won't you get down and have supper with me?

She was instantly on the ground, yanked the saddle from the back of the pinto, and turned him loose. Then she went over to the fire and leaned above the pan.

"You ain't feeding very rich," she said gloomily.

He suggested that he had some other provender in his pack—some more bacon, some corn-meal flour, some potatoes, a few cans of tomatoes, and other essentials.

"Huh!" said the girl. "All that chuck and you eatin' like this? That's tenderfoot, I'd say. Look here, you got everything except what you need to tie them fixin's together. And I've got that!"

She went back to her saddle and produced the limp body of a headless jack rabbit of some size.

"We'll have rabbit stew, partner," said she. "Hustle up some wood. I need a fire, not just a plain smoke like you got here?"

He obeyed; obedience was his habit, and now the fire rose to seasonable proportions, but her own flying hands were working miracles. She tore the skin off the body and then with a long, blue-bladed hunting knife she slashed the meat into convenient chunks. A can of the tomatoes was confiscated, potatoes peeled with wonderful dexterity, slit into morsels, some bits of bacon added, and the whole mess dropped into a pot which she produced from her pack.

"Looks like a load, don't it?" she remarked as she fixed the pot above the fire, wedging it safely against capsizing. "It *is* a load, too. But it's a dog-gone handy thing, partner. It beats a fryin' pan more'n a mile. A fryin' pan fills up your stomach with grease and half-cooked dough. This here pot gives you a meal."

By this time the roaring fire made the contents of the pot begin to simmer around the edges and the fragrance which it gave off seemed to Allan a heavenly thing. She sat by with a peeled stick of wood to stir the contents from time to time, and all the while she blazed forth questions at Allan. She wanted to know from what place he came, what was his destination, what he had been

41

doing, what was his name, his age, his purpose in life. He told her, in reply, that he was Allan Vincent, that he had grown tired of living in a city, that he had come West to find what he could find, and that he was gradually beating his way West. For the rest, he had neither purpose nor destination. He wanted to hear her own story. She told it gayly and briefly enough, stirring the pot from time to time.

"My name is Frances Jones," said she, "by rights. But folks call me Frank. Dad named me after a fightin' dog he owned when he was a kid because he said he could see by my eye that I had a fightin' nacher."

She grinned at Allan, but he did not smile in return; he was regarding her seriously and gently.

"My dad loved fightin' dogs and buckin' horses," she went on. "He wouldn't have no hoss about the place that didn't have a little pitchin' in its system. He used to say that a hoss was like a man; if it didn't have a little devil inside, it didn't have no good, neither. My dad had both! But bad luck beat him. Mother died before I could remember her. The rest of the time dad was fightin' wild hosses and a mortgage. He could beat the hosses, but he couldn't beat the mortgage. He used to say that a mortgage was like bad rheumatism: you couldn't get it out of your system. Things was so bad that my big brother, Jim, he pulled up and went West, one day. That was three years back. Dad kept on goin' down-hill. Six months ago he lay down and died."

She paused here and stabbed at the pot with her stick—a little blindly, thought Allan.

"I stuck on, got things on the ranch fixed up good enough to sell the place, and when it was sold there was just enough money to leave my pinto and this here outfit. I tried to get in touch with Jim, but he'd disappeared. What I'm aimin' at now is to locate him. And here's the stew ready to eat. Get your plate ready, Al!"

It seemed to Vincent Allan a most sumptuous feast; even the tough flesh of the rabbit had been boiled to a state approaching tenderness. He ate it with relish.

"But," said he, "I've been wondering how you were able to catch it?"

"The rabbit?" said she.

"Of course."

"I'll tell you how it is," said Frances Jones. "When you see a rabbit jump across your trail, all you got to do is to sit fast and look it in the eye. It gets plumb hypnotized. All you got to do then is hop off your hoss and grab it by the neck."

"Is that really the way?" asked Allan fascinated.

"Mostly around these parts," said the girl gravely. "That's the way they catch 'em. But some folks that ain't got the time to spare just uses a gun."

"Ah," said Allan, "I don't suppose that a girl like you could handle a gun?"

"Can't I just!" said she. "Lemme show you with your own Colt."

"I don't carry a gun," said Allan. "I've never shot one in my life, you know!"

At this, she was reduced to staring, and he knew that he had sunk to the lowest possible point in her estimation. In fact, she said not another word, but sat back with her chin in her hand and allowed him to clean up the utensils without proffering the slightest assistance. He hardly noticed this oversight on her part, however, for his mind was full of another thought which matured slowly and did not come to expression until his work was ended. The sun had long since set when he turned to her at the last. The red in the west had paled and there was only orange and palest green along the horizon.

"Traveling by oneself is a lonely thing," said Allan. "Don't you suppose that we could go on together—until you reach your brother?"

At this she lifted her head sharply, and the last of the sunset light fell upon her features; they seemed to Allan of a most dreamlike loveliness.

"That brother of mine is a gun-fightin' man getter!" she declared.

"Well?" asked Allan.

"What would he think, Al, if he knowed that I'd been travelin' alone with a man?"

Allan considered all the possibilities that might arise from such a thing.

"Why," said he at the last. "I suppose that he'd be

43

mighty glad that you had company on your ride. Don't you think so?"

He heard a faint gasp from the girl.

"You got the world beat!" she stated at last.

"Is anything wrong?" asked Allan.

"How many girls have you teamed around with?" she asked, and he thought the question most surprising.

"I have never had time to see them," he said frankly.

"H'm!" said she. "I thought not."

"I've always been very busy," he confessed. He swallowed! it was bitterly hard to let her know the whole truth, but there was something about her that drew it from him. "I was always so slow in school," said he, "that I had to work at home every afternoon and evening to keep up. And then when I went into business it was the same thing over again; there was so much to learn. Besides," he continued, with a growing embarrassment which he could hardly explain, "one must know a great deal to talk to a girl."

"You seem to be talkin' pretty free and easy to me," she stated.

"You're more like a man—or a boy!" said Allan. It was a discovery which he was glad to get into words; it cleared his own mind. He came an enthusiastic step closer to her, smiling. "You're easier to understand," he said. "You aren't always laughing at me, you know!"

He broke off with a sigh of disappointment, for at this very point she had burst into ringing laughter. She mastered it with an effort. Then she sprang up and found his hand and shook it heartily.

"You're queer," she said. "But I guess you're all right. I'm goin' to turn in on the other side of the hill. Gimme a call at breakfast time, will you?"

With that, she was off up the hill. She whistled, and the pinto fell in at her heels like a dog. He saw her against the stars on the crest of the hill; then she disappeared and all at once the very thick of the night closed about him. He became desperately lonely, even more so than when he had rolled out of New York, Boston-bound, on the night of the tragedy which had changed his life so utterly. All that he could do, at first, was to refresh the fire, but when it blazed most brightly it only served to make him conscious of the limitless dark around him, and of the chilly distance to the stars. He left the fire and went for a walk. Mustard would not follow at his heels as the pinto had followed the girl. He stumbled gloomily among the rocks and found no content. Then a new thought came to him when a wolf bayed far, far away, a terrible and lonely voice in the night. Other wolves might come. Maybe they were hungry.

Suppose, then, that danger should come upon her when she slept? Plainly it was his duty to guard her, and the thought warmed his heart. He hastened up the hill and went cautiously over the crest, for he must not alarm her with his approach. It needed half an hour of laborious searching. Then he made her out where she was rolled in her blanket in a sandy hollow surrounded by rocks; by leaning very close he could make out even the glimmer of her features and the whispering sound of her breath. He listened to it for a long time with an inexpressible delight; then he sat down with his back against one of the rocks and began his vigil.

The night grew cold; he sat his jaw and braved the chill from his blood. Sleep came upon him step by step, numbing his brain. He shook it off. There was an immense and quiet excitement in his heart with the feeling that he was serving her in this fashion, silently, unknown to her. Suppose, however, that among the soft shadows in the hollow below them a lurking wild beast should be stirring and should rush ravening upon them both? It made his blood run cold, but he gripped a heavy rock near by and weighed it in his hand. Such a missile would smash the skull of any living creature and for the sake of Frank, he told himself, his aim would surely be straight. All the loneliness had left him now. The very touch of the air against his face was friendly; the stars were familiar eyes above him. And when he tired of sensing these things, he could fall back upon rich stores of memory. Tucked into the corners of his mind there were infinite pictures, and even the sound of her voice, so plainly recalled that it vibrated through his body.

The rock put forth an angle which hurt his back; he shifted into a more comfortable position, his chin resting upon his breast, and almost instantly heavy sleep rolled over him. A vague feeling of guilt struggled against it for a moment; then he was lost.

He was wakened by the lifting of the hat from his head which allowed the level splendor of the newly risen sun to strike against his face and cover his eyes with a mist of red. When he looked up he found the girl standing before him, half stern, half astonished.

"What are you doing here?" she asked him bluntly.

"Oh," said he stupidly. "I'm so sorry I fell asleep. But I thought it would be better to be near you in case—in case something——"

"Jiminy, Al!" murmured the girl. "You come here to take care of me, maybe?"

He rose to his feet, a little red. "I thought it might be safer."

It seemed to him that a faintest gleam of a smile crossed her eyes, but it was gone at once.

"Let's hustle breakfast," said she. "I'm hungry as a wolf!"

CHAPTER 6

JIM JONES IS WANTED

Breakfast was finished and the saddling completed before the great problem came into the mind of poor Allan. How was he who could not sit the saddle on his horse to keep pace with the rider of the agile pinto? He told the girl with much dismay òf the difficulty, and her amazement was extreme.

"D'you mean to say," she breathed, "that you're travelin' with a hoss that you can't ride?"

"I'm trying to learn," said Allan. "I try her every morning and stay on a little longer each time."

"A hoss like that," said the girl, chuckling, "is like tobacco without no matches. Lemme see you try her out?"

He obeyed. There followed an earnest fight which lasted three exhausting minutes. But, at the end of that time, Mustard began to swing in a circle and slung poor Allan headlong from his seat.

"You see," he said as he staggered to his feet, "that it's better than it used to be. She used to knock me off.in a second."

The girl had not yet stopped laughing at the picture

of Allan tumbling head over heels in the sand. But now she dismounted from the pinto, fitted her toe into the stirrup of Mustard's saddle, and whisked into place as lightly as a bird. Allan stood agape with every muscle tensed, expecting to see her skyrocket through the air at any instant, afraid to shout a warning for fear that the noise might excite the mare. To his unspeakable amazement, Mustard merely tossed her head in the air and then jogged obediently off. She turned in a circle and came back.

"Let out the stirrup leathers on the paint hoss," called the girl, busily shortening those of Mustard. "You can ride pinto to-day."

"What did you do? How did you manage it?" panted Allan.

She looked him calmly in the face.

"Hosses is a good deal like rabbits," she told him. "You got to catch their eyes; then they're easy!"

It was an explanation which needed to follow the subject further. Besides, to be explained, but he was too mystified behind her eyes, behind her silence, he guessed at laughter which was bubbling very near to the surface. As for the pinto, he merely grunted and kicked a few times at the unexpected weight which dropped upon his back, but being as sturdy as he was fine looking, he presently shook his head in resignation and trotted off by the side of Mustard. Poor Allan was too full of bewilderment to talk for half an hour, and at length he put his state of mind into words clearly enough.

"There are a great many things which one can only learn from experience," he said. "I thought that the country would be simpler. But after all, I'm afraid it isn't."

"Except the girls," she suggested. "Which they're a lot easier to talk to in the country."

He considered her for a moment. He rarely answered a remark hastily or offhand, and now he concluded by shaking his head.

"If I had known you then as well as I know you now," said he, "I should never have dared to begin talking to you at all."

At this she broke into laughter. Mirth must have been stocked up in her for a long time, so hearty and so continued was her outbreak. But, since it was by no means the first time in his life that he had been laughed at, he did not mind the mockery. No doubt she was putting him down as a fool and a weakling, but at least there was no positive dislike in her manner. How little she thought of him as a man was revealed before long by her questions. She wanted to know how he expected to make his way in this wild country, and he answered that he had worked his way so far and hoped to be able to do so again. Could he handle a rope? Did he know anything of cows or sheep? He did not! What had he been doing up to this time? He had worked in the hay, loose and baled.

"Did you stand up under that?" she asked, and under her casual manner he could read her surprise.

"I managed it," said Vincent Allan a little tersely.

But, in his heart of hearts, he had a foolish and childish wish that she could have been present at Casey's when he had beaten Bud with a punch! In the late morning a rabbit jumped from behind a cluster of out-thrusting porphyry rocks at the top of a dike and raced across the path before them. He had a chance then to see her hypnotism. It came in the form of a Winchester snatched from the holster of the saddle on Pinto, which she leaned across like a flash to reach. She whipped it to her shoulder. He saw the muzzle slowly follow the flight of the rabbit for an instant, then the gun spoke and the poor victim leaped into the air and ran no more.

"The head, Al! The head, I guess!" cried the young savage and spurred Mustard furiously to the place. She had reached it, dismounted, and was holding up the prize in her hand when he came up.

"Look!" she cried, and he saw that the rifle bullet had passed clean through the head of the jack.

That was their noon meal when they made a dry camp, a short halt, and then pushed ahead once more. He asked her then how she had been able to learn to shoot so very well, and before she could answer she had to pause, squirming carefully down the trail.

"I'll tell you, Al," she said at last. "You get a look at the target through the sights—then you—you *wish* it dead, and pull the trigger!"

And her whole young body quivered with savage exultation. He wondered at that. Indeed, he went through the whole day with a continual bewilderment in his mind and the feeling that she was far, far beyond his mental horizon. That night he had indubitable proof that her feeling for him was only pity. For sitting beside the camp fire she opened her heart and told him that he was out of place in this region. He should go back to the cities in the East, where good-natured men had the law to take care of them. He saw her lip curl a little when she mentioned the law. It was plain that for her part she had little use for it; but for him she considered it a necessity.

That night was far different from the first one. He hardly closed his eyes from dark to dawn, so miserably did the sting of her contempt torment him; and if he dozed a few moments by chance, it was to dream of a wild centaur racing over the mountaintops with a brandished rifle in her hand and her laughter streaming down the wind behind her. Yet, when she was cooking breakfast the next morning, as if to baffle him the more, she showed him her first trace of real feminine weakness.

"Suppose when we get to El Ridal—suppose that Jim ain't there and that there ain't no trace of him. What'll I do?"

She made such a gesture of helplessness that his heart leaped in him, but at her new remark his heart failed him again. He asked when she expected to reach El Ridal, and she said that they must be there a little after noon of that day. That day, then, would be their last together, unless Jim failed to be there. Upon that possibility he set his heart. Before they started the day's ride he made a desperate effort to conquer Mustard and a little more of the girl's esteem, but it was not to be. Mustard turned himself into a figure eight and in half a minute shook her master dangling into empty space. When he stood up, the girl was not smiling; she was shaking her head in a slow disapproval.

"I'll never make a rider," said he hopelessly, and she only responded with a cold: "Oh, I dunno. Lemme try her again!"

She tried Mustard not only quietly, but with quirt and spurs. Mustard fought like a maddened thing. There was a five-minute struggle which left Allan staring and shouting; but Mustard was thoroughly beaten. The girl flung herself out of the saddle. The battle had shaken her terribly; her face was white and her eyes glaring, but she bit her lip and called up all her gallant spirit to keep herself from staggering when she walked.

"Try Mustard now," she said a little hoarsely. "I guess she's got the pepper out of her now!"

So up the trembling, sweat-dripping side of Mustard he climbed and settled himself gingerly in the saddle. Behold, there was not even a kick! Mustard flattened her ears, shook her head, and then accepted the inevitable. She had had enough out of one clinging piece of humanity that day; she wanted no further lessons. But if her spirit were crushed, that of Allan was completely broken. He who wished to appear as the protecting hero had been forced to accept charity, as it were, out of the hand of the lady of his heart. He groaned inwardly when he thought of it!

All morning they climbed through the foothills and into the mountains themselves. They journeyed through the cedar brakes of the hills; they came among the giant forests of pine where the beds of dead needles received the fall of hoofs with a softened crackling; and so they reached, by noon, the view of El Ridal.

Down the face of the mountain to the west a snow-fed torrent ripped its way, white with foam like a streak of snow itself, or shaken into veils of mist where it plunged over lofty precipices, and where the stream reached the foot of the mountain lay El Ridal at the head of a narrow valley with the dark hosts of the pines marching down to it on either hand. It was only a small village. Perhaps there were three-score buildings in it, and though they were still an hour's ride from the place, Allan could count every roof.

Down the steep trail they hurried, now, until the trail widened to a road, chopped into ruts and hollows by the wheels of buckboards, and so they raised the dust of the main street of the town itself. Before they entered it the girl drew rein.

"This here town," she said cautiously, reading his face, "has a lot of pretty hard men in it. Are you dead sure that you want to come in, Al? They got a way of talkin' with their guns!"

His humiliation was so great that he dared not look into her face.

"I'll take the chance," said Allan huskily, and so they went on side by side until they came before an old, unpainted shack of large proportions across whose front was inscribed the sign: "Empire Hotel."

The girl cried out at the sight of it. "That's Jim's headquarters!" she said. "I've always sent his mail care of the Empire."

"Wait here," said Allan, and dismounting from Mustard, he went inside.

Times seemed to be dull in the Empire. There was no lounger on the veranda in front. There was no one in the hallway which served as a lobby also, saving one fat fellow who leaned far back in his chair with his boots propped against the face of the tall stove which stood in in the center of the space.

"I wish to find the proprietor of the Empire," said Allan in his most pleasant voice.

The fat man ran a thumb beneath the single strand of a suspender which crossed his shoulder, sinking deep into the soft flesh.

"I'm him," said he.

"Then," said Allan, "perhaps you will be able to give me some information."

"P'r'aps," said the other.

"I wish to find Jim Jones," said Allan.

The proprietor kicked the door of the stove clanging open, and kicked it clanging shut again. Otherwise he made no answer.

"I wish to find Jim Jones," said Allan a little more loudly.

"Might you be a friend of hisn?" said an ominous voice, though the head still failed to turn toward him on the puffy neck.

The nature of Allan, as has been seen, was as mild as milk and honey, but something began to grow taut in him.

"Can you or can you not tell me where I may find Jim Jones?" he asked for the third time.

"Who wants to know?"

"A lady. His sister," said Allan.

The proprietor did not deign an immediate answer to this remark, but after a time he said deliberately: "I wish that all of Jim Jones' friends was in purgatory, where he'd find 'em soon!"

A film of red floated across the eyes of Allan, as though he were looking at the noon sun through closed lids. He leaned, put his hands on the arms of the proprietor's chair, and lifted him lightly around, chair and all. Then he repeated his question. The proprietor had turned purple, all his face puffing with fury, and his big, pudgy hand squashed over the butt of a Colt. But he did not draw the gun. He was considering another fact, which was that his weight, the last time he waddled onto a scales, was nearly two hundred and eighty pounds, that the chair in which he sat must weigh twenty pounds more, and that the man before him had raised all that clumsy burden as lightly as though it had been a stuffed toy and not a reality of flesh and fat. The proprietor thought of these things, and some of the blood departed from his face.

"Why might you want to know about Jim Jones?" he asked. And he studied the face of the other hungrily, curiously. It was not the face of a man of violence. And the eye which looked down to him was a mild and gentle an eye as ever looked forth from the brow of a maiden of seventeen who has not yet learned to doubt the world.

"I've already said that Jim's sister is here inquiring," said Allan.

"Dog-gone me if I don't hate to have ladies take long trips for nothin'," said the fat man, "but as sure as my name's Bill Hodge, she wasted her time. She ain't goin' to find no Jim Jones here!"

"He was here formerly, was he not?"

"He was."

"But he left?"

"He did."

"Do you know where he is now?"

"If I knowed, would I be sittin' here now? No, sir, I'd be hell-bendin' to get at him, and I wouldn't be ridin' alone. Nope, they's a sheriff an' a dozen other gents around this here town that's plumb anxious to see that young gent ag'in!"

The joyous, expectant face of Frances came before the memory of the other, and he asked sadly what her brother had done.

"Nothin' but beat me out of a month's room and board. That's all, aside from shooting the sheriff's boy, Charlie, and dog-gone nigh killin' him, and makin' us all waste horseflesh tryin' to catch him, an' stealin' a hoss from Hank Moon, an' most likely playin' in with Harry Christopher's gang of murderin' hounds! Outside of them things he ain't done nothin' to speak of!"

CHAPTER 7

ALLAN'S GREAT BLUNDER

Allan went back to Frances Jones with a singular mixture of outward gloom and inward happiness—selfish inward happiness because he was sure, now, that he would still have an opportunity to prove to her that he was a man in spite of all of his failings, and because no brother could take her suddenly away from him. She needed only one glance at his face; then she slipped from pinto and ran to him.

"What's wrong?" she cried in an excited whisper. "What's happened? Is Jim hurt?"

"No. He's sound and well," said Allan as cheerfully as he could.

But she stepped back with a groan of anguish.

"It's worse than that, then," she said instantly. "Jim has busted loose at last and tore things up. Is that it?"

"There's been a little trouble——"

"He's been drove out of town. I know! Oh, dad had it in him, but he got married young, and he fought it down inside of him. And now everything that he didn't do Jim'll be doin' for him—an'—an' I wish I'd never been born! I wish I'd never been born!"

Her grief was so wild that Allan could not even attempt to comfort her. Sorrow in most women had always seemed to him very like sorrow in a child—pitiful, perhaps, but never tragic. But grief in Frances Jones was like grief in a man. No tears fell from her eyes, but her body trembled and her voice seemed to tear her throat.

When the spasm left her, she leaned a hand against a pillar of the veranda, still shaken, exhausted, despairing.

"What'll I do now?" she said, not appealing to him but to herself.

"We camp right here," said Allan. "There's very little chance that we'll be able to find him. If the other people in El Ridal knew where he was, they'd be out hunting for him. So it's plain that they can't tell us what we wish to find out. We can only wait here and hope that Jim will find out where we are and then try to come to see you. That's logical, I think."

She gave him a look of surprise, as though such intelligence in him startled her, but it was so plainly the only thing for her to do that she nodded.

"Except," she said, "that I'll have to sell the pinto to pay for my board."

"I've got enough to see you through a few days," he offered.

"I don't take no charity," said she coldly.

"It's not charity, you see, Jim will pay me back when he comes."

At least, there was nothing better for her to do than to accept for the time being, but when he had carried her roll of blankets up to the room which Bill Hodge grudgingly assigned to her, she hesitated at the door of the chamber with one hand upon the knob and the other laid lightly on his arm while she looked up into his face.

"Al," she said, "you're a square shooter—the squarest I ever seen."

And she slipped inside the room and shut the door in his face before he could make any answer. In the meantime, he had twelve dollars to support them both, and mountain prices ran high. For lack of a better source of information, he went straight to Bill Hodge.

Hodge, to his inquiry about work, squinted a pair of fat eyes at him. "What kind of work might you be able to do?" he asked. "Can you handle an ax or work a drill and a single jack, or ride herd, or——"

"I know nothing about these things," confessed Allan. "But if I can do something which needs only patience and strong hands, I'll do my best. Is there such work around El Ridal?"

It was impossible for Bill Hodge to believe him. Men who talked a pure form of English and looked one in the eye as they spoke, did not ask for mucking jobs. He thought it wise to wink at the young man and tell him that the sort of work he was looking for would come along in due time.

"Them that want work always get it, he said. And them that want trouble," he added significantly, "mostly get what they want, too!"

Upon this wise suggestion Allan brooded for some time. Then he started out on a tour of the village, but a rumor had spread with the mysterious speed of whispers before him. No one needed his two strong hands, it seemed. He came to the blacksmith who was cursing an inefficient helper and letting the latter hold the tongs while he himself worked with the sledge.

"Can you use another man?" asked Allan from the doorway.

"Man?" thundered the blacksmith, shaking his gray head, darkened almost to black by the soot which had collected on it. "There ain't no men in these days. The old brand of men has gone out of style. They got nothin' but clipped coins circulatin' these here days!"

"I don't know what you mean," said Allan mildly.

The blacksmith waved his helper toward the forge with the bar of iron on which they had been working.

"You don't know!" sneered the smith, whose gray hairs gave him liberty of speech. "You're like the rest of the young men of these here days. You don't want to know. Sweat ain't honest enough for the young gents, and the old ones has busted their backs raisin' a flock of good-for-nothin's! How tall was your dad?"

To that sudden question Allan answered that his father had been an even six feet in height.

"That's it! He was six feet! What're you? Old story— they've shrunk up. Nothin' but runts, these days, and them that are big are weedy! Look yonder by the door. I was a young man when that barrel was put there, son, with as much scrap iron in it as there is right to-day, and no more. I wasn't more'n thirty, then, and El Ridal wasn't no more'n a pup of a town. Well, sir, I took hold on that there barrel and lowered it down by myself clean out of the back of the wagon that brung it. Where's there a man in El Ridal to-day that can budge it? Where's there a man?"

Just then the thrill of his own might ran warm in the arms of Allan. He stooped and fixed his grip on the barrel. His knees sagged, his shoulders gave, then straightened, and the barrel rose from its settled place in the floor, rose with clots of moist dirt clinging to its bottom. It ascended until it was waist high. Then the bottom burst and the iron junk rained upon the floor.

The blacksmith had run forward with a shout of amazement; he halted in mid-stride and stared at the youth who had torn to shreds the pride of his own herculean youth. For in the old days the might of the blacksmith had been a thing of wonder, and men had traveled many miles to look upon him. Still, in his gesture, there was revealed a speaking suggestion of the power which had once clothed his arms and of which age had robbed him. He looked upon Allan, now, as though that youth had been personally guilty of the crime. But his ill humor left him almost at once. Like most men who work with their hands and feel the curse of Adam in the actual sweat of the brow, there was a broad vein of honesty in him, and now he began to nod as he looked at the young man.

"Takes an exception to prove a rule," he said not unkindly. "But what might you be looking for with me, friend?"

"Work," said Allan.

The other smiled and then shook his head, "I've heard tell about you, partner," he said. "Friend of Jim Jones ain't here in El Ridal lookin' for the kind of work that I can give 'em to do. The pay is too slow."

With that cold comfort he sent Allan away, and the latter went back to the hotel. Affairs were now serious indeed, for his funds could not hold out for more than two days at the most, considering that he had the girl to provide for as well as himself. At supper they sat at the end of the long table which the Empire Hotel set out for its guests, and he told her nothing of his unlucky adventures. There were half a dozen others at the table, all rough-dressed, rough-mannered men, but Allan could not help but admire their tact. They were hungry with curiosity concerning the sister of Jim Jones, yet they veiled their glances and seemed to study her from the corners of their eyes only. Had she possessed nothing but her pretty face, she would have been stared at in any other place, he thought, but here they treated her as carefully as though she were an old woman! He observed these things and admired. But he had little room in his heart to pay attention to them. He was himself full of the subject of Frank, and full of the face which smiled at him across the table. He was full of the charm of her grace, of the slenderness of her round wrists, and of the taper delicacy of her fingers. He was full, too, of that strength of mind which kept her from so much as mentioning her anxiety for her brother. His name never came upon her lips; not even a shadow of trouble was allowed to appear in her eyes. For all her bluntness and her carefree ways he felt what he had felt before—the very aroma and radiance of gentility.

They sat together on the veranda after supper, in a far corner, away from the rumbling voices of the men. They spoke seldom, because of the trouble in the heart of the girl, and because of the content which was growing in the heart of Allan, for he could feel them growing closer and closer together; he could feel her thought resting upon him and tuning toward him. Once she said: "After all, Al, a woman is pretty weak, I guess."

He could finish the rest of that sentence to his own satisfaction, and finish it he did. When she said good night, he still remained on the veranda, lost in thought, brooding on the rough-headed mountains where they pressed up among the white hosts of the stars, and listened to the far-off rumble of El Ridal falls, a tremor which was felt by the mind rather than heard by the ear.

Afterward he went for a stroll, because there were so many things in his heart that he could not keep them to himself and felt that, before long, he should have to talk to his nearest neighbor, uninvited. Once or twice he walked up and down in front of the hotel. Then he turned away and entered the trees which filled the empty lot at its side. And here it occurred to him that from this place he could see the very window of her room. It gave him a foolish thrill of happiness. He checked it off from the front of the building—the third from the very end, now vacant of any glow from within—a black rectangle glittering with a single starry high light. He saw that, and he saw in the next moment a dark form of a man climbing the side of the building. He had barely cleared the ground, and his destination might be any one of half a dozen windows, but all that Allan thought of was that the window of the girl's room was just above the head of the stranger.

It did not occur to him to make an outcry. Or even had he wished to do so, he was possessed of such a fury of anger that it filled his throat and choked him. He raced straight for the hotel, caught a dangling foot just as it reached up for a fresh hold, and plucked the night wanderer to the ground.

The fallen man leaped from the ground with a cry, and Allan saw the dim wink of steel in the starlight. He had no time to see more. The fastest of all gunmen could not draw a weapon as fast as the naked fist can strike, and the fist of Allan was already on the way. It landed somewhere on the body of the man and sent the stranger reeling away. His gun exploded; a bullet sang into the distance; and then Allan had him in his hands.

He had no thought in his mind except that this fellow might have intended to reach the room of the girl, and that thought filled him with a brutish desire to rend limb from limb. He fumbled for a hold, found it, and felt the form beneath him go limp while many voices turned the corner of the building and rushed toward him. They swarmed about him and lifted him up; his victim came with him.

"Jim Jones!" cried some one. "It's Jones, sheriff!"

That name had turned Allan sick and weak, and he staggered back from them, relaxing his grip. He saw a little man, with a tuft of gray beard, leaning above the prostrate figure on the ground.

"I thought this gent was a friend of Jones," he heard the little man muttering, "but if we hadn't got here pronto, boys, Jim Jones would of been so doggone dead that a rope around the neck couldn't of done no more for him."

He straightened and faced Allan. "You get the reward for this, son," he said. "Was that the game that you was playing with the girl?"

Allan could not answer. She, too, would think that. She, too, would feel that he had been playing a game, and for a reward collected on the head of her brother!

CHAPTER 8

TO RESCUE

They carried the limp form of Jim Jones to the veranda
of the hotel, and there they laid him down. The sheriff
had handcuffed the wrists of his prisoner and removed
no less than two pairs of revolvers from his person. Thus
stripped of weapons and secured, they seemed to feel far
more at ease, but even so they were restless, and Allan
could see them peering up and down the street as though
they expected a rescue party to rush upon them at any
moment. For his own part, he was busy only in watching
the face of the unconscious man. There was no doubt as
to his relationship with the girl. There were the same finely
made features, the same nervous, clearly cut lips, the same
bigness of eye, the same resolute square to the chin, the
same curling blond hair. But whereas the girl was small
even for a woman, her brother was big even among men,
a strong, lithe body which seemed formidable even in this
utter repose. A purple splotch covered his throat. There
was no doubt where the terrible grip of Allan had rested
upon him.

Now he stirred, opened his eyes, and groaned. They

waited for no further recovery, but lifted him at once and with a man on either side, the sheriff walking with drawn gun behind, they escorted him toward the jail.

It was a little frame shack which contained two cells made of steel bars and a small office in front which was used by the sheriff as his place of business. In one of the cells they placed young Jim Jones who, from the time his memory had returned to him, had not uttered a syllable.

"What will happen to Jones?" asked Allan of the sheriff.

The latter made an unmistakable gesture, as of arranging a noose around his neck.

"Hanging!" breathed Allan, full of horror.

"I'll tell a man!" said the sheriff. "Now, you'll be wantin' to know when you get that reward, son. That'll be fixed up inside of two or three——"

"Darn the reward!" burst out Allan, and hurried from the jail, feeling that he would stifle if he remained longer within its walls.

At the very door he met Frances Jones, white, anxious, and in haste. There was no doubt that she had heard what had happened; there was no doubt that she had learned his part in the capture, for she gave him a look of horror and of scorn as she passed, that withered on his lips the words he would have spoken. He stumbled out into the night trying to bring this matter right in his own mind, but the more he thought of it the more he cursed his own stupidity.

He should have guessed who that stranger was, climbing the wall of the hotel. It was the very thing which he had himself suggested. The news of his sister's arrival would bring down Jim Jones to the town to see her; that had been his idea. It was only that the coming of Jim was so sudden that he had been unable to believe that the stranger might be he.

In the meantime, El Ridal was coming to life. There was a humming and a murmuring throughout the town. People appeared in clusters, here and there, wandering toward the jail, and fragments of their talk came to the ears of Allan. It was he of whom they were all talking. They had learned of his feat in the blacksmith shop that afternoon; they linked it with his capture of Jim Jones and made him out a Hercules. He sat down behind a tree to try to fumble his way through this misty difficulty, and as he sat there he heard two voices approach and pass him on the farther side.

"He looked," said one, "like a doggone tenderfoot."

"Tender the devil!" said the other. "That gent is a detective. You can lay to that. A darn foxy game he played, too. He meets up with Jim's sister. He's got an idea that she's tryin' to meet her brother. So this gent, Vincent, they call him, lays low to grab Jim when he shows. And doggone me if he ain't done it. He'll make a nice bit of money out of that!"

"It was a low thing to do!" cried the other of the two.

"Sure," said his companion, "he ain't nothin' but a skunk with a strong pair of hands. But did you hear what he done to Jim Jones in about five seconds?"

"Near tore him in two, I understand."

"I seen Jim afterward. Looked like a grizzly had been pawin' him."

The two drifted farther down the street, and their voices became an indistinct blur in the ears of the listener; he had heard enough and more than enough. If those who were only strangers to Jim Jones felt like this about him, what a white fury must be that of the girl? She would never forgive him—a thousand times never! Not unless he should take Jim out of the danger into which he had thrown him. Not unless he should bring Jim safely from the jail where he was now locked.

Of course that was to ask for a miracle which could not be performed!

He began to walk up and down behind the southern row of houses which straggled along the main street of El Ridal. Half a dozen times he measured the distance back and forth; then he came back wearily into the street itself, intent only on reaching the hotel and getting into his bed before anyone could see him. When the morning came, a long rest might have brought an idea into his mind. He passed the jail on the way and found it quiet at last, with only a single light burning in the front window of the little shack. But when he came to the hotel he found that another center of interest had been found. It was a tall bay stallion which stood in the street, flattening its ears at the strangers who pressed so closely around it, sometimes dancing with its hind feet, as though preparatory to lacing out with them. It was a glorious animal, mounted with a fine saddle and with a profusion of chased gold on the bridle and saddle.

"No wonder," said Bill Hodge, "that them rascals that hang out with Harry Christopher can jump down here on us and then get away again without our bein' able to catch 'em. They put enough money into hossflesh. That there hoss might be a racer, from the lines and the legs of him! What becomes of him?"

The voice of the sheriff made answer: "He stays right yonder in your stable till we get young Jim Jones sentenced. Then we'll put the horse up for auction."

All of this was enough and more than enough for Allan. He went sadly away through the night to ponder the problem over again from the start. An irresistible attraction brought him back to the little jail, and there he peered through the barred window and saw the captive seated on his cot, holding a cigarette with his iron-bound hands and even whistling a tune as he finished the smoke and dropped it under his heel. He seemed to Allan the best-looking, the finest-spirited, the most courageous man he had ever seen. And that he himself should have betrayed such a fellow into the hands of a law which would destroy him was indeed too terrible! All the labors of a long life could never unbalance such a calamity. He would owe the world a debt which he could never repay if he were the agent of the fall of Jim Jones.

These were the heavy thoughts of Allan as he went back toward the hotel again. He found all quiet there by this time. The gossips had at last scattered. Only one light burned in the whole face of the big, rambling structure, and all the other windows were blank and black. Allan, entering, went softly up the stairway and came to the door of the room of Frances. There was no sleep for her on this terrible night, of course, and her door was raggedly framed with pencilings of yellow lamplight. All the money that remained to him he put together, folded it thin, and slipped it cautiously under the door. Then he withdrew in a panic, his heart in his mouth, expecting the door to fly open before him at any instant and the girl to be raging at him. To her he was a traitor, the coldest and the most malignant of scheming traitors, and he dreaded meeting her more than he would have dreaded the passage through a living wall of flames. But fate was kind to him in this instance.

He went from the hotel to the barn, and there he saddled Mustard first, and afterward the magnificent horse of Jim. Then he led the pair behind the houses until he reached a cluster of saplings near the jail, where he left them. Mustard would stand so long as her reins were thrown. That was almost the only good feature among her manners. And the stallion he tethered to Mustard. There remained nothing, now, except to storm the fort itself, and he looked sadly and gravely down from the hillside where he stood toward the little squat shadow of the jail.

Two expert warriors, two gallant men of gun and battle, were seated in the sheriff's office to guard the prisoner, and guard him they would with the last drop of their blood. Even one of them would have been too much for Allan to master, he felt, for all his strength could be made into nothing and unstrung by the touch of a single bullet. They were men of fire and steel; he was a thing of wood which they could easily blast from existence.

He took note, before he started, of the blue blackness of the sky, of how the mountains were roughly sketched in with spotted lines of stars, of how the great, soft masses of black forest curved in around El Ridal, and of how El Ridal river flashed and rumbled in the distance, springing down the breast of the mountain.

Allan begán to grow cold. Where would the bullet strike, and how would it feel tearing the flesh or smashing through bones? He thought of all the faces of all the men and women and children who had ever come within the narrow circle of his small life. He saw them clearly, and a sneer of scorn seemed to be upon the lips of all, and their eyes were blank with indifference. If the men in the branch bank where he had served so long could have heard of his fall, they would only smile and shrug their shoulders and declare that a house dog should not try to be a wild wolf! That was what they would say, and having said it they would forget him. However, they would never know. All that the world would hear was that an obscure young man who called himself Allan Vincent had perished while attempting to liberate an outlaw from the jail.

He looked still further. He saw his grave dug. He saw his body carried unhonored to the place and lowered into the eternal cold and wet and darkness of the pit. But with that, the first warm glow of light came across his mind. For beside his grave there would be at least one sincere mourner, and that would be the girl with tears in her eyes and sorrow in her heart for she would know by the very act of his last moment of life that he had not willingly betrayed poor Jim.

With that last picture to cheer him, Allan felt a sort of glory fall upon him. It became so ridiculously easy to die that he almost laughed aloud, and indeed he was smiling steadily as he passed through the darkness toward the jail.

CHAPTER 9

ALLAN GETS GUN PRACTICE

Since the events of that night have become of historic interest and since the tale is told over and over again with many variations, it is well to be most careful and begin at the foundation of the narrative, that is to say, with the two men who, on that night, sat guard over the person of Jim Jones.

It may be taken for granted that they were not ordinary fellows. Even had Jim Jones no allies in the town, he would have been guarded with particular care lest he should have broken his way through the rotten bars of the El Ridal jail. But Jim Jones was not unaided or unseconded. Certainly he had allies in the very town itself, since it could only have been through a townsman that news of the arrival of his sister had been brought to him. Friends he had in the town, then, and outside of the town it was freely rumored that he had most efficient helpers who were no other than the ruffians who rode at the bidding of infamous Harry Christopher. Such friends as those villains made to one another were to be dreaded by all who tampered with a single member of the gang. Men were not sure, but it was guessed that Jim Jones must be one of the crew. Therefore the extra precautions were taken to guard the prisoner. Under all ordinary circumstances, either Walter Jardine or Elias Johnston would have been considered more than ample security for the safety of any prisoner, or of any half dozen prisoners, for that matter.

For they were both famous as men of war; each distinguished as an upholder of the law, dauntless in the face of all odds. Each was many times proven. Neither had ever been beaten in fair fight, and among the citizens of El Ridal it could be said that no three of the fiercest and the most determined gun fighters could have stood for a moment against these two warriors. Such were the two against whom Allan was now proceeding.

He rapped at the door of the jail which was presently opened, and there stood before him, dim in the shadow, a small man with a thin face of which the only important feature was a very long and thin nose whose end was a brilliant red—a color so intense that it was almost painful. He recognized the visitor at once and nodded to him with a grin.

"I been waitin' for you to show up, Al Vincent," he said. "Dog-gone modest for you to keep away while the crowd was hangin' around, I'd say!"

He waved Allan inside.

"I'm Elias Johnston," he said by way of introduction. "I'm mighty glad to meet up with the gent that caught Jim Jones. I always been figuring that it would take a whole crowd of us to land that Jones. Here comes a stranger and takes him with one hand, might say!"

His admiration was wholly genuine and unaffected. He was a little man, hardly above five feet in height, and as thin as he was short, but short time as he had been in El Ridal, Allan had heard of some of the feats which those bird-claw hands had accomplished, and he regarded the little man with the glistening nose and the pale eyes with much admiration.

"I was lucky," he said frankly to Elias Johnston. "Besides, if it had come to a gun fight, I could have done nothing. I know nothing about guns."

Elias stared at him as, in another part of the country, one would stare if an apparently cultivated gentleman, announced that he was unable to read or write, or signed his name with a cross. So Elias stared at Allan, blinking, abashed, unable to speak. Finally he said weakly: "Come on inside. My old partner, Walt Jardine, is inside."

Presently Allan stood before the second and the greater of the pair. He was a round dozen years younger than Johnston. He was in his early twenties, but his record was already long as a man of violence. From beneath a smooth, rounded forehead a pair of dull eyes, like the eyes of a bull in a quiet moment of grazing, looked forth at Allan. And even the great president of the bank in the midst of his highest burst of eloquence had never seemed so formidable or so great to Allan as did this rudely clad cow-puncher hardly out of his teens.

"Here's the gent that caught Jim," said Elias Johnston. "He tells me that he got Jim by luck, Walt."

Walter Jardine smiled. His smile made his face seem foolishly fat. Then his smile changed to a chuckle, and the laughter forced out the thick blue veins upon his forehead and along his throat. He heaved out of his chair, squat, huge of torso, and yet with a wonderful springiness of foot. For after all, the very greatest of all sprinters are heavy, low men. So it was with Walter Jardine. Allan felt of him that there was no feat beyond his power. Their hands met, and over his fingers those of Jardine closed

68

softly, more firmly, with increasing pressure, then as his own grip began to resist, Jardine used all his might—a might which made his right arm quiver to the shoulder. And he said to Allan at the same time: "I'm mighty glad to see you, Vincent. I guess it ain't luck that landed Jones here. I've heard about what you done in old Dan Marberry's shop with the barrel of junk iron."

So he spoke, holding the hand of Allan as though in great cordiality, so that Elias Johnston looked on with smiling pleasure to see this kindly greeting between two men so famous for physical might. He could not detect the stir and quiver of laboring muscles up the forearms, drawn taut and more taut until they threatened to tug the tendons out of place. It only lasted for an instant, after all—that strange trial of strength. Then Allan, who only now understood the game which Jardine was attempting to play with him, closed his hand steadily, easily—as one might close one's hand through resisting butter. So he pressed the power out of the famous right hand of Walter Jardine and made it relax and brought the metacarpal bones crunching together. In another effort he could have broken them, perhaps. But now, when resistance had ceased, he also ceased, and without a word released the hand of Jardine.

The latter instantly shoved his right hand into his pocket and sat down, whistling a tune. But above the puffed cheeks and the merry run of the notes his eyes were like those of the bull which lifts its head from the grass and sees, far off, the leader of a rival herd breaking down the fence and coming into its own preserve.

All of these things came about in the passage of ten seconds, in quietness, and the murmur of pleasantly spoken words, but Allan knew that he had gained for himself the most implacable of enemies. Something moist in the palm of his own right hand made him look down. It was a red smear of blood, not his own, but blood which had spurted from the finger tips of Walter Jardine!

"Dan Marberry will never get over havin' his best story spoiled—about what a dog-gone strong man he was when he was a kid! No, sir, he'll never get over that!"

How grateful was Allan to Johnston for making talk

during that brief interim when neither he nor Jardine was able to speak!

"But, take it by and large," went on Elias Johnston, "dog-gone me if I see how a gent like you, that can do the other things you've done, can get on without knowin' how to handle a gun!"

"Ah!" murmured Walter Jardine. "Ain't you much with a gun, Vincent?"

"I have never so much as fired one," said Allan.

"And you wear no gun now?" said Jardine, staring.

"No."

"With Harry Christopher and his gang lyin' low an' waitin' for a chance to get at you? Vincent, El Ridal ain't no place for you! You better be movin' along!"

"Wait!" said Elias Johnston. "Take this here Colt, partner. Take a grip on it. No! Dog-gone me if it ain't easy to see that you never handled guns before! Hold her like you loved her. You can't dance good with a girl that wants to hold you off at arm's length. Ain't that right? You got to get sort of close. Well, old son, it's that way multiplied with ten with a gun. You got to grab onto 'em. Squeeze that butt like you was shakin' hands with the best friend you ever had in the world. And you can lay to it, that a sweet, clean, straight-shootin' Colt like that one is as good a friend as anything that ever wore flesh. It's a silent friend; all the talkin' that it does is right to the point!"

He laughed as he spoke, and in the meantime, he was arranging the hand of Allan on the butt of the revolver, arranging it with the utmost care, and at the same time qualifying his first instructions. The gun was to be held firmly, but not with such a strain that the muscles of the forearm would begin trembling or twitching.

"The main part of usin' a gun, some folks say, is ten years practice. I ain't one that agrees with 'em. Ten years of *wrong* practice ain't worth one week of *good* practice. And that's a fact. They's two things needed by nacher—an eye that can see straight to a mark, and a hand that ain't got no shaking in it—a hand like the hand of Al Vincent. Look at that, Walt!"

Allan was holding the weapon out at arm's length when

his instructor stepped back with an exclamation of surprise and admiration.

"Look how steady that is, Walt! Look at the streak of the light along the barrel. There ain't no tremble to that line of light. That gun is more steadier'n rock!"

Walter Jardine had leaned forward out of his chair. He now removed his right hand from his pocket. The blood had been wiped from the fingertips, but the entire hand was swollen and discolored by the terrible grip of Allan. Jardine hastily returned the hand to hiding, and shifting a little in his chair he dropped his left hand upon that hip of the gun which hung upon that hip. For he was a two-gun man, in the true sense of the term. That is to say, many wear two guns for the sake 'of having a second to fire when the first is emptied, but how many are there who can fire accurately with both hands at the same time? It was this ambidexterous talent of Jardine which made him celebrated among his compeers as a dreadful fighter indeed. He now studied the steady hand of Allan with a sort of hungry interest.

"He's steady," he admitted presently.

Johnson looked sharply at his partner, surprised at the apparent reluctance which was in the voice of the younger man.

"He's steady," said Jardine again with a little more heartiness, "but how fast is he?"

"Give him time to learn how to pull a gun."

A faint and disagreeable smile came upon the lips of the other. He took from the wall a cartridge belt with a revolver hanging in the holster. This he buckled about the hips of Allan. Then he stepped back.

"They's a man with two guns standin' in the doorway right behind you ready to fill you full of holes! Stop him, Vincent!"

At that sharp cry of Jardine, with a little start of fear, although he knew well enough, reasonably, that it was a test and not a fact, Allan wheeled and snatched the Colt from the holster. It seemed to him that he acted both smoothly and swiftly, but before he had finished wheeling or dragging the Colt forth, the rapid voice of Johnston was barking: "Dead! Dead! Dead! Dead! Turn back ag'in, Al. Nope, you ain't fast! You don't think that way"

"What should I have done?"

"Dropped flat for the floor, twistin' over while you fell, twitchin' out the gat while you was in the air, and firing once or twice before you ever hit the boards. That's what a real fast man can do. That's what I've seen Walt Jardine do. Of course you ain't had practice. But still you're slow. You'll always be slow."

He shook his head sadly, as though the masterpiece which he had guessed at and which he had been striving to realize as a fact, had now been blurred and spoiled past all recovery.

As for Walter Jardine, the disagreeable smile was at the corners of his lips again, and his bold eyes looked through and through Allan as though he were saying to himself: "This fellow has strong hands, but what do the strongest hands in the world matter compared with a a forty-five caliber slug in action—or six slugs flying all at once!" Such were doubtless the thoughts of Jardine, but little Elias Johnston was already upon another track.

"Speed ain't the main thing, Walt."

"What is, then? A kind heart, old-timer?"

"Don't get hard. I say, straight shootin' is bettern's slow shootin'."

"But straight fast shootin' is better'n straight slow shootin'!"

"Sure, but is there any gent that can really be sure of where his guns are workin' when he's makin' a fast play?"

There was a little pause.

"I reckon there is," said Jardine soberly at last.

His companion shrugged his shoulders.

"I seen a time when Laurie Blackmore and Tom Gant and Bill Greening and some of their pals was all throwed into one saloon up on old Gaffney Creek about five year back when that little gold rush started—I mean the time they started for gold and didn't get none! Well, havin' rushed and got nowheres, they was all set for trouble, and when the lot of 'em was jammed into one room it was like putting giant powder into a fire. They exploded.

"I was about two blocks away. The shootin' kep' up all the time that I was running to the saloon. Must of been two hundred shots fired. When I got through the doors, the crowd had scattered. The saloon was wrecked. The mirrors was junk. The windows was bashed out. Even the flooring was all splintered up, not sayin' nothing of the ceiling bein' all raked across.

"One man was sittin' in a corner, tyin' up a cut in his left arm where a slug had grazed him. There was a dead dog in another corner.

"There's what come of fast shootin'. A dozen gents that had used guns all their lives was jammed into one room. They all started out to massacre everybody else as fast as they could pull their triggers. All they done was to bust furniture—and kill one dog! Yet there wasn't a man there that couldn't of killed three men in six seconds if he'd took his time. Nope, slow work can be the best work. You're slow, Al. Maybe you'd ought to be glad of it!"

At any rate, in that speech he had given to Allan the nickname which clung to him ever after.

CHAPTER 10

ON THE BACK OF MUSTARD

Such a conclusion would by no means be accepted by a man so famous for the lightning celerity of his draw combined with amazing closeness in shooting. Jardine frowned and shook his head.

"Besides," he said, "they ain't one man in twenty that can work slow without losin' his nerve. Suppose that you and me was to fight. You're fast as chain lighnin', say, and I'm mighty slow. Before I get my gun unlimbered, you've planted a couple of slugs in me, or else I've heard one slug chew into the floor and another whistles by my ear. Maybe you think that'll help me a lot? Maybe you think that I'll be able to take a cool, easy aim, partner? Nope. I'll tell you what, Elie, the gent that's fast with the draw has always won out nine times out of ten, and he'll keep right on winnin'."

"I ain't denyin' that," said Elias Johnston slowly. "I guess that you got the right of that, old-timer. But hear me what I say: If there was a man that took his time, that stayed all calm and cool and didn't tighten up none when the time for the fight come, he'd kill the fast gent nine times out of ten. Am I right?"

"You're askin' for a gent that ain't been born yet and that never will be born," insisted Jardine. "They ain't nobody that can stand up to close gun fire without startin' in to dodge."

"I dunno," said Elias. "I couldn't. Maybe you couldn't. But they's a terrible lot of queer folks in this little old world, son. You don't want to forget that. Wait a minute. It's time to take a walk around the shack and see that all's clear. I'll be back in a jiffy, and we'll talk some more."

So saying, he planted a sombrero on his head and swung away through the door; his heels tapped lightly on the front steps; and then the sand could be distinctly heard gritting under his feet as he walked about the place. So flimsy were the walls of the jail and so small was the circuit around them that he would hardly pass out of hearing at the farthest point in his journey. But in the slight interval, Allan knew that he must make his attempt. He must make his efforts against Jardine while little Elias Johnston was away from the room. But Jardine alone was enough to puzzle him. He stared down at the floor, wondering how he could begin; and while he stared down, he felt the glance of Jardine fixed steadily upon his face, reading it rapidly, hating him with all his heart because of the defeat which he had suffered in that mute duel of strength a few moments before.

"Hear me talk, Vincent!" cut in Jardine at last. "They's something on your mind. What is it? What d'you want?"

At this, Allan looked up and he saw that the other was grinning in a savage mockery at him, as though all of his hopes were clear to Jardine and were despised by him. Only one retort, and that a brutal one, came into the mind of Allan.

"I was wondering when you would wish to shake hands again?" he asked.

The veins swelled again in the face of Jardine. "A darned trick!" he said. "But there's more than one trick in the world, old son!"

"Try with the left hand, then?" proffered Allan, rising.

"Darn your hands!" snarled Jardine, his fury now showing in the ferocity of his eyes. "Keep off from me, or I'll—"

He had no time to say more. The left hand which Allan had extended toward him and from which he had drawn back, now thrust out. The fingers condensed into a compact fist. The fist struck Jardine low on the ribs. Soft and casual as that blow seemed to be, it had behind it such crushing weight that it expelled the wind from Jardine's body and doubled him up. He clawed at his revolver with his sound left hand, but even as the fingertips touched the butt of the gun, he was struck heavily across the temple and dropped into darkness.

One half—and what seemed at the instant the greater half of Allan's work—was now accomplished. The famous Walter Jardine was helpless on the floor. It only remained to secure him completely and then to turn to the reception of little Elias. But there was very little time—hardly a moment in which to work. He managed to twist the victim upon his face, snap a pair of handcuffs over his wrists, and then wedge a bandanna between his teeth. So secured against any violent movement and against any warning outcry, he wheeled from Jardine and leaped to the door just as Johnston stepped inside.

There was no time for Johnston. The flying danger was already in the air, hanging above him and swooping irresistibly down at him as young Allan, desperate with haste and resolution, flung himself clear of the floor and swept at Johnston with extended arms. Yet in the tenth part of a second which remained to him, the little man thrust out a stiff left arm to ward off the attack and snatched out his revolver. His hard little bird-claw left hand struck sharply into the lunging face of Allan. But before his revolver was clear of the holster he was crushed under the avalanche.

At the first touch he ceased to struggle. He felt himself taken by hands which were not human—they were flexible steel. To wriggle against the grip of those fingers was simply to bruise one's flesh. Therefore, in another moment, he was secured by handcuffs exactly as his companion had been. He was placed against the wall. A rifle was laid between his legs and the legs of Jardine, who sat facing him. Then they were secured to the rifle with intricate lashings of many-folded rope. The gag remained in the teeth of Jardine. But with Johnston, Allan struck a bargain.

"Johnston," he said, "when I say that it makes me sick to have to do this, I hope you'll try to believe me. I had rather have injured almost any man than you."

Elias grinned and nodded, as much as to say: "This is really very foolish bluff, and what can it bring to you in the way of an advantage?"

"Give me your word that you will give no alarm," said Allan, "and I'll use no gag on you."

"That's fair," said Elias Johnston quietly. "But tell me what in the devil you're after, Al Vincent?"

"Where are the keys to the cell?" asked Allan.

"Yonder, in the right-hand upper drawer to the desk. But what the deuce do you want to do with the prisoner?"

Allan made no reply. He opened the drawer, found out his bunch of keys almost at once, and then went toward the cell room followed by the horrified, whispering voice of Elias Johnston.

"Al, you ain't goin' to do a murder on a helpless man?"

Allan went hurriedly through the doorway into the cell room, and there he saw Jim Jones rise stiffly from his cot at the sight of his captor. Allan had no time to examine facial expressions, however. His fingers had to fly, now in the trial and the selection of the right key to unfasten the cell door and the right key to unfasten the manacles which confined the hands and the legs of Jim Jones. In the meantime, the two most famous men of El Ridal sat in the adjoining room bound with ropes and with iron, but what would these avail for very long against their flaming wits as they struggled to gain freedom? There must be fast work indeed. He could only gasp as he rattled at the cell door: "Jones!"

"Well?" snarled the captive, his voice full of hate as he saw the man who had captured him.

"If I can get you out of this jail and put you on your horse, will you swear to do nothing thereafter except what I shall advise?"

"Is this a fake?" cried Jim Jones.

Allan opened the door to the cell at that moment, and, kneeling, he began to work at the irons which locked the ankles of the prisoner together. With two such famous men as the two who were now in the sheriff's office and with so much strong steel to contain and hold one man, surely El Ridal had done its best to keep its prisoner secure!

"Does it look like a fake?" asked Allan, thinking of the two fighters in the next room and trying key after key with desperate speed. "Promise me, Jones!"

"To do what?"

"Nothing except what I tell you to do after I get you out of this jail."

There was a gasp from the prisoner. "If you get me clean out of this," he panted, "I belong to you, partner, if you got any use for me!"

"Your word of honor?"

"My word of honor ten times over!"

The key turned in the lock. The ankles of Jones were free, and now the liberator turned to the handcuffs, but at the same time there was a knocking at the front door of the jail, and then a voice which called: "Hello, Walt Jardine! Johnston!"

The key turned; the handcuffs fell jangling to the floor.

"Now a gun—quick!" pleaded Jim.

"No shooting! Come with me!"

He led the way at a run out of the cell and to the rear window of the jail.

At the same time the front door slammed open and

77

there was a confused shouting from the front of the little building. The window itself was jammed. Jim Jones kicked the pane to smithereens and then slid through to the outside, and as Allan prepared to follow, he saw the door fly open which led into the sheriff's office. There stood the sheriff himself, and behind him another man. Their guns were out in a flash. Two reports boomed through the room, two heavy shocks struck against the wall inches from the body of Allan, but then he was through and stood on the ground beside Jim Jones. No matter how eager that man might be for freedom, he had waited for his liberator, true to his word, and the heart of Allan warmed suddenly to his companion. Perhaps Jim was guilty of all the crimes of which he was accused, but certainly there was a strength of loyalty in him which was worthy of the brother of Frances.

Allan began to run at full speed for the saplings where the two horses had been left. Behind them there was a sound of stamping feet, guns exploding, wild shouts. Someone slid through the window by which they had made their exit and raced in pursuit. Others were coming around the jail, yelling to rouse the town.

But in the meantime they reached the clump of saplings, and Allan groaned with dismay. The horses were not there!

It was the despair of a moment only. Then, very few yards away, he saw they had strayed slightly from the first spot. Jim Jones was instantly in the saddle upon the bay stallion. Allan scrambled onto the back of Mustard and was presently fighting a furiously bucking horse. Twice he almost lost his stirrups; twice he was nearly whipped from his place. Then the leader of the pursuit came shouting up and opened fire. It was the discharge of that gun which saved Allan, for, frightened, by the explosion, Mustard began to run as fast as her stout legs would bear her in the rear of the flying stallion.

CHAPTER 11

JIM'S STORY

They had not covered a quarter of a mile before the entire town seemed to have awakened and taken to horse behind them, so great was the uproar and the rush of hoof beats out of El Ridal, and the hopes of Allan fell every moment, for though Mustard might have iron endurance, she could not hope to escape the first burst of speed of many fast horses and determined riders who knew the ground which lay before them, even by starlight. Still, though the mare was slow, Jim Jones did not give up his rescuer. Twice he reined back beside the struggling mare and entreated Allan to urge her to greater effort.

"You ain't followin' a plough—you're ridin' for your life, partner!" cried Jim.

Which was not news to Allan, for he well could imagine that his shrift would be short if they could catch him. He brought the roan mare to the highest point of her efforts, but still it was not fast enough, and the men from El Ridal swarmed closer and closer.

To take them where speed would count less than strength, Jim had led the way straight up the steep side of Mount El Ridal. He now drove the bay stallion through a tall clump of shrubbery and dismounted, ordering Allan to do the same. When he obeyed, he found himself in a narrow triangle of level ground, a tiny shoulder of the mountainside with a deep dark gulf of black beneath them. No horse could descend that precipice. Not even a man could have climbed it save with the greatest effort. Yet toward the corner of the dropping-off place Jim Jones, calling upon Allan to follow, led his horse and presently disappeared!

But the yelling men of El Ridal were pressing in fast from behind, and it was as well to meet death in one way as another. So Allan went ahead, dragging the snorting, rebellious Mustard behind him until he discovered that the corner of the little plateau did not come to an abrupt end, as he had thought, but continued in a narrow ledge which ran around the corner of the mountain's shoulder and out of sight. Here was the explanation. It was plain that Jim had led the bay out of sight in this direction, and Allan prepared to follow.

It required all his courage to so much as set foot upon that dizzy path. It seemed to him scant inches wide, and it consisted of crumbling stone which threatened to roll underfoot or perhaps to break quite off. He could not have proceeded in any other situation, but with those riders yelling up the trail, he found the nerve to go on. With his right hand he led Mustard, snorting and trembling in the rear. With his left hand he gripped at the receding upper face of the cliff. So, leaning his weight inward, he went ahead with his teeth set and a sick feeling in the bottom of his stomach. Once his foot slipped. It was a scant half inch, but it seemed to take Allan halfway to eternity, and, glancing down he saw beneath him only the emptiness of air to receive his body, the polished ribs and jutting fragments of the cliff dripping with starlight, and far, far beneath the white streak of foaming water through the heart of the night. He had to stand through two or three deadly seconds before the trembling weakness left him and his brain cleared. Then he pressed ahead and in half a dozen strides turned the corner onto a level spot large enough to have built a house upon. There was Jim Jones, with the end of a cigarette pulsing through the dusk and putting two glinting high lights in the eyes of the bay stallion which stood nearby.

"Why are you stopping?" cried Allan. "Don't you hear them yelling up the trail? Every second counts! Why don't you go on?"

"Need wings to go on from this place," said Jim Jones calmly. "This here is a little trap that I happen to know about."

Allan could only gasp: "You're joking, Jim!"

"I ain't, though. I figured that we couldn't ride away from that gang with a slow hoss like Mustard. Thought that we'd dodge in here, let 'em swarm by, and when they got tired chasin' and yellin', we could slip out and keep on our trip."

"But does no one else know of this place?"

"Sure. Twenty-five men out of El Ridal most likely know about it."

Allan groaned. He could feel, already, the pressure of a muzzle against his ribs.

"Then we are lost, Jim. They'll be sure to come. Perhaps they're filing along the ledge now!"

"Maybe," admitted Jim with the most singular calm. "Maybe they're coming and maybe they ain't. It's all a chance. We couldn't get away with heels like Mustard to run with. Only thing that we could do was to sit tight and wait."

Waves of cold were passing through the body of Allan, but he did not exclaim again, for he was beginning to see that the whole thing had been done for his own sake alone, and it was a revelation in unselfish courage on the part of Jim. That he could have risked so much when freedom and safety were his by simply loosening the reins on the matchless bay stallion, seemed a wonderful thing to Allan; but after all, that was the sort of stuff of which his sister was made. From that instant it was impossible for him to believe that any crime of cruelty or brutality could really be charged against young Jones. There must be extenuating circumstances. Now Jim was explaining quietly that it was quite possible that many of the pursuers might think of searching the ledge and the little shut-up to which it led, but there was a fighting chance that they might not. Indeed the place was so well known that perhaps no one would credit the two of them with such folly as to take shelter in this trap.

There was hardly a doubt that this was the case, for now the hunt could be traced clearly as it wound up the mountain's face high, high above the place where they waited. A salvo of guns roared; then excited voices clamored; more guns exploded.

"They're killin' shadows, now," chuckled Jim Jones softly. "When they begin to do that, they're about ready to quit the trail."

"And then?" asked Allan humbly, seeing that the wisdom of this youth, about such matters, was far greater than his own.

"Then we'll go back along the ledge, climb onto the hosses, and start ridin'. But lemme know how you managed to get to me in the jail that way? I thought there was two in the sheriff's office? I thought that them two was Jardine and Johnston? Was I wrong?"

"They were there," said Allan. He paused a little, thinking back to all the emotions with which he had approached the jail, expecting death. This was surely far better than death—to sit back in the lap of the mountain watching the stars and listening to the muttering of the river beneath them. "But while I was talking to them," he went on, "Johnston went out to walk around the jail and see that no friend of yours attempted to come up to the building from the outside, do you see? As soon as he was gone, I saw that I had my opportunity, and I was able to take it. I knocked down Jardine, handcuffed and gagged him—"

"Knocked down Jardine!" cried the other in astonishment which was almost consternation. "Knocked down, Jardine! Handcuffed and gagged him!"

"And just as I finished, Johnston came in. Of course, he is so small and I was taking him by such surprise that it was easy to master him. After that I took the keys—"

"Him bein' so small. So's a rattlesnake small! You took on them two one another and cleaned 'em up—with your bare hands, Al?"

"Of course," said Allan. "I can't use a gun, you know."

To this his companion returned no remark, and they sat for a time in quiet listening to the noise of the pursuit which was spending itself far up the mountain. Small groups of horsemen, besides, were hurrying up from El Ridal, and to any one of these it might occur to search the trap.

"When we leave the trap, where do we go?" asked Allan.

"Al, have you heard of Harry Christopher? He'd be mighty glad to have you with him!"

There was an exclamation from Allan. "I've heard of him. He's the last man we'll join, Jim. We'll simply ride out of this section of the country—"

"I can't, Al."

"I have your word," said Allan slowly.

The other groaned. "Al," he said, "dog-gone me if I ain't a skunk, but when I told you that I was your man for keeps I sure forgot somebody that come before you. I've swore to Harry Christopher that I'd do what he said for this year—ride, or fight, or—"

"Or steal?" said Allan heavily.

"Or steal," admitted Jim with a sigh.

"Jim, tell me how you happened to join such a fellow as Harry Christopher?"

"I'll tell you the whole thing. It's a bad mess; but I'll keep nothin' back."

He made a pause, rolled another cigarette, and in the interim a squirrel which had been disturbed in its sleep, chattered angrily from a stunted pine which clung to the steep mountainside above them.

"It come out of gambling," said Jim gloomily, at last. "When I hit El Ridal first I was doin' fine, savin' my money, hopin' to be some sort of a help to the folks back home. But then I learned poker, and that was my finish. Every month my pay went across the table to some gent that had slicker fingers or better luck than I had. And there was always some such gent around. I got in deeper and deeper. Same time I was payin' attention to Marie Prevost. Maybe you heard about her in El Ridal?"

"I was there only a few hours, you know."

"Mostly you hear about Marie before you been there ten minutes. Marie Prevost is the queen of the town. One look at her would make you plumb happy for a half a year. And that ain't exaggeratin'."

He said it soberly, and the face of Frances rose in the mind of Allan. He could well understand how one glimpse of a woman could make a man happy, or wretched, for half a year.

"Things between me and Marie was goin' along fine," said Jim, "until I met up with her brother at a card game one night. I had a bit of luck while he was playin'. In an hour I cleaned him out of five hundred bucks and busted him flat. He left, lookin' black and fumblin' at his gun, but I'd seen gents do that before, and it didn't mean nothin' to me. I kept on playin', and they cleaned me out just as bad as I'd cleaned out Charlie in the beginnin'.

"That was that. The next night I went to call for Marie to take her to the dance over to the schoolhouse, and while I was sittin' downstairs waitin' for Marie to finish the powderin' of her nose and the last tryin' out of her smiles, down comes Charlie.

"When he seen me he give a start, like he stepped on a tack.

"'Might I ask,' said he, talkin' real soft an' mean, 'what you're waitin' for here, Jones? You got a line on one of the hired men that's got a chunk of money to lose?'

"It was considerable talk to take from anybody, but I managed to swaller it. Him bein' the brother of Marie, I'd of let him just about walk on my face, for that matter. I told him that I wasn't there to make any trouble; I says that he'd lost his money fair and square the night before, just the way I'd lost mine after he left the place.

"'They's kinds and kinds of crooks,' says he at that. 'I ain't got any doubt that some crooks has more brains than you got.'

"That was getting me pretty hot.

"'Shut up, Charlie,' says I. 'I ain't here to start a fight. Not in Marie's house.'

"'Come outside,' says he. 'There's plenty of room there.'

"'Charlie,' says I, hangin' onto my temper as hard as I could. 'I ain't goin' to fight.'

"'You're yaller,' says Charlie.

"And when he said that, I heard somebody snicker. I dunno who it was to this day. Maybe it was Marie's little kid sister, Ruth. She always had a way of hangin' around to hear what the growed-up folks had to say to each other. Anyway, I didn't wait to think. I only knowed that somebody had stood by and heard me takin' water. I forgot whose brother he was. I just out with the ten best cuss words I knew and tossed 'em all in his face. Before I got half through he was after his gun. It came out fast as a wink, but mine came out a shade faster. I beat him by a wink, and he went down when I shot.

"That was enough for me. I figgered that I'd killed him sure, and I run out and made a grab for my hoss. I made such a dog-gone fast reach for that ol' hoss that he threw up his head and bolted. And I could hear old man Prevost yellin' and cussin' and hollerin' murder on the inside of the house.

"Seemed to me like all of El Ridal must be hearin' him. I jumps across the street to the hotel. I didn't wait none to ask questions. I could hear old man Prevost yellin': 'Murder!' right behind me.

"They was a line-up of hosses at the rack in front of the hotel. I picked out the best with my eye as I come flyin'. Long as I was to be a hoss thief, I might as well steal a good one.

"That sounds like fool talk to you, I guess. You're a plumb honest man, Al, and I suppose that you would of stayed and stood your trial and took your chances of provin' that you was no worse than the gent that you'd shot. I *tried* to make myself stay. But it looked like stayin' to die, and I wasn't ready to stay and die—not even for Marie's sake!

"I picked out old Hank Moon's cream and made the saddle in one jump. Then I skinned out of El Ridal before they knowed that I was more'n started. That's how I come to leave El Ridal. I'd shot a man and stole a hoss—I dunno which is much worst to of done."

"Did Charlie Prevost die?"

"That's the joke. Sure he didn't die. It was only a graze. He's got a scar on his face and a dog-gone good will to kill me one way or another if his luck don't play out on him. He spends his time workin' out ways of snaggin' me. You can lay to it that he was ridin' in the lead when the boys hit the trail after me tonight!

"That's the joke. Because I thought I'd killed young

Prevost, I busted loose and went rampagin' around. When a gent has killed a man and stole a hoss, it don't make so much difference what else he's done—and a little thing like jumping your old board bill—that don't amount to nothin'—you see?"

"I see," said Allan.

How very perfectly, indeed, he understood all that had passed in the mind of the unlucky fellow!

"First thing I know, I get cornered by two different posses squeezin' in on me from two sides while I'm ridin' about takin' my pleasure of the country. I rode the old cream hoss ragged. It was near dead, and they was sure to catch me when here come a gent leadin' a hoss—a big, strappin' bay hoss. He comes up to me, gives me the hoss, and him and me, we slide away from the rest of 'em like they'd been anchored to the ground.

"That was Harry Christopher. D'you wonder that after meeting up with him like that, I'd give him my promise to follow him for a year, anyway? I wanted to make it a lifetime, but he said that a year was enough. If I liked the life after that, I could sign up for the rest of the time. You see? Now you come, partner, and tell me that you'll give me a new grip at life if I'll promise to do what you want me to do. I didn't think of my promise to Christopher while you were talkin'. That's the straight of it, partner!"

It was impossible for Allan to doubt him. Good faith and sincerity rang in his voice as truly as the hollow voice of El Ridal River spoke of death and danger in the deep of the valley before them.

"How long do you have to stay with Christopher?" he asked at last.

"Five months more," said Jim Jones.

"Then," said Allan, "I have to stay with you!"

CHAPTER 12

"YOU'RE AN ACE"

It was in vain that Jim plied him with arguments, questions, and even with entreaties.

"If it's ever knowed that you've rode with Harry Christopher and his gang," said Jim finally, "it's enough to lynch you in nine states west of the Rockies. I know what I'm talkin' about!"

"Why, then," said Allan, "I suppose I'll have to take care that I'm not caught in any one of those nine states. Is that right?"

"But what in the name of Heaven makes you want to come with me? What good will it do you, Al?"

There was one of those pauses which were very frequent when any one talked with "Slow" Allan, or Slow Al, as he came to be better known by that name.

"It'll give me a chance to become a friend of yours, Jim."

"You're that now, if ever a man proved that he could be the friend of another. Look what you've done, Al!"

"I've only undone the trouble that I made for you myself. There's no credit coming to me for anything like that. I've played an extraordinarily foolish game. But we begin now at evens. In fact, Jim, I won't let you shake me off!"

"What started you feelin' so dog-gone friendly to me, old-timer?"

There was another pause, while Allan slowly pushed the name of Frances out of his mind.

"When I learned that you were so young, Jim; and when I saw how brave and quiet you were in the face of the danger that I had left you in, I couldn't help admiring you for that. So I decided to help you if I could. And the more I see of you, Jim, the better I'd like to have you for a friend. You go back to Harry Christopher. You can't help that. But I'll go with you, if Christopher will let me come into his gang."

"You'd play a game with that gang of crooks on account of me, Al?"

"If you'll let me stay along."

He heard Jim mumbling softly in the darkness.

"You're a queer one," said the other at last. "But I'd rather have you with me than ten fightin' men," he added, chuckling: "I got a reason. I've felt the grip in your hands!"

With that, he prepared to venture across the narrow ledge and out of the trap again, with Allan walking close behind him, leading the roan mare. For the sounds of the pursuit had died out; it had broken into two streams, sweeping across the head of the mountain and still combing the night for the fugitives. The passage across the ledge was almost easy, now, after the first grim rehearsal had been finished, and now they sat the saddle on the farther side, with two fresh horses under them, and no enemy in sight. Jim Jones led straight down the mountain.

"But that's toward El Ridal!" objected Allan.

"Sure," said Jim. "That's the last place they'll be lookin' for us."

Allan set his teeth to keep from gasping. He felt, on the whole, like a small child following an older and adventurous brother through unknown perils, compelled to keep up simply because he would be too ashamed if he failed to keep pace with the other. Yet so serene was Jim as he rode down into the den of his enemies from which he had barely escaped, and so recently, that he whistled softly as he jogged along with the stallion turning his beautiful head anxiously from side to side as though he understood the burden of peril which his master accepted with so light a heart.

Not only did they aim straight at El Ridal, but when they came near the town, Jim skirted recklessly behind the houses until the shambling breadth of the hotel was spread before them. There he dismounted. To the hasty question of Allan he replied that having failed to see his sister in the first attempt, he would double back among the very teeth of his foes and attempt to see her a second time. The piece of arrant foolhardiness left Allan speechless for an instant, and before he had recovered, Jim was lost in the black of the night.

There began a long vigil between the two shacks where he held the horses, straining his eyes through the night, straining his ears to catch every approaching sound. Once a dog bayed and was answered with mellow music by two or three of its kind; whereat he thought, with a shiver, that they were surely trailing the fugitives with hounds. But the dogs became quiet.

Still, though it was far, far past the usual sleep-time of El Ridal, voices and lights stirred through the town. At length horsemen began to come in from the mountain. They were the riders returning. He could hear the older citizens calling out for news; he could hear the grumbled answers of the riders, disgusted with the failure of their quest.

The door of the house just before him opened and a woman came out bearing a lantern at the same time that a rider, doubtless her husband, came through the yard. They both approached the shed to the right of Allan, and he groaned in his quandary.

He could not draw back with two horses without making enough noise to betray himself; and if he had to flee again, Jim was cut off without a means of escape from the town. Yet if he stayed where he was, the chances were great that one of the two horses would neigh or stamp or in some other manner draw attention. He stood, therefore, with the head of a horse caught within each arm, whispering softly to them while they pricked their ears and nosed cautiously at him. Fear, being the most vital and the most common of all the emotions is also the one which dumb beasts understand the best, and these two horses knew very well that the master who held them was afraid. So they nosed at him gingerly, asking with glittering eyes and sensitive nostrils what the danger could be and still listening to the faint cautioning hiss of his whispers.

The sliding door of the shed had been banged open. The woman was holding the lantern, and across the side of the shack, through the great cracks, he saw the shadows rise and fall in waves as her husband unsaddled and fed his weary horse, whose panting was plainly audible.

"We give 'em a hard run up the mountain," the man was saying in response to breathless inquiries. "Pretty nigh to the top. Tom Gilbert seen the pair of 'em scooting through the shadows of a bunch of trees. He turned loose his gun at 'em and called to the boys. We made a rush and burnt a lot of powder, but I guess we didn't hit nothing. The trees an' the light was ag'in' us."

"A pretty piece of work," said the woman, moaning. "This'll get us all murdered in our beds by Harry Christopher."

"There's got to be a change," said the citizen. "We got to get together and run down them wolves."

"Johnston and Jardine have got a pretty good deal to answer for!" said the wife. "Do you think maybe that they was bought off?"

Her husband groaned. "There ain't no use in thinkin'," he said. "What beats us all is this Allan Vincent, as he calls himself. There's some that thinks he's Lew Ramsay!"

"No!" breathed the wife.

"I dunno. That's what some says. Don't look like there's nobody but Ramsay that *could* handle Johnston and Jardine—unless them two was bought off first. But what did Vincent mean by catching Jones if he wanted to have him loose afterward? It looks all kind of mysterious. None of the boys can work it out. But Jardine and Johnston says that they'll keep on the trail of Vincent a hundred years if they have to, but they'll run him down in the end; and they sure talked like they meant it. I guess that they wasn't bought. Somebody seen Jardine's right hand. It was all swole up and mashed and purple lookin'. And he had a big lump on the side of his head."

"I seen this Vincent. He don't look none too big."

"He can do big things, though, and that's what counts. Come on back to the house."

The sliding door was slammed again. They went up the path to the house with the man carrying the lantern, now and his legs changed into immense, stalking shadows that swept the trees at the side of the yard with light and shade. The screen door to their kitchen jangled behind them, and they were lost to the eyes of Allan, who had been watching closely and listening carefully.

They left him with enough food for thought, however. For if Jardine and Johnston were determinedly upon his trail, his life was not worth a counterfeit dollar unless he hurried from that region as fast as a horse could carry him. Such a retreat he could not make. He had given his word to young Jim, and that word he must keep.

To that point in his reflections he had arrived when there was low-voiced: "Hands up!" behind him.

He wheeled, ready to dive at the knees of the enemy, when he saw the handsome face of Jim laughing in the starlight.

"Frontways ain't the only ways that danger comes," chuckled Jim.

And he vaulted lightly into his saddle. In another moment they were weaving along through the dark behind the town, with Jim chatting constantly and gayly. He had gone up the side of the hotel at the very place where he had been climbing before when the strong hand of Allan plucked him down like a dead branch from a tree. One tap had brought his sister to the window and through it he crept. In the gloom of her unlighted room they had embraced, and there they had talked.

"She told me a pile of things," said Jim, laughing to himself so that he could hardly continue. "She told me about the way some gents can watch and keep the coyotes away while they're sound asleep; and how a rabbit can be caught by hypnotizin' 'em; and how to ride a buckin' mustang; and how's the best way to slide money under a door for a girl that ain't got none to go on. I'll say that was mighty decent of you givin' her money that a way. But I've give her plenty now so she won't have to worry none for some little time to come."

He fell silent. The face of Allan was hot with shame, and he blessed the covering curtain of the darkness.

"I told *her* about some things," said Jim, much more soberly. "I told her about how a gent could be took out of jail by a man that only used bare hands against two that had guns. I told her about a man that would find a friend in just half a day and know him well enough to go outlaw with him. Well, Al, before I got through what d'you think she done?"

"I have no idea," said Allan faintly.

"Dog-gone me if she didn't bust out cryin'. Can you lay over that?"

"Well," sighed Allan, "she seems to be a person who's full of contradictions."

"She's worse'n that. She's a Sunday newspaper riddle," declared his friend. "After that she says to me: 'Ain't he the most wonderful man you ever met, Jim?' I allows that you got your points. 'They's nobody like him!' says she. 'Just as simple as a girl, an' braver'n any man!'

" 'Well,' says I, 'I'll go down an' get him and bring him up to see you again, if you feel that way!'

" 'Jim,' says she. 'How can you talk that way?'

" 'What's wrong?' says I.

" 'It ain't modest,' says she, 'to see a gent in a lady's bedroom.'

" 'I ain't goin' to disappear,' says I.

" 'Besides,' says she, 'I don't want to see him.'

" 'Why didn't you say that first?' says I. 'You kind of rattle when you talk tonight, Frank.'

"She didn't say nothing, but sits there beside the window, lookin' plumb sad and plumb happy all at once. The way ma used to look when dad was sick in bed and all in her hands.

" 'You got to send him away, so's he'll be safe,' says she to me, after a while.

" 'He looks like he's able to take care of himself better'n anybody I ever met,' says I.

" 'Jim,' says she, 'you talk like a fool! He ain't no more'n a baby! He dunno how to fry bacon, even, without burnin' it!'

"She jumps up and grabs hold of me.

" 'Jim, Jim!' says she, all teary, 'you promise me that you won't leave him!'

" 'I'll stay as close as he'll let me,' says I. 'What's the matter with you? You act like you was in love with this gent?'

"I thought she was, too, the way she was actin' and carryin' on about you. But now she pushed herself away from me and says: 'It ain't gentlemanly to talk like that to your sister, Jim, and you know it.'

" 'Dog-gone it, Frank,' says I, 'what's wrong with that I said?'

" 'He ain't no more'n a stranger to me,' says Frank. 'Besides, I really don't care if I never see him again!'

"That was too much for me. After her carryin' on about you bein' the best gent in the world, it beat me. Don't it beat you, Al?"

Allan sighed again. His heart and his brain had been in such a dizzy whirl during this related conversation that he had hardly been able to draw a breath; now the ending let him down so abruptly that he could hardly believe what he was hearing.

"I'm afraid that I could never understand her, Jim," he said.

"Forget her," said Jim, chuckling. "She was always that way. You never could get her cornered. She was meant to be a man. She rides like a man and she shoots like a man and dog-gone me if she ain't as square as a man!"

"Ah, yes!" said Allan. "I would wager my life that she is all you say."

"By the way, before I left, she scratched a couple of words on a piece of paper and give them to me to give you. Here they are."

He took an envelope from his pocket which Allan received with trembling hands and opened gingerly, as though precious gold dust might be wasted from the interior if due care were not used. He spread out the sheet of paper which was contained within, lighted a match, and therein he read only this:

DEAR OLD AL: You're an ace.

FRANK.

This cryptic document he perused thrice over, with blurred eyes, until at last he folded the paper carefully, inserted it in the envelope, and replaced the letter in his pocket.

"After all," said Allan thoughtfully. "there are some things which one hardly cares to understand. Don't you think so, Jim?"

CHAPTER 13

SLOW ALLAN MEETS CHRISTOPHER

Two days later, Allan sat with his back against a scrub oak, watching roan Mustard nibble at the tough, sundried grama grass; and when he tired of watching Mustard, he turned his attention to his target practice. For he was working assiduously and had been for two days, to master the intricacies of gunfire with a long-barreled Colt. Young Jim Jones, a master indeed with all manner of firearms, had taught him methods of sliding a revolver swiftly out of the holster into the hand and firing so that the draw and the explosion of the gun came at one and the same instant, so to speak. But Allan could not imitate the smooth, lightning flash of which Jim's draw consisted; he was not one of those who have within them stores of nerve energy, like static electricity, ready to flash into convulsive action. His draw was terribly slow, and he knew that it always would be slow. But another trick had been successfully taught him by Jim, and that was to point his gun instead of sight it.

It is an old trick, after all, and as a rule is not a particularly good one. It varies in value according to the person who acquires it. It is based upon the fundamental truth that most people, when they point at an object, point quite straight—an unstudied directness. Some indeed, are remarkably accurate and a few will point with a forefinger as certainly as an expert can level a rifle and, of course, much more easily and swiftly. For these the trick has the greatest value. When a revolver is drawn from the holster in close fight, there is not time, of course, to raise it shoulder high and drop it on the mark. As a matter of fact, a great many gun fighters have filed the sights entirely off their guns, so as to be reasonably sure that there will be no friction in drawing the Colt from the holster. Before a man could raise his revolver high and discharge it—in a close fight—he would have received at least three bullets in his body. And Allan, fatally slow in the draw itself, must at least fire from the hip the instant his muzzle was clear of the holster. That became possible for him when it was discovered that he was one of those fortunate people who point straight naturally. The forefinger he placed along the barrel of the weapon as he fired, pulling the trigger with the second finger of either hand. And, as straight as he could point, so straight could he shoot.

The results were amazing. His snap shooting had been as ridiculous in aim as in speed until the idea of pointing was explained to him by Jim. Then, at a distance of thirty feet, he planted four out of six shoots somewhere in the body of a tree which was hardly more than a foot in diameter—and this while working the trigger as fast as it could be pulled!

Of course it was by no means a very brilliant display— except for a beginner. And when it came to firing at very small or very distant objects, Allan was uniformly poor with a gun. With a rifle, in fact, he could do nothing. It was only with a revolver, shooting at close range at a fairly large object, that he was effective, but when all the conditions favored him, the results were truly surprising. He became so expert that as he and Jim cantered down a trail and fired for practice at the trees nearby, he actually struck the targets more frequently than his tutor! But if he lamented his inability to shoot at distant marks, Jim Jones gave him the grim reassurance that men did not die in open battle under the sky but by sudden explosions of hatred or rage across a card table, or on meeting in the street. A ten-pace duel was generally a long-distance one! For the simple reason that the duels were always impromptu.

Thus encouraged, Allan devoted every spare moment to the perfecting of his newly acquired art. How much he might have to depend upon it no one could tell, since he had taken upon himself the duty of protecting the brother of Frances. Nor was that all, for since he broke open the jail at El Ridal he was outlawed from the society of all law-keeping citizens as much as Jim Jones or even Harry Christopher himself.

So, as he rested his back against the tree trunk, he worked diligently. Over and over again he twisted the gun as fast as his fingers could fly, out of the holster, covered a target without raising the weapon above the height of his hip, and fired. His targets consisted of a black-faced rock which scarred white whenever a bullet drove against it, a rotten fence post whose fellows had long since disappeared, and the trunk of a sapling

The nearest was within twenty paces, and the farthest within twenty-five, yet in twenty rounds, he scored only one miss and was telling himself with a sort of quiet savagery which was new to his nature, that had there been men before him they must all have been struck down. Then suddenly, he felt, rather than heard or saw, something stirring behind him.

It must be Jim, returned from the head of the valley to which he had ridden on before to see Harry Christopher and arrange for the bringing in of a recruit. But when Allan turned, he saw not the handsome features of Jim, but a swarthy, broad man-with a weary expression.

Altogether, there was a shade of the profoundest gloom on his brow. He leaned against one among a cluster of tall rocks, his arms folded. Seeing that he was observed, he nodded to Allan not a greeting, but a concession to the habit of courtesy.

"Keep right on, son," said he.

He could not have been more than three or four years older, and yet his tone and his manner was that of middle age. To be sure, his hair was gray, and his face deeply lined, but he had the unmistakable appearance of ruined youth rather than of broken-down middle age.

"I'm through shooting," said Allan, putting up his revolver.

"You don't clean a gun when you've finished usin' it?" asked the stranger sharply.

One might have thought that the weapon belonged to him and that it was a personal injustice to him if the Colt were not treated in the correct manner. However, Allan made no difficulty about answering the most impertinent questions. Besides, this man looked like one who had been a little unhinged, mentally, by the falling of many sorrows upon his shoulders.

"I'm told not to clean my guns," said Allan, "until I'm by myself—or with people whom I know."

His mildness made the other only the more irritable, to all appearances. "Meanin' that I'd cut your throat if your back was turned to me, I suppose?"

This was ill nature so causeless and so gross that Allan lifted his head and stared at his companion; he did not reply a single syllable. Yet his restraint was by no means favorably noted by the gloomy man:

"Talk out what's bitin' you," he commanded. "Don't sit there mopin' about it. You don't like what I said?"

"Friend," said Allan, still as gentle as ever, "you seem to have been in trouble lately. I'm a peaceable man, sir, and I have no wish to add to your troubles."

"Add to 'em?" thundered the other, red with irresponsible rage. "What could *you* add to me?"

Again Allan was forced to be silent.

"Some of you kids," went on the other sneering, "have a way of thinkin' like that. You blaze away with a Colt for a couple of hours and you think that you know some-thin' about it. Lemme tell you that handlin' a Colt right is like paintin' a picture. Partly it's born inside of you and partly it's got to be learned with half a lifetime of dog-gone hard work."

"I suppose so," said Allan. "For my part, I make not the slightest pretext of being an expert with weapons. I only feel that I'm extremely lucky to have hit the targets as often as I have just done."

"Targets? What targets?" roared this implacable quarreler.

Allan pointed them out.

"Them ain't targets," snarlingly came back the stranger. "Why not start in shootin' at the hills themselves?"

"But," said Allan, "those targets are as large as men. In a fight——"

"You'd be able to do a murder. There ain't any doubt about that. But gents don't practice all their lives so's they'll be able to use a gun; they practice so's they'll never *have* to use it!"

Over this peculiar maxim Allan brooded for some time, without hurry, deeply involved in the intricacies of the suggestions. At length he nodded and regarded his companion with much admiration.

"That's a peculiar way to put it, but I think I understand."

"I say you practice so's you won't *have* to shoot to kill. Suppose you, now, was to try to make a gun play agin' me. Would I kill you because I'm faster on the draw than you? Nope. I'd simply put a ball through your hip that'd teach you not to talk so smart to the next gent you met up with."

And, stepping forth from the rock a little, he looked with a sort of cruel hunger upon Allan. The latter dared not reply. In the first place, he had not the slightest doubt but that this fellow was capable of shooting him to bits. In the second place, a chilly atmosphere breathed from this stranger. There was no encouragement for rash advances when one was in his presence.

"Here," said the gloomy stranger, laying a hand upon the butt of his gun, "is what I'd call shootin'. Look yonder at the bird on that dog-gone branch——"

He jerked his head in the designated direction and he

saw that a bird, perhaps frightened away from the place in the beginning by Allan's fusillage directed against the three targets, had returned to discover the cause of all of this noise and its cessation.

"Are you going to kill it?" asked Allan sadly.

"Not without givin' it a fightin' chance. I ain't no murderer—not even of birds!"

So saying, he whipped out his gun, fired, and the little twig on which the bird had been sitting fell to the ground. The bird itself dropped a foot or so into space before it recovered and darted off. Once more the gun spat and tossed its nose. The bird dodged sharply; two or three tiny feathers, knocked adrift, floated downward as slowly as if the still air had been a well of water.

There was an oath from the marksman; there was a sigh of relief from Allan.

"By heaven!" thundered this strange fellow. "I think you're glad that the darn bird got away!"

Mildness, as it has been seen, was the leading feature in the soul of Vincent Allan, but now he felt an electric irritability spring up in his heart. He found himself examining the stranger carefully and focusing his attention upon two points—the pit of the stomach and the point of the jaw. Little nervous ripples ran through the striking muscles along his arms and his thick shoulders twitched. But he only sighed again. For he told himself that to attack this fellow, no matter what the latter's insolence, was to invite death. Yet it would almost be worth death to have the privilege of striking him once. His conduct was almost intolerable.

"You're angry," said Allan. "You're trying to pick trouble with me; but I don't want to have any trouble."

"I knowed that you wouldn't," sneered the other, with obvious meaning.

"In fact," said Allan, rising to his feet, "I think I'll leave you."

"Wait a minute," said the bully. "I ain't said that you could go."

There was a shortening of breath in Allan; by the peculiar sensation in his cheeks he knew that he was smiling, although he had no desire to, and blood surged into his brain until his temples throbbed.

"My friend," said Allan, measuring his words and his voice, "it will be much better for me to go now. I have no desire to do you any harm."

The other gaped at him. "You ain't got—no desire—kid, have you gone dippy?"

"Keep back from me," said Allan.

"D'you mind telling me *how* you could do me any harm?"

"With my hands," said Allan a little huskily, and he took half a pace forward. "With my hands, sir!"

"And how would them hands get a chance to grab me?"

"I am not ignorant of your skill," said Allan, "but if the first bullet did not instantly kill me—if I lived to place my hands upon you—I assure you that you would die with me."

Something made the other leap suddenly back.

"Heaven help me!" he cried, half laughing, half astonished, and certainly with an entirely new voice. "I believe you mean it, and I believe you could do it. Hey—Jim! Come call him off!"

And here Jim Jones came hastily from behind the rocks, smiling, but a little pale.

"You ran that race too dog-gone close to the finish to suit me," he said. "D'you believe what I was tellin' you?"

"I do," said the stranger solemnly. "And you might introduce us, Jim."

"Al, this here is Harry Christopher. Harry, this is Al Vincent."

They shook hands, looking one another closely in the eye, as men do who have seen enough of one another to respect what they know and desire to know more.

The manner of Christopher had become greatly altered. He was still smiling as he shook the hand of Allan.

"When Jim come up with word that you wanted to join us," he said, "I figured that I'd come down and try you out. They ain't no place in a gang like mine for a gent that ain't got some iron in him. Well, Al Vincent, you look like the right stuff to me. If you want to join us, come in and welcome. We'll drink to him now, Jim, eh?"

He drew a flask from his pocket, tipped it at his lips, and then passed it to Jim, coughing and choking over the fiery strength of the stuff. Jim, in turn, pledged the new member most heartily, and the third turn was that of Allan. But he paused with the flask in his hand.

"What's wrong," asked Harry Christopher. "Are you changin' your mind, Al?"

"I never drink," said Allan. "It makes my head so dizzy, you know!"

CHAPTER 14

TRUE SPORTSMANSHIP

There were six blanket rolls around the edges of the room, but there were only five men seated about the stove, a patched and shattered stove, eaten through with rust here and there so that the flames gleamed now and then and puffs and curls of smoke were constantly rising. Above it the pipe staggered up to the roof, bound about and secured with bits of wire. But for all the smoke which rose from it, the stove was the most necessary bit of furniture in the chamber. Even when it was kept roaring day and night, the dampness soaked up through the boards of the flooring and cold wet winds, filled with the harvest of cold which they had gathered from the snows of the summit, swept in under the big pines and whistled through the chinks of the wretched walls of the shack, stabbing the men with icy drafts which made them shudder from time to time.

An hour of work would have patched those walls and made them proof against the storm, but the five had greater things to occupy their minds than the mere patching of a rickety house. They preferred to alternately roast and shiver in this damp house while they conned over and over the scheme which held them there. And though the cold weather might be unfortunate, at least they were secure, here, against a greater danger, and that was from the long arms of the law which were reaching out for them, fumbling constantly to find them. Here near the crests of the mountain, wrapped about in the gloom of the pine forest, they could develop their plans and let the law fumble and reach in vain toward them.

Jim Jones was the least significant of the five. Next to him was the long and lank form of Hank Geer, perpetually swallowing a triangular, jutting Adam's apple which perpetually rose again. He was a famous man, was Hank. He was useful in the extreme to any criminal society for the very good reason that there was nothing which he would not attempt. He was reckless, it might be said, by calculated principle. For when a man has the burden of half a dozen murders upon his head he knows, as Hank Geer knew, that the recompense is coming and will not be long delayed. He had done enough to warrant many deaths; therefore he was willing to keep on doing, convinced that to reform would now be impossible and that to hide from the law was also too great a task. Sooner or later he must be searched out and he must go down; in the meantime, his one overmastering desire was to die in action. He dreaded not the death by a pistol shot, but the death by the rope, with the trial, condemnation, and the grisly wait in the condemned cell. Upon these things his mind constantly brooded; they would not out; and the more dare-devil the adventure which was proposed, the better he liked it; for even if he failed in all else, he would gain if he could find death in action.

Beside this gloomy figure was the yegg, Lefty Bill Mason, who had cracked safes in every part of the country and who was convinced that there were many more which must succumb to his wits. He had a magic way with steel doors. And some men said that those pointed, foxlike ears of his were able to read the heart of a combination! He was a bundle of good nature and nerves and the vital soul of every enterprise which he entered. His companion on the other side was no less a person than Sam Buttrick, who had graduated from the ranks of the prize fighters and brought his small head and massive blunt jaw to greater works of art. Guns were not altogether at home in his huge hands; the knife was his favorite weapon, but better even than the knife was it to get his square-tipped fingers upon an enemy. He was outlawed not because he loved crime, but because he needed the stimulus of terrible danger. Sitting about a house he was a most lethargic individual, but when the time came for the commission of the crime, he blossomed like flowers under a warm May sun and became most gay. It might be said of Sam Buttrick that he was not vicious out of malice but because viciousness was inborn in his nature. The last member of the group was Harry Christopher.

They sat in a semicircle before the stove with a large piece of paper upon the floor which they dwelt upon with their eyes. There was a map sketched upon it by the skillful hand of Lefty Bill Mason; from time to time he stooped to make some alteration. He seemed more interested in the map as a work of his art than in the crime which they were now projecting with such consummate care.

For all things were done carefully under the management of Harry Christopher. He succeeded by the detailed elimination of evil chances.

The scheme now under consideration was of the first magnitude. It embraced an attempt upon a cash shipment of three quarters of a million, and the minor details had been arranged to the last stage. Harry Christopher delivered a brief resumé.

"Here's where we got to get in our work," he said. "When the train hits Gully, they're goin to switch the guards, and one of the new guards is Tom Morris. Understand?"

"Who done that?" asked Sam Buttrick. "Who got Tom in as a guard?"

"One of the smartest gents in the world," said Harry Christopher. "His name is Money."

He tilted back on the boy which served him as a chair, chuckling with the greatest satisfaction.

"I'll tell you what money can do! It can pass a gent through the eye of a needle, if it wants to. It can make black look white. It bought the news about how much money was goin' to be in this here shipment. It bought the news about what train it would be shipped on, and how many would guard it and what would be their names. But almost the most important of all was to get one of my boys named among the guards; and what d'you think? It cost only a hundred bucks!" He laughed with a venomous content. "It ain't what you spend. It's the way that you spend it. I've put out twenty thousand in flat cash here and there to get the news that I wanted; but only a hundred was all that I needed to put Tom Morris inside of that car as guard."

"Twenty thousand!" said Sam Buttrick, whose brute mind had paused to grasp only one particle of this statement. "Twenty thousand for *news!*"

"That ain't nothin'," answered 'Lefty' Bill. "Mostly the boys have to pony up with a quarter to a third of everything they haul down to the gents inside that furnish the lay to 'em."

"They got no cash," responded Harry Christopher scornfully. "Them poor, drivelin' fools is workin' for the sake of the fun in it, not for the cash. Take one of them bums like Twister Matthews or Lew Shawney that's talked about so much—what do they get out of their work? Just enough to keep 'em with a taste of high life in their mouths, that's all. They're hired, you might say, by the skunks that lay back and take none of the chances. I'll show you how they work it. Suppose that I'm on the inside of an office. I know about a big money shipment. Well, I send out to a bird like this Twister or Lew, and they say, 'Here—you take half and gimme half, and we'll call it quits. I'll take my share after you've pulled down the stuff.' "

"How," asked Buttrick, rubbing the back of his hand over the bruised and flattened button which served him as a nose, "how can the gents on the inside be sure that the gents like us, after we got our paws on the coin, would live up to our promise and give 'em a half?"

"Because," said Harry Christopher promptly, "the minute that one of 'em was double crossed, the word would spread around among the whole of the gents that handle coin, that Twister, say, is crooked. The minute that that news gets around, Twister couldn't get enough real news about shipments and such things to be worth five cents. He might as well go out of business. But as I was sayin', most of the boys have to do business on credit. They say: 'Tell me where to pick up fifty thousand and I'll give you half.' But that ain't my way. I pick out a gent that needs coin bad and that knows what I need to know. I wait till his rent comes due, and his kids needs clothes, and his wife is down sick. That's what I wait for. Then I slip around to him and I say: 'Kid, all you got to do is to open your trap and say six words; an' I'll pay you a thousand a word. Are you on?' That's all there is to it. Simple, if you know how to work it!"

"Suppose they won't kick through?" asked Sam Buttrick, his jaw dropping, so profound was his interest in the details of these criminal maneuvers which were beyond the ken of his brute mind.

"If they won's kick through, try somebody else that might know. If you can't get somebody else, you go back to the first gent. His doc has told him by this time that his wife had ought to have a trip to Florida for the winter. You know that line? You take him and say: "Ten thousand cash! Here it is in my hand!' "

"That always gets 'em?" muttered Buttrick.

"*I* ain't ever failed," answered the chief sneeringly.

"Well," said Lefty suddenly, "where do we get at the train?"

"Don't rush," said the captain with the same tone of contempt. "I got all the details worked out. But I want you all here before I tell 'em to you. Where's the kid?"

"Al went for a walk, I think," said Jim.

"I told him to keep close," said the captain. "What'n the devil does he mean by leavin' the place?"

"I dunno," said Jim. "I guess he got sort of restless. He'll be careful."

"He dunno enough to be careful," put in Hank—the first word he had spoken in an hour.

"He dunno enough to do nothin'!" responded Buttrick. "He don't look much to me—that kid."

"What he's doin' with you, Harry," said Lefty Bill, "beats us all, and that's flat. Jim is a good kid, and I suppose that Al Vincent is his friend, but what Al can do that figures him in with us, I dunno!"

"He rides," said Hank, "like an old woman on a plow hoss. He can't shoot none. He can't talk none. He don't know nothin'. He acts like a boob and dog-gone me if I don't think that he *is* a boob!"

"What's the word, chief?" asked Buttrick.

"When the time comes," said the chief, "you'll see him come through well enough. At least, he's a strong man."

"Lemme work two minutes alone on that kid," said Buttrick sneeringly, "an' I'll mash his face in for him. That's what I think about him bein' strong. I don't worry about his strength!

"You've heard what he's done?"

"I don't give a darn about hearin'. I care about seein'. I've heard a lot of queer things since I come West, but I ain't seen much that was worth seein'. Let the kid *show!*"

Hank and Lefty Bill nodded their heads and the chief, after a survey of their faces, nodded likewise.

"There's the kid now," he said. "I can hear him whistlin'. Sam, you think that you can handle the kid. Well, we'll leave you in here alone with him. You do your best. But, mind you, don't try no gun play or knife play, because if you do, though you might kill the kid, I'll tell you sure that he'll kill you, too, before he's ended. He can't be stopped!"

He uttered this last warning in a tone so solemn that all were impressed; and even Sam Buttrick seemed a little abashed.

"It ain't because I doubt your judgment that I doubt the kid—" he began.

But Christopher shook his head in token that he wanted to hear no more. He had seen the doubts of his crew concerning young Al Vincent, as the latter called himself, growing darker and darker from day to day, and he knew that there was only one thing to do, and that was to let the "kid" fight his way into some sort of recognition.

"You've made your choice," he said darkly to Buttrick.

"You're forty pounds heavier than the kid. You've had your turn in the ring. You ought to be able to handle him easy. And you say that all you want is a chance at him. Well, Sam, you get your chance. We're goin' out, all of us. We'll wait outside for ten minutes. That ought to be long enough for you and him to settle up your troubles. So long!"

With that, he turned upon his heel and left the place and the others trooped out after him. They passed Allan nearing the house, waved to him, and watched him go on with that peculiar effortless, ground-covering stride which was typical of him when he walked.

When he had disappeared into the shack, they took up a position to the windward of the place and waited. With the wind combing through the old building, it carried to them, in general, all the noises which sounded from the interior. Waiting there, they were not long in hearing the trouble begin. The front door had scarcely slammed behind the "kid" before the great, harsh voice of Sam Buttrick began to bellow.

"That won't last long," said Jim Jones to the others. "And if you want Sam to come out of this with a whole skin, you'd better step back there and be ready to bear a hand!"

The chief, however, merely raised a hand for silence. The others were lending all of their attention to the scene within the house of which they could not pick up, however, any intelligible words, but only the throaty roars of Sam Buttrick and, after these, the mere murmurs of Vincent Allan in response. This continued through a long two or three minutes, then stopped.

"Something's happened," said Lefty Bill. "Let's go in and see!"

"We'll stay here," said Harry Christopher. "We promised Sam that he could have ten minutes, and we'll give him all of that time."

"Whatever's happened is wound up already," said Jim Jones. "And it lasted so dog-gone short that I figure it must of been knife work, chief. Sam has slipped his knife into the ribs of the kid—and if he has——"

"Stay where you are," said the chief sternly. "If I got the say in this company still, you'll all stay put right where you are. If Al couldn't stave off Buttrick—we don't want him with us. If he was fool enough to get knifed, we'll bury him all decent and proper, but there ain't goin' to be no hand laid on Sam. We invited him free and easy to step into this fight. He ain't goin' to collect no bad consequences. That's flat and that's final!"

There was no gainsaying Harry Christopher in such a black humor. In his heart of hearts, Jim Jones suspected that the chief had never forgiven Allan for the first encounter between them when, it might be said, Allan had called the former's bluff. At any rate, they waited now in the rear of the shack until the whole length of the ten minutes had elapsed—and like an eternity it seemed to Jim Jones before the signal was given. Then he was in the shack in a trice with Lefty Bill at his heels and the others following hard.

What he saw was a scene peaceful enough. The huge form of Sam Buttrick lay stretched upon the floor and beside him kneeled the "kid," busily bathing his face and his breast with cold water and then fanning him vigorously with an old magazine.

"Sam stumbled and hit his chin on the floor," said Allan mildly, and looked gravely up to the faces of the others.

They leaned, astonished. There was a large purplish welt along the side of Sam's jaw. There was a lump on the back of his head. And across the knuckles of the right hand of Allan there was a flush of red.

Here Sam opened his eyes suddenly, gasped, choked, and then swayed to his feet. With one hand, strong as rock, Allan caught him under the pit of the arm and supported the reeling form.

"I was telling them," said Allan gravely and loudly, "how you stumbled and hit your chin on the floor. You understand, Sam?"

Some of the cloud of pain, fury, and astonishment cleared from the swollen face of Sam Buttrick.

"Mighty queer thing," said Sam Buttrick, now recovering rapidly. "Caught my toe on a board on this fool floor and come down slam on my chin. Darn queer. Never had it happen to me before."

So saying, he glared about him at the circle of listeners, and they dared not grin in return.

"Looks kind of funny, though," whispered Lefty Bill a little later, "how a floor could of hit him on the jaw and the back of the head at the same time!"

CHAPTER 15

THE LETTERS FROM AL

The partnership of Walter Jardine and Elias Johnston had become indissoluble, for having been friends and co-helpers in many triumphs, they were now riveted together by the disgrace of a failure which involved them both. Having lived on a mountaintop of glory for many years, they were now brought down to the dust of the common-place and surrounded by the amusement and the shrugged shoulders of those who had always stood in awe of them.

Lesser men would have sped away from El Ridal and gone to distant parts of the country where men did not know their shame. Rasher men would have plunged head-long onto the trail of Allan. Indeed, this was the advice of Jardine, but Elias Johnston would not hear of it.

"If it was this tenderfoot himself and just him," he said, "I'd be for trailin' him. But it ain't him. He's throwed in with Jim Jones and Jones is with Christopher. Even if we get the trail of Al Vincent, it would only lead us into the Christopher gang."

"What could be better?" said Jardine.

"I can think of better ways of dying," said Elias Johnston. "We might drop three or four of 'em, but they'd be sure to get us in the long run."

"What'll we do, then?"

"Set right here in El Ridal."

"And hatch a lot of laughter," said Jardine. "I'll be doin' a killin' if this here keeps up much longer. That old fool Carpenter laughed plumb in my face to-day."

"You won't do no killin'," said Johnston. "I say that we'll set right here and wait."

"For what?" said Jardine.

Johnston became a Socrates. He sat up on the edge of his chair and jabbed his questions at his companion briefly, with a pointing forefinger to give them emphasis.

"How did young Al come here?"

"On a hoss, I suppose."

"He'll come back on a hoss, too. But who brought him here?"

"Why, the girl, I guess."

"All right, what happened?"

"You ought to know."

"I'm askin' you."

"Words is cheap. He come here and grabbed Jim Jones while Jim was tryin' to get in to see his sister."

"Why did he do that?"

"To get the name of it and the coin, of course."

"What did he do afterward?"

Jardine grew purple. "I ain't goin' into that."

"Did he get Jones out of jail after he'd put him in?"
"He sure enough did."

"What make him do it?"

"I dunno. I ain't no prophet, and I can't read the minds of fools!"

"He was a fool to do it, then?"

"He was."

"He changed his mind about keepin' Jones in jail and gettin' the reward?"

"Sure. It looks that way, don't it?"

"What makes a fool out of a man?"

"Booze, I s'pose."

"Booze first. Right! What next?"

"Women, then."

"Right ag'in. You got a head on your shoulders, Walt. Well, then, was Al drinkin' while he was in town?"

"Not that I heard about."

"Did he have a breath when he come to tackle us at the jail?"

"The darn smooth-talkin' hypocrite—no!"

"Then booze didn't make no fool out of him, but women did."

"Maybe that follers."

"Who was the woman?"

"You mean—'Frank' Jones—Jim's sister?"

"I mean her, I guess."

"What makes you think so?"

"Is she pretty?"

"Like a picture."

"Is she dog-gone nice to talk to?"

"She sure is."

"Well, then, she's the kind that makes fools out of men. Look here. Who would Al please by settin' Jim free?"

"Jim and his sister, I guess."

"He done it to please the girl, then."

"I guess so."

"Then he's lost his head about her."

"Maybe so."

"If he's lost his head about her, will he stay away from her?"

"I guess not."

"Where is she now?"

"Right here in El Ridal, I guess."

"Then will he come right back here to El Ridal?"

"Not unless he's a fool."

"We've already pretty nigh proved that he's a fool, ain't we?"

There was an exclamation from Jardine. "You mean that we hang about and watch the girl."

"She's our bait, old son. We watch her and we catch the sucker!"

"How'll we do it?"

"Go right to the hotel and put up there. If folks talk, let 'em talk. We'll watch her and we'll watch her mail."

"How can we do that?"

"When does the mail train come in?"

"Once a day, about eight o'clock, evening."

"Soon as it's sorted, is the mail that goes to the hotel took up there?"

"Sure."

"What happens to it?"

"It's brought around and put under the door of the rooms."

"Well, son, when mail comes for Frank Jones, we'll be handy around to get it before she does. Ain't that sense? And you can lay to it that some of that mail will be comin' from young Al!"

Upon these suggestions Walter Jardine agreed to act, and the two of them promptly rented a room in the hotel where they lived very quietly, letting it be known that they were getting ready to do some trapping among the mountains. They had two occupations. One was to follow Frank Jones at a distance every day, no matter where she went or what she did. One was to watch the evening mail and see what letters came for the girl.

It was a program simple to execute. There was no more suspicion in Frank than there might have been in a child. She lived very quietly and, apparently, contentedly in El Ridal. In the day she rode her pinto through the hills in the morning and in the afternoon she visited friends in the town, for she had not been there three days before she knew every one in the place. At night, she went to bed early. And when she rode out, Johnson or Jardine were sure to pick her up shortly after she left the town and trail quietly behind her. At night, too, when the mail came in, and when it was distributed to the doors of the guests in the hotel, though the proprietor who executed this mission usually rapped at the doors, he never disturbed the girl. Her mail was left pushed half through the crack beneath the door, and here Elias Johnson, light-footed as a gliding snake, came to steal it and carry it away to his room. There they steamed open the flap and slipped out the folded sheets which were contained.

There were many letters, after the first few days, and nearly all of them were from girlhood friends who lived in the home country of Frances. Now and again they came across the stiff and stilted letter of some youth from the same district, someone far more eloquent with a quirt or a rope than with a pen. Through these labored scrawls they waded laboriously, and night after night, having completed their tasks, they carried the letters back, having carefully resealed them, and replaced them beneath the door of her room.

Both of them had moral scruples. But Elias Johnston hit upon a bit of sophistry which eased their consciences.

"What we're doin'," he said, "is to try to keep her away from this gent. It ain't nothin' in our pockets but trouble. But it means maybe that we'll be able to keep her from bein' foolish with a crook. That's the only way to look at it."

Here was a sufficient excuse to put them both entirely at their ease, and when the haul came, it could be relished with an undiminished joy. There was nothing remarkable about the envelope except the almost feminine precision and delicacy with which the address was written. So carefully drawn were the letters that all character disappeared from them.

In fact, Elias Johnston was for returning the letter unopened.

"A big-handed gent like Al," he said, "wouldn't push a pen as plumb pretty as that."

"We ain't missin' no chances," said Jardine, "though it's a cinch that a girl must of wrote this."

So they steamed open the flap and drew out the contents and read:

DEAR FRANK: Jim thinks that it's better for me to write to you because his handwriting might be known in El Ridal. This is to let you know that we are safely in the mountains. Jim is happy and looks very well.

It seems at present that we are to come down toward El Ridal before long. Not to stop there, but passing near by it. In case we do, one of us or both of us will try to come to the town to see you. That is, if we are passing during the night. If you hear two short whistles and then

113

two long ones, you'll know that one of us is beside the hotel. Then if you'll come down from the hotel the back way you'll find one of us or both of us waiting behind the sheds among the brush. Yours faithfully, AL.

Jim misses you a lot and talks about you all the time.

The treasure was in their hands, it seemed, at last, and a great recompense for their long torture and their long waiting.

"But it sure don't look like he would bust himself wide open to get down," said Walter Jardine. "Love? That don't have no sound like love to me, Johnston. 'Yours faithfully' is a devil of a way to wind up a letter from a gent to the girl he loves. Ain't that so?"

"Have you ever wrote one?" asked Johnston, grinning.

"I have," said Jardine brazenly. "I've wrote a pile of 'em. And the finish of the dog-gone worst of the lot was hot as lightin' compared with the finish of that there letter. If that's love, I'm simple in the head. Look at the wind-up. 'Jim misses you a lot.' Sounds like the letter was dictated by Jim, not wrote out of the head of Al. Sounds just about as warm an' kind-hearted as a letter that a brother would write to his sister."

Upon these observations Elias Johnston brooded for a time. But he said finally: "You can't tell. This here love is a queer kind of a disease. Sometimes it makes a gent laugh. Sometimes it makes him cry. Sometimes it makes him talk like a fool. Sometimes it makes him shut up like an owl. There ain't no way of figuring it. I've tried before. What he says about Jim missin' her most likely is meant for himself."

"You do a pile of guessin'. It don't buy nothin'," insisted Walter Jardine. "Leastwise, we can lay and wait for 'em, and they's one chance in ten that it'll be the gent we want. Even if it was only Jim Jones, it'd be a lot better'n nothin'."

"It would," admitted Elias. "But I'm here to state that I'll lay ten to one that the gent that shows up will be young Al himself. Will you take that?"

Walter Jardine regarded the other calmly out of his bull eyes. Then he rose from his chair, crossed the room, and from his coat plucked forth a wallet.

"I got five hundred here," he said. "You can cover that with five thousand if you got it, partner."

CHAPTER 16

CHRISTOPHER
HOLDS A GRUDGE

The problem which lay before Harry Christopher and his men, though on the face of it simple, had complications which were most severe. At the town of Gully, Tom Morris was to become one of the guards. Between that point and the town of Cranston, there was a district of low, rolling hills. Beyond Cranston, the train descended into the flat, open country. If the train were not held up before Cranston, the robbery would have to be performed in the midst of a country where towns were comparatively thick and populous and where a complicated network of telephone and telegraph would carry the tidings from one place to another and a hundred bands of pursuers would have an excellent opportunity of cutting off the retreat of the plunderers, supposing that all went well with them in the actual robbery. It was necessary, therefore, that the holdup should take place between Gully and Cranston.

This was in itself a considerable stretch, but even here there were difficulties. It was a farming rather than a herding country. Little villages were numerous. The same difficulties, in short, which threatened the robbers in the flatlands beyond Cranston, were still a danger between Cranston and Gully, though those dangers were to a certain extent lessened because the ground was rougher and because there were, here and there, bits of forest to shroud the pursued and in which they could take at least momentary refuge if they were too closely pursued. Still, if an alarm went forth, from many and many a farm units would ride forth to swell the posses, which were sure to be both numerous and determined. There were reasons behind this surety. In the first place, half a dozen crimes of some magnitude, including a train robbery of the first importance, had actually occurred in the region within the past two years and the men had been given an opportunity to learn how to work together to cover their district. More than that, they had not only been trained, but the pack had been well blooded. For of the half-dozen crimes, in four cases the pursuers had overtaken the miscreants and run them to earth. They were naturally proud, therefore, of such a high percentage. They boasted that the crime wave had died out in their vicinity and that criminals sought other and easier hunting grounds.

Besides, the people of Cranston County were capable men of action quite beyond the average of the usual agrarian populations. They lived in a foothill district as has been said, with streaks and stretches of forest hither and yon, and just above them the mountains swelled up to great heights, with the big Cranston River rushing down toward the plains. Over those rough foothills and through the upper mountains, the men of the county hunted in the autumn of every year. They were men born with rifles in their hands, so to speak, and their marksmanship was as keen as their hunting trips were frequent.

Yet it was in this district that the train must be intercepted. There was no help for it, and Harry Christopher frankly warned his associates in the band that with their work they were almost sure to raise up a most formidable nest of hornets that might sting them all to death. Neither were his followers so foolhardy as to consider the risk

116

small. They were all of sufficient experience to realize the danger that lies in the strength of honest men and supporters of the law banded together even against the wits of the most expert and hardened lawbreakers. But the prize was great. There was three-quarters of a million dollars in hard cash to be distributed among them if they won.

That sum would be divided, all told, among about nineteen men. These were Tom Morris, who would be aboard the train as a guard, Jeff Stevens, who would board the train at Gully, ride as blind baggage toward Cranston, and on the way, at the appointed place, climb over the tender, and hold up the fireman and the engineer; and in addition to these and the five men who were with Harry Christopher, Steve Yerxa was bringing up ten old adherents of Christopher from the south and these would draw to a head at a convenient place where they could await the last-minute instructions of the chief out of whose brain the entire scheme had been born. Nineteen men made a considerable band, but to attempt the holdup with fewer might be difficult, considering that there were heavily armed guards in the treasure car and that the train might well have aboard it thirty or forty Westerners, each with a revolver which he knew how to use and, if occasion offered, *would* use. The passengers would have to be marched out of the cars and lined up, partly that they might be plundered in detail and partly that they might be under the eyes of the robbers, every man, while a detail of the assailants sacked the rich booty in the express car.

Nineteen men, under these considerations, would not be too many. And there was really plenty of spoil for them all. To the leader, Harry Christopher, there was to be assigned no less than a quarter of the entire proceeds, and even after he volunteered to pay off the expenses of the expedition which had to be met before the robbery was so much as attempted, he would still have no less than two hundred and fifty thousand dollars as his single portion! But to every one of the others who were joined in the attempt, there would accrue a magnificent reward of more than forty thousand dollars in money!

To poor Vincent Allan, the very attempt to conceive such a sum was an effort which strained his mental powers.

He had been accustomed to think of money in an impersonal manner. While he often handled large sums in the bank in Manhattan, still those sums had little more meaning than if he had read of them in a book. They had no relation to him. All that he knew of coin was the beggarly small stipend which he received at the end of each week in an envelope. But the prospect of receiving forty thousand dollars—and more—was a dazzling thing.

Not that he would keep it. Of course he could not do that. But if the daring scheme succeeded, which he greatly doubted, he would take his portion of the profits and send them back to the company which would have been so boldly robbed. Not if the prize had been a million would it tempt him for an instant. For honesty had been ingrained in his nature as deep as his simplicity.

He had only one purpose and that was to stay as close by the side of Jim Jones as possible throughout this affair and protect him in every manner. That would be a small answer in the eyes of the law, he knew. But it would be a great thing in the eyes of Frances, and it would be a great thing in his own eyes, for he had come to love Jim.

Thinking thus of the possibilities of the action that lay before them and of what it might mean to him in the end, he was amazed to see men so hard headed and so experienced as "Lefty" Bill, for instance, now most light-heartedly calculating in what fashion he could spend his portion of the loot. He and all the others were as confident as though the money was already actually in possession. They talked almost as though the deed had already been performed. There was only a single exception, and that was Harry Christopher. The captain never varied in his gravity. And sometimes it seemed to Allan that he could detect the leader sitting back, as it were, and studying and judging with contempt these lesser creatures who did his bidding and whom he despised for their obedience and their blindness to the dangers which were before them. Once, indeed, that flash of insight was confirmed in a startling manner by Christopher himself who took Allan aside and said to him:

"Now, Vincent, what's your plan for the spending of this here forty thousand that you got—"

"I haven't seen it," said Allan.

"You'll see it, old son. There ain't no doubt about that!"

Allan shrugged his shoulders. "I'm not counting on it until I see it," he said.

The chief scowled at him, "If they was all like you," he declared, "there wouldn't be no holdups; there wouldn't be nothin' done exceptin' sittin' tight at home and sleepin' and eatin'."

It was plain that he did not approve of such reserve on the part of his assistants. What he wanted was a number of headlong adventurers, willing to confidently undertake any risk, no matter how great, and out of their confidence he could find an energy which would turn his schemes into real action. There could not be more than one doubter in any party. But in Allan a second conservative was provided. And, from that moment, Harry Christopher looked upon him with a dark eye. He disliked his new follower for some of the very qualities which he most prized in himself!

At this Allan could only partly guess. But to actually understand and appreciate the mind of Harry Christopher he felt was a task far too great for his powers. The brigand was like a star; and Allan conceived him only by glances at very clear moments and could not even follow him for a moment at other times.

They started for the work when there still remained a week before the appointed day of the robbery. They had a considerable distance to cover, however, and the leader was strict that the horses should not be tired out by a forced march to the scene of the crime when the full strength of every animal might be needed to take them to safety afterward. They did not proceed in a solid body. Instead, each man went by himself, and the routes they followed all differed according to the taste of the individuals. There was only one couple, and that consisted of Jim and Allan, who were linked together partly at the request of Jim and partly because Allan really needed a guide through the unknown districts through which he was expected to journey. They parted, then, with little ceremony. The captain, as he dismissed his men, made them a little speech. It was not at all polished and it was not at all emphatic, but it was to the point.

"Gents," he said, "you got seven days to get to the place where you're goin' to meet me. What happens to you in between is your business. You pick out your own trails. If you get into trouble on the way, of course you don't figure in on this game. And a gent that gets into trouble *before* a party is pulled off, I don't want to ever have with me ag'in. When I see you come in at the right place and at the right time, I ain't goin' to look at you at all. I'm goin' to look at your hosses. If they look plumb fresh, I'll know that you've took your time, made a good easy march every day, and that you're going to be in shape to work for yourselves and the rest of us *after* we've done the job on the train. But if I see a man of you comin' in with a hoss that looks all ga'nted up and tuckered out, he don't figure in on the party at all. I don't care if he's my brother, I'd tell him to start ridin' and get out of the neighborhood because I didn't want to have him around me any more. Well, so long gents, and good luck to the whole of you!"

With that, he had left them, riding off down a trail on his finely shaped brown mare which had been his companion in every adventure of the past five years, during which he had made his fortune. She was as famous, wellnigh, as was he. Allan went off at the side of Jim, thinking over the speech of the leader.

"One would think," he said at last, "that Christopher didn't care whether his men showed up or not."

"He don't," answered Jim promptly.

"Suppose that so many of them disappoint him that he can't hold up the train.?

"Then he'll lose his time, his twenty thou' that he's soaked into the job, and all his hopes. But he'd rather have a loss like that, I've heard him say, than have a whole bunch of blockheads around him that he can't depend on. You understand? If he's got a man around him that's weak, he says that it's like having a weak link in a chain—it may drop the whole load one of these times! He wants nothin' around him but men that he knows are the true steel, old-timer!"

He added suddenly: "What's wrong between you and Harry?"

"I don't know," said Allan. "Nothing, I hope. I've followed orders."

"Something is wrong, though."

"What is it?"

"Well, I've watched him looking at you sometimes and I could of swore that he was tryin' to study you out and not bein' able to understand. I could of swore, Al, that he was sort of afraid of you!"

Allan pondered this remark quietly. And then he thought of a solution which was amusing and simple at the same time. It might very well be that the chief could not understand because, for the first time in his life, he had in his band an honest man. At least, the thought was pleasant. He wondered if this was the explanation.

The next remark of Jim's was not nearly so pleasing.

"And if I'm right," said Jim, "you want to look out. If Harry Christopher is afraid of you or any other man he won't rest until he's done 'em up. That's his way!"

CHAPTER 17

AL DARES DANGER

The course toward Gully which Jim mapped out carried close past El Ridal, as Allan had hoped it would, but when Jim himself said nothing of attempting the dangerous visit to the town in order to see his sister, Allan had not the courage to make the suggestion. It was the third evening of their journey when they pitched their camp on the lip of the gorge and looked down through the trunks of the pines to where the yellow lights were beginning to shine in the blue heart of the valley. How Jim could see those lights without feeling an impulse like a whip urging him down toward the hollow, Allan could not understand until he remembered that after all Jim was only her brother.

In fact, young Jim had not a word to say concerning his sister while they pitched camp and hobbled the horses and cooked their supper over a fire of the most gingerly small proportions. His own thoughts were so firmly fixed upon that topic, and that topic alone, that he heard what Jim had to say only dimly.

Coming so close to El Ridal, naturally enough, Jim

was thinking and talking of those two famous men of battle from whose hands he had been torn by Allan. So he sat with his shoulders cradled against a hummock of earth and told tales of great deeds which each had done singly and of the still greater things which they had accomplished by working together.

"But the queerest thing of all," declared Jim, "is that here we set as pretty as you please on the top of the house laughin' down at the both of 'em!"

"Maybe they're trailing us now?" suggested Allan.

It brought a shudder from Jim; he could not help glancing suspiciously at a stir among the moon shadows which lay thick and soft beneath the pines. But it was only the sway of a sapling, cuffed by the wind.

"They ain't after us," breathed Jim. "Old Christopher is keepin' tab on 'em, and he gets word regular from El Ridal. They're still there settin' quiet and turnin' their thumbs one around the other. What's in their heads? What's their little game?"

But Allan was now so lost in the contemplation of another subject that the last questions had to be repeated and with violence before he said: "Perhaps they're afraid, Jim."

It was a random answer, spoken because he did not wish to bother his head with the subject, but the effect was to make Jim gape at him.

"Afraid?" echoed Jim. "Them two dunno what fear is. That word ain't got any meanin' for 'em! Afraid? Of us? Listen to me, old son, they'd eat a dozen like the two of us and figger that they hadn't had a fight."

But even this threat could not disturb the mind of Allan for very long. In another moment he had returned to his meditations; and Jim, giving up all effort at speech with such an unsociable companion, at length twisted himself in his blanket and lay down to sleep on a bed of thickly heaped pine needles. He had hardly stretched himself out with a preliminary groan or two of comfort, when his breathing became thick, slow, and heavy.

So, in a trice, Allan found himself left alone in the middle of the mountain night. That sense of immeasurable bigness, the aching distances from the ground to the lofty tip of the pine tree, from the tree to the mountain summit, from the mountain peak to the cold white stars hanging in the thin immensity of space—this sense of prodigious size had at first weighed upon his brain and the first impulse had been to withdraw from it, to find shelter in a house, or to bend his eyes upon the ground. But, by degrees, his mind expanded to this prodigious frame. Those who dwell in cities cannot know the sky. They are only aware, now and again, of a pleasant blueness against which the bricks of some distant wall make a line of red; or they see, as they look up from an open carriage, a whirl of stars flowing through the heavens in a narrow street fenced in by the shadowy walls of the great buildings on either side. This is all that city dwellers can know of the sky. It was all that Allan knew. The sky was a place chiefly of importance when it poured down rattling hail, or rain, or soft, cold snow.

It was not in the same category after he went West. He sat now upon the ground with his head fallen back loosely upon his shoulders and stared upward with an earnest wonder and an ardent happiness. He felt, most of all, a sense of utter folly that he should have lived so many years with such wonders about his head and yet have paid no heed to them. He was like a man who sees that his neighbor's daughter, suddenly has turned the corner of her life, as it were, and become a woman with a certain electric significance, something new in voice and hand and eye, something which can be studied long and long but the mystery never quite understood. So it was with Allan in the clearing among the pines on the edge of El Ridal Cañon. He was tasting the lonely beauty of the mountain night as a new thing; he was growing drunk with it; and the more his heart swelled with this new delight the more impossible it became for him to drop his thoughts from the heaven to the black earth except to one place and to one person.

He had only to bend his head. The starry host slid out of his vision; the forested mountains swept up against the sky; then in the heart of the cañon he was staring at the little cluster of yellow lights which were El Ridal. By day it was a wretched little village indeed, for then one could see its actual buildings, unpainted, ramshackle, as though made hastily and thrown down without design in the great cañon at El Ridal. But at night all one could see was the gleam of its windows, which seemed to represent the mind of man, not less mysterious and magnificent than all the glory of the stars and the mountains.

So it seemed to Allan, not clearly, but in a vague emotion which enthralled his brain; and when he thought of humanity, it looked back to him out of the bright eyes of Frances for she was yonder among those yellow lights in the hollow!

With this, the dreamer looked at his companion, listened for an instant to the deep, regular breathing, and then rose carefully to his feet. Half an hour down the slope would take him to El Ridal. An hour would take him back again. And surely days and days before this, she had received the letter in which he had sent her the signal. He would be down and back long before morning, long before Jim awakened, sound sleeper that the latter was! Now that the idea had hold upon him, it increased in strength. It pushed him forward in frantic haste as though he were running a race until he reached the outskirts of the town, and stood among the trees beside the hotel. There he whistled his signal twice and went back behind the sheds, as agreed, to await the coming of the girl.

He had no thought, now, of those two formidable champions who so filled the mind of Jim Jones, yet he was wonderfully full of fear. It held him there among the trees with his breathing short and a dizziness in his mind; and it was the girl herself whom he so dreaded!

For, when he saw her, at last coming through the shadows, a pale form, his heart grew so small in him that he had to stretch out his hand and support himself by leaning against the trunk of the nearest tree. He could not speak until she had come straight up to him, for she seemed to locate him by instinct even in the darkness. He could not speak even then, except to murmur an unintelligible word. Neither did she give him any greeting for a long moment, but seemed to be studying his face and in so doing came so close that her own features were no longer blurred. A high light glowed on her brow. It made her eyes seem marvelously deep and dark and gave her all the dignity of added years of age. Allan had been as eager as he was afraid; now, however, he only wished to turn and flee from her.

She said in her usual matter-of-fact manner: "I knew it wouldn't be Jim. Jim's sound asleep right now, I s'pose."

No joy at seeing him, then; only profound regret because Jim had not come to her!

"He didn't know that I intended to come," said Allan feebly. "I slipped away without waking him, you see."

She nodded again. "I understand Jim. But what did you come to tell me?"

The panic of Allan increased; he searched his mind and could find nothing. "I don't know," he said.

The girl stamped her foot. "You've come down here and taken a chance that might get you half a dozen bullets for a free present. I guess you know that!"

"I hoped the danger would not be so great," said Allan.

"You *knew* it'd be. But you come anyway. Tell me why?"

He could only sigh.

"Did Jim have a message for me?"

"No."

"Al, you're actin' sort of simple. What's wrong? D'you mean to say you've come down here for—fun! You?"

Her bewilderment and her dawning scorn, it seemed, put a cruel whip upon the shoulders of Allan.

"It was to see you," he said at last, simply.

At this she gasped. Words were ever ready on her tongue, but now they failed her.

"And I really," he explained in his own heavy way, "thought that I would have something to say when I saw you, Frank."

"Look here," said the girl, "are you on the level about this, Al? You come down here and take a chance on bein' blowed in two just for the sake of saying 'Hello' to me?"

"It sounds foolish," said Allan. "I'm sorry."

"Jiminy!" breathed the girl. "It's crazy. Plain batty. Go back right now and get on your hoss and ride as fast as you can to get clean shut of El Ridal. This ain't no private hospital for you. Quick, Al! Where's your hoss?"

"Where I left Jim," he answered lamely.

It brought another furious outbreak from the girl. "You walked in? Of all the poor, bogged down—but listen to

126

me, Al. How are we goin' to get you out of this?"

"We?" murmured Allan. "Don't you worry about me, Frank. I'll manage for myself."

"H'm!" said she. "It don't look to me like you was none too good for managin' your own business. Well, now you've seen me, and we've said hello, and I know that Jim is well and too mean to come to see me himself— there's nothing left except for you to start back the way you came."

She was so quick with her words, and so matter of fact, that poor Allan could not make his brain function with a response. He could only stammer: "There's one thing more—"

"What is it?" she snapped out.

"Al, what's wrong with your head?"

"It's slow," he broke out desperately. "There's something inside of it that I want to tell you, Frank, but it won't come out."

She began to nod, and he could see her smile.

"Good old Al," she said, putting a kindly hand upon his arm. "You're better a million times than any of these smooth-talkin', smart-actin' boys. Take your time. Then tell me what's wrong."

All through their interview she had seemed to be growing older and wiser; he had seemed to himself to be dwindling into youth and insignificance, but now the burden of her pity was an added load which almost crushed him. Besides, he knew now that he could never, really, put what was in his heart into words. So he shook his head and said, rather sadly: "It's no use, Frank. It seemed to me, five minutes ago, that when I saw you I'd have a thousand things to say. But they've all disappeared."

"But at least you know the main drift," said she.

"Chiefly about you, Frank. I wanted to tell you of the ways in which I have been thinking about you." He drew a great breath as he remembered all the times of wretched loneliness. "I wanted to tell you that it seemed more than a year since—"

At this, with a little, startled cry, she caught him by both arms and drew him forth out of the shadow of the

127

tree so that the light of the heavens fell dimly upon his face.

"Al!" she whispered to him. "Are you tryin' to make love to me?"

"Love?" murmured Allan aghast. "I've never thought of such a thing in my life! No, no—it isn't love, Frank."

"H'm!" she said. "I got to take your word for it. Of course—I'm glad that my guess was wrong. But if it isn't that, what *is* in your head, Al?"

"It would only puzzle you, Frank, as it has puzzled me."

"Give me a try."

"But how could you know? You're only a girl, and a young girl, you see."

"Listen to me, Al. There never was a girl so dog-gone young that she didn't know all about every man in the world."

"Is that so?"

He asked her so seriously that she looked up sharply into his face with a quizzical little smile on her lips to meet the sarcasm of the expression which she was sure must be his; but then, seeing him all sober and all sincere she had to bow her head and Allan saw her shoulders shaking.

"Are you sick, Frank?" he asked in the greatest alarm.

She answered in a choked, explosive voice: "No, no!"

At any other time, he would have sworn that this was the voice of one who struggled against immense waves of laughter.

"But you are unhappy, Frank. There is something that I have said which has made you desperately unhappy. I can feel the pain in your voice, and here you are shaking from head to foot. Oh, what a stupid brute I have been. But I would rather have torn out my heart than to have hurt you. Will you try to believe that I mean what I say?"

Her answer was a stunning blow. It was a blow, indeed, after which he could never quite recover his mental poise so long as he lived. For she, starting a little back from him, cried out: "Al, what a silly, silly baby you are!"

And with that she broke into the heartiest laughter which, because it had to be controlled in sound, almost choked her.

CHAPTER 18

HANDCUFFS ARE NEAR

Allan, staring and wondering at her, wished himself a thousand miles from the spot. Yet, though she might be laughing at him, she was so lovely in her mirth that he would have changed his mind and wished himself back again.

Here she managed to gasp out: "Dear old Al. Excuse me; I couldn't help it!"

He said as simply as ever: "It doesn't really matter. No one ever has taken me very seriously, you know."

"But *I* take you seriously, Al."

Alas, she was still shaking with suppressed mirth as she spoke to him, and the anguish of his soul made his heart burn and his brain grow cold. All those twining muscles of arms and shoulders and breast and back of which he had become so newly conscious now wakened each into a life of its own. His fingers began to curl a little. What he wanted was to lay his hand upon some living thing and crush and tear the life out of it. He cast two or three baffled glances around him to find a prey among the shadows.

Then the girl was close to him again, fumbling to take his hand.

"Dear Al," she said, "now you are angry. I shall never, never forgive myself if I've hurt your feelings. But you know how girls are. We laugh at anything. I'm sorry, sorry, partner!"

"It's nothing, really."

"Tell me every word about what brought you here."

"If it had been love, Frank, do you think that I should have the courage to stand here and tell you about it? No, no!"

"What *is* love, Al?"

"I don't know, exactly. But it's something beautiful, of course."

"D'you think so? But go on," she was saying more blithely. "Tell me all about it, Al."

"Well, it's like homesickness, Frank. Except that I have no home to go to now. So it can't be homesickness."

"Ah!" said she.

"Does that mean anything to you!" he asked.

"Gimme time, Al. What else?"

"Nothing. Except that I have been constantly thinking of you. It has been a most wretched experience."

"Thinking of me?"

"Because, whenever I see you, you are smiling at me in a very peculiar way; as if you understood all about me and didn't want me to know how well you understand. Of course I've been used to having people treat me in that way. But for you to do it hurt a great deal more. I don't know why. That's all I can tell you—except—"

"Except what, Al?"

"You have no idea of what queer things go on inside of me as I stand here and watch you now. A little while ago you held up your head. Do you mind doing it again?"

She obeyed him without a word, looking at him through her lashes.

"Now with the starlight on your face, you are wonderfully beautiful, Frank."

She started a little. "I think you've said enough, Al," said she.

"But there is a great deal more."

"Like that last thing about starlight?"

"Oh, no. Even the way the hair curls at the nape of your neck, or the sound of your voice, Frank, are marvelous to me. And when I sat beside you in the desert that night as you slept, the sound of your breathing was such a delight that I had never known anything like it before."

"Hush, Al."

"Have I said a wrong thing?"

"About twenty of 'em, I guess."

"I only wanted to tell you the truth. I wanted to explain this peculiar thing to you."

"This thing that isn't love?" she said.

"Yes, of course."

She sighed. "You're either terrible smart or terrible simple, Al."

"Of course I'm simple. Everyone has always known that."

"Everyone don't know nothin' at all about you, old son. Everyone is a block head. But I'm beginnin' to guess things—I'm just beginnin'—"

She slipped suddenly close to him until her body touched him and he could hear her hurried breathing.

"Al, there's something sneakin' up through the shadows right straight behind you. Where's your gun?"

"I didn't bring a gun."

"Here. I always carry one. Act as if you didn't suspect nothin'. Take this gun. When you shoot, shoot plenty low. Shoot to kill, or they'll kill you!"

He took the gun with his right hand. He put his left arm slowly around her.

"Don't be a crazy man—your life, Al!" she whispered.

But when she strove to slip back from him, it was like leaning back against an iron beam.

"Jump for the trees!" she whispered.

He merely leaned and kissed her quietly, unhurried, and at the same instant a quiet voice was saying out of the darkness: "Look this way, Al Vincent!"

"Dive for the ground!" cried the girl. "Shoot as you drop."

Instead, he turned slowly toward the voice.

"You fat-faced rat—you skunk!" snarled the voice of Walter Jardine in the darkness. "Here I am. There you are. Start the party with your gun."

"I'll never be guilty of murder," said Allan gravely.

"Murder? I say, fight, or I'll fill you full of lead."

"Al!" cried the girl, frantic. "He'll kill you! Walter Jardine! Walter Jardine! If you shoot this man, I'll swear that he hadn't raised a hand to defend himself. I'll have you hounded as a murderer—"

"If you won't fight, you dog, drop the gun you got and put up your hands."

"And be sort of quick about it," added Elias Johnston from a position immediately to the rear.

Then Allan could understand. Jardine wanted the first opportunity to kill his man. But if Jardine failed, Allan still would not have been the victor, for that deadly little marksman Johnston would have remained to shoot him from the rear. He thought of this as he raised his hands closely above his head.

The two were instantly beside him.

"Have you got the cuffs?" asked Johnston.

"Right here."

"Get 'em on his wrists pronto. I'll keep him in hand while you do it."

So Elias drove the muzzle of a revolver into the pad of thick, soft flesh which covered the ribs of Allan and in a savage whisper invited him to dare to stir an inch in any direction.

"The first time you so much as twitch your hide like a hoss shakin' off a fly, I blow a chunk out of your liver, old son. You lay to that."

The handcuffs were prepared and held forth.

"Al, Al!" the girl was sobbing. "It would have been better to have fought them till you died."

"How did you know that I had come?" asked Allan curiously.

"There is whistles and whistles, old son," said Johnston, proud of the clever device by which he had discovered the signal.

"Then," cried the girl, "they've been opening my mail! Oh, you low, cowardly—"

What name she would have found for them in her wrath was never to be known, for at this instant a gun cracked from the trees nearby and the hat was jerked over the eyes of Jardine. He whirled with a curse of rage and surprise; at the same instant, the gun muzzle was removed from the ribs of Allan. It was only a fraction of a second as Elias involuntarily twitched away to face the new and unseen danger. But that slight interval gave Allan a chance and he used it. The back of his hand smashed into the face of Elias—a blow as fast as the flick of a cat's paw, as crushing as the battering forepaw of a grizzly, that most terrible of boxers. It flattened the nose of Johnston and knocked out three unfortunately too prominent teeth. At the same time it drove him off his feet. He floated against the trunk of the nearest pine tree, rebounded, and rolled limp upon the earth.

In the meantime, his strangled cry as he felt the stunning blow, made Jardine turn merely in time to meet the flying danger. It was only a grazing punch, but it flattened him as though it had been a cannon ball caroming from his skull. Before the echoes of the shooting had died away, before the voices from the hotel and from the street of El Ridal had had a chance to begin their alarm calls, Allan was in the thicket and at the side of none other than Jim Jones.

"You square head!" was the unkind greeting of Jim, and then wasting no more breath, he turned upon his heel and they fled through the darkness as fast as they could.

Halfway up the wall of the cañon toward their camping place they paused and looked back toward El Ridal. They could hear the voices of the confusion plainly enough. They could see lights stirring as men ran from house to shed with lanterns. They could hear the crash and rattle of the hoofs of galloping horses. But wildly as the horsemen rode, they did not come in that direction. They fled out from El Ridal along horse trails, and not in directions where a man would have to climb by foot.

"What's beatin' them is what near beat me," said Jim Jones after looking on for a time. "You goin' to El Ridal on foot. I claim that's the dog-gonedest fool thing that was ever done—or else the smartest."

"How did you know——" began Allan.

"There wasn't nothin' to that," said Jim. "I woke up the minute you got up. I seen you stand. Then I seen you start sneakin' away as plumb soft and easy as a hoss walkin' through gravel. So I decided to foller along. I got pretty scared when I seen you drivin' for El Ridal. But I kep' on. I didn't want to be outdared. But Al, what the deuce did you have to say to Frank that was worth runnin' the risk of Jardine and Johnston?"

There was no reply from Allan. But to his heart of hearts he was confiding a firm belief that it had been eminently worthwhile.

CHAPTER 19

THE HOLDUP STAGED

Where the railroad track cleft through a sharp-backed hill the trap had finally been laid, and the bandits had been carefully arranged on both sides of the cut. They worked in units of two.

"Any pair of fools might lick one dog-gone good fighter," said the captain as he made his arrangements. "But two good fighters workin' together and watchin' the backs of one another could stand off twenty or thirty blockheads."

Each pair, then, was instructed with the most minute detail. For a whole day they had camped in a hollow near the chosen place. The twenty-four hours were used to send word to Gully, in order that the two assistants of the gang who were on the train at that place might know where to make their attempt; and the rest of the time was spent in the most assiduous rehearsal of the parts which they were to play. One unit was to master the engine and see that the fire box was flooded, so that the train could not at once speed on its way and so rush a signal of danger to the nearest station. Other units were to turn the passengers out of the long line of coaches. The chief fighting men and brains of the whole body, in the meantime, were to concentrate on the attack upon the car which held the safes in which the cash was protected. Here Harry Christopher would in person lead the attack to destroy the guards; Tom Morris would be expected to play his part from the inside when the crisis should have arrived; and after all, the problem of the safe itself would be solved by the dexterity and the "soup" of Lefty Bill. Such was the general plan. The part which Allan was to play was merely to help turn the passengers out of the cars and help in the work of going through their pockets for their personal effects. He was only delighted that he should not be called upon to share in any gun work.

So all the preparations were made, and half an hour before the train was due to arrive, they were all in their hiding places, stowed back among the shrubbery on the slope of the cut, or else hidden high on the lip of the pass. The last cigarette was smoked. The last pipe was put out. All became quiet. For there had been a last announcement of all from Harry Christopher:

"The gent that makes us lose this here game—"

It was a threat which did not need to be completed, for the drawn, solemn faces of each man's neighbors made a sufficient warning. He whose single fault should cause the scheme to fall through would be murdered on the spot. There was no doubt about that. The tension was too great among them all. For they knew the character of the men of Cranston County. They knew that even if the robbery were successfully carried through only a small portion of the danger had been overcome. They had been pondering for days upon the risks which they were advancing to face. The result was that the nerves of every man had been drawn to the breaking point. Jim Jones lay beside Allan and the latter watched his face curiously.

The cheeks were pale; the lower jaw thrust out. He looked like a man who already faced a leveled gun.

As for Allan himself, he felt that he was in the middle of a strange dream. It was a bright warm day, with hardly enough wind even in the height of the heavens to give the clouds motion. It was now mid-afternoon, and the air had grown hotter steadily since noon. Upon the unshaded back of Allan the sun, beating down, pressed through the coat and burned against his skin. Heat waves shimmered and danced over the edges of the hills. The lizard on the brown, flat stone not a yard from Allan did not move during all the time he lay there.

Then the rails began to sing. Only in such a perfect silence could so small a sound have been heard. It grew louder and louder, a thin vibration which, as the engine swept around a nearer curve, increased to a sudden roaring. Here it was in sight, black, huge, with a plume of smoke cutting sharply back behind the smokestack. Allan could see the monster sway with its speed and its power as it took the curve into the cut and then—the grind of brake suddenly applied, a shudder down the great line of coaches, and the train slid to a halt just before them.

A single voice raised a sharp cry. That was Harry Christopher. Then his whole pack of wolves raised the answering yell as they swarmed down to their prey. Allan saw the engineer and fireman climb down out of the cab with their hands stuck high above their heads and a squat little fellow with a masked face following them, his revolver poised and glittering in the sunlight. He himself, scrambling to his feet behind Jim Jones, pulled down over his head the mask which he had cut from the black lining of his coat. He drew his revolver; he was part of the active little crowd which was rushing at the train.

Jim Jones raced in the lead. "Stay out here. Stick 'em up as they come up!" called Jim, and leaped up the steps into the first coach.

A woman screamed somewhere in the train, a wild, long cry that kept working among the nerves of Allan long after it had stopped. It stayed in his brain for days. He saw many faces appear at windows, flattening against them, and then quickly drawn back as though they felt that the gun held was leveled at each square of glass. Such is

136

the omnipotent power of a gun that if it is leveled on a hundred it seems meant particularly for every individual in the throng.

Now the passengers came tumbling down the steps, some cringing women wringing their hands even while they held them above their heads, some frightened men, others nervously careless. From the front of the train there was a thundering fusillade of gun fire. It was over in a moment; then the wild voice of Harry Christopher:

"Good work, old boy; Brain the——"

They had won the treasure car, then!

In the meantime, he dared not look to see what had happened. He had his part to play, carefully outlined, carefully rehearsed, and as the passengers came out, he barked at them: "Turn your faces to the car! Line up. Not too close. Keep your hands away from your pockets. Steady now. My job is to keep you quiet. I have bullets to do that job if words aren't enough. You there in the gray hat, get those hands higher—*above* your head!"

How like sheep they were, obeying, though there was enough man power in the passenger list of that single coach to have ground the entire band of Christopher to pulp! There was a savage pleasure in being one of the controlling minds in such a time as this had come to be. They watched him from the corners of their eyes. The whole line cringed when he made a gesture with his weapon.

This car was emptied. From other cars the same procession was pouring forth. Jim Jones came, fairly dancing with gay excitement.

"Good work, old-timer!" he called to Allan. "Keep 'em stiff as cardboard. I'll go through 'em. Empty your pockets, gents. Turn them pockets inside out!"

He went up the line with a sack under one arm. The other hand deftly went through the clothes of those who were too slow in tumbling for their possessions. The sack swelled larger and larger and fatter and fatter with the stolen treasure. Now and then came a whimpering cry from some woman who saw her rings stripped from her fingers by that rude, strong hand. Sometimes a man groaned as the fat wallet was brought forth. There was not money and jewelry only, but also more than one weapon came to light. Out of even the car in which Jim had first entered, five revolvers—no fewer—were taken. But all of these armed men, courageous enough under circumstances when they were prepared to face danger, had been unnerved and made helpless by the very audacity with which a single man dared to enter the car and turn them all out as though he carried a machine gun and not a six-shot revolver in his hands.

They were like sheep indeed! Just such a sheep had Allan himself been, and he wondered if, in the time to come, he would not return to the fold once again and wonder at those reckless days as though they were things in which his ghost alone participated.

Now the work neared completion. The sacked passengers were herded meekly back into the coaches. They had hardly disappeared within them when there was a hollow deeply-muffled report from the front of the train, followed by nervous shrieks from a dozen women through the cars. But even the untutored mind of Allan knew what had happened. Lefty Bill had proved his skill, and the door had been blown from the safe; the treasure was at the mercy of the bandits, and Harry Christopher had at last brought his scheme to consummation.

It seemed as though the explosion had roused endless echoes down the cut. The hollow roaring continued. Instead of dying away, it grew steadily, and then the explanation came suddenly. The rear guard who stood lookout on the upper lip of the cut while all of this work was being executed, galloped along the crest shouting.

"Another train! Quick, boys!"

Here it came, speeding and crashing down the track. It came prepared for mischief, too. One could see men standing on the lowest steps of the two coaches which composed the train, and in their hands was the terrible glitter of sunlight slipping up and down rifle barrels. In some way an alarm had been given at the town of Gully after the first train left, and perhaps this train load of protectors or avengers, as the case might be, had been dispatched in all haste.

Half a dozen men with sacks of some size under their arms or thrown over their backs were rushing from the treasure car with Harry Christopher standing behind them, guarding their retreat, bellowing orders at the rest of his men. Those orders commanded every man into the saddle with all speed, and the whole little brigade streamed up the slope, scrambling as fast as it could.

The passengers began to issue. News that the second train was approaching had spread like wildfire. There were even two guns which had not been taken in the plunder, and with these the passengers opened a hasty fire. There was too much venom in their minds and too little steady care in their hands, however, to make that fire effective. It only served to spur on the flight of the plunderers.

A far greater threat had now developed, however. With screaming brakes jammed on, the second train came to a rattling stop. From the steps leaped the citizen posse, and the metallic clangor of rifles began. They advanced like soldiers attacking a fortress, pausing to put in a shot and then running forward again at full speed. They fired at anything, everything, but the bandits were over the edge of the cut without injury and the rifle fire must perforce cease until the posse had climbed up to the ridge. Before they gained it the entire party was in the saddle and scooting for shelter as fast as spurs could drive the tortured horses. The dipping hills did the rest. There was a long-range scattering of shots as the last of the fugitives galloped out of sight, but presently the whole band drew down to a canter and the leader gathered them together for a brisk examination of damages sustained.

In the entire party there was only one wound and that was a scratch across the left shoulder of Lefty Bill where a rifle bullet had nipped him. It was bandaged on the spot, and while the bandaging took place the leader issued his orders.

A band of such a size could not hope to cross Cranston County without running into the law. Consequently they were ordered to split into two divisions. Nine men, with Lefty Bill in charge, were to make for the mountains through one pass. The remainder under the direct command of the chief were to head for another opening into the higher lands where they could hope to dodge pursuit. In two minutes the affairs were detailed and the points of rendezvous were appointed. Then the two divisions, with waved hats and shouts of farewell, separated. Lefty Bill with his contingent headed south and east. Harry Christopher with the others drove toward the north and east. Both directions were obliquely aimed at the mountains.

With Christopher rode Allan and Jim Jones. And Allan rejoiced that at least his lot had fallen in with that of his friend. Moreover, he had no doubt that they would now break through to safety. Counting the leader, they were ten in all, well mounted, well armed, and if they were pursued, the chances were great that they could outride their pursuers except so few that their numbers would avail to crush the men of the law as fast as they came up.

On the whole, Allan felt only relief. But the big weight upon his conscience was that one man had died in the attack on the train. He was one of the guards who took charge of the treasure car. He had been treacherously murdered from behind by Tom Morris, and at this attack from within, the other two guards had thrown down their arms. That was the secret of the easy fashion in which the treasure car had been mastered.

CHAPTER 20

PURSUIT

They rode steadily until dusk. Then they halted for coffee and crackers and bacon, which was eaten in raw slices sandwiched between the crackers. It was dark when they started on again, and yet it was not dark enough, for a rising moon began to ride above the eastern mountain-tops and an unkind flood of white light painted the faces of these buccaneers in silver and black. They pressed ahead without speech, with only the squeaking of leather against leather, the faint jingling of spurs, the snort and the trampling of the horses.

They had the consolation of being already among the foothills, however, and the chances were bright that they would be among the upper mountains by the dawn, if all went well. Harry Christopher, therefore, decided to abandon caution for a time and pressed straight on along the main highway, abandoning the wearisome and slow crosscuts over the countryside which were sure to leave them deep in the heart of Cranston County when the morning came. They took the highway and had jogged a full two miles along it, with their spirits rising every moment, before they encountered a traveler in the opposite direction.

He was a good-natured chap who wished to pause for gossip.

"I got no time for talk," said Hank Geer, cutting him brutally short. "We been out chasin' the gang of crooks that held up the train. I'm tired. So're the rest of the boys. Might as well of chased a lot of shadows. They'll never be caught."

"Ay," said the countryman. "That was Harry Christopher's work. He was recognized by the hoss he was ridin'. They ain't catchin' Christopher until a blue moon comes along, I guess. Well, so long, boys. Sorry you had bad luck."

He disappeared down the road, waving his hand to them. But his horse was no sooner around the next corner than they heard it break into a furious gallop. Harry Christopher instantly drew rein and the others paused likewise.

"You hear that gent ridin'?" said Christopher. "Well, he smelled a rat. He smelled a rat, you can depend on that!"

"Lemme go back and tag him," said Hank Greer grimly, pulling his long rifle from its holster. "They's moon enough shinin' for me to see a yaller hound by!"

"You stay put," said Christopher coldly. "Killin' is your line of trade. Money makin' is mine. We got to use our hosses more than our guns this night. Which I say, ride like the devil, boys. Trouble sure comin' behind us!"

Straight up the highway they galloped at a round pace. Not racing, for considering the distance which they had to travel, it would have been folly to trust to the speed of their horses at a springing gait which would soon wear them out. A full half hour was passed in this fashion. Allan watched the others busily at work. They were shifting the weights of their packs. More than one deliberately threw his blankets away. Others changed the saddlebags. All were making grimly ready for a hot pursuit and Allan did his best to follow their example.

"What'll happen?" he ventured to ask Jim.

But even Jim had no words. He merely turned a grim face upon his companion. Speech was to no purpose at

142

a time such as this when no man could tell what might come in the next five minutes.

When the half hour ended, however, they had the first indication of danger hurrying up in their rear. Hank Greer, whose ears were prophetically sensitive and sure, checked his horse suddenly and raised a hand. The whole party followed suit, and the instant their horses had stopped moving they could hear far back down the road, a sound like the beating of a rain storm.

"Hosses!" said Hank Geer calmly. "This here night we're goin' to ride."

There was a short, earnest consultation. The general vote was for heading straight on down the road, and though Harry Christopher voted to take to the cross-country trails at once, he allowed himself to be persuaded. Their horses were still in good condition. They might be able to distance the pursuit which, perhaps, was burning up horseflesh by a too frequent use of the spurs.

"Keep on ridin' steady. Don't whip no hoss and don't liven 'em up with no spurs," directed the leader. "Take all of this mighty easy. They ain't goin' to be no spurt until we got their bullets whistlin' around us. And then maybe we can whistle back a little bit.

On his own magnificent horse he now took the lead to regulate the pace and struck away at a swinging canter which the others could easily maintain. In the meantime, that noise like rain increased behind them, swelled large, and finally, looking back down a straight stretch, brilliant with the increasing moonlight, they could see the party behind them.

It was a sight to make the hearts of the stoutest quail. For, packed closely together across the road and stretching far down it there were no fewer than two-score horses. They came fast, but not recklessly fast enough to burn out the hearts of their horses, for one could tell by the fashion in which the group held together that all of the animals were kept well in hand. This was the meaning, then, this resolution and this system, of the saying that crimes were no longer profitable in Cranston County.

"I didn't know," snarled out Hank Geer, "that there was that many fighters in Cranston County. Dog-gone me, they ride along as slick as cavalry."

Like cavalry, indeed, they came, and the hearts of the fugitives failed them when they saw that resolute charge of such a body of fighting men. Perhaps in the mind of each rose up those other lurid tales of how the men of Cranston had ridden down criminals and having cornered them had meted out justice of their own for fear that justice in the court of the law would not move swiftly enough. The whole troop of the bandits began to push ahead with frantic haste. Even the sharp voice of Harry Christopher, raised in command, could hardly keep them back to a reasonable gait—such as that maintained by their pursuers, for instance.

"And they all got *hosses!*" shouted Jim at the ear of Allan. "Old son, we're in for it!"

For truly the posse held the pace with wonderful ease and still crept up on the outlaws little by little. Before them now appeared a long, narrow cut between two ranges of hills, a cut as narrow as though it had been gouged out by a river, and perhaps a river had indeed done the work in past ages, since when it had run dry.

Once in the throat of this pass, where the moonlight left a steep, thick shadow on the eastern side and the sharp walls cast back the echoes of the hoofs in thunder, the party fell into two divisions on account of the narrowness of the trail. In the first flight were Harry Christopher at the head and then five others. Behind came a considerable gap, for there was the slow pace of Mustard to contend with—Mustard, who had become weary of the running in spirit rather than in the flesh and desired, now, to slacken to a most moderate canter. A prick of the spurs merely made her run stiff-legged, with a humped back. In vain the companions behind Allan cursed both him and his horse. In vain they strove to get past, for on either side of the narrow trail the boulders jutted up like great teeth. And the rest were kept back.

Allan heard the raging voice of Sam Buttrick in his rear yelling: "Knock the fool kid in the head, Hank, and we'll bust by him! He's sellin' us all for a nickel, this way!"

"Get out of the way!" thundered Hank Greer, the terrible. "Get out, if you can't ride your fool nag no faster'n a walk!"

But Allan had no time to act according to this gentle advice, and perhaps he would have received the bullet which had been advised by Buttrick had not the sharp voice of Jim cut in: "The gent that pulls a gun on my pal Al gets pulled on by me!"

Perhaps that warning saved Allan in the first place. In the second place he was protected by an incident over which none of them could have had the slightest control. There was a loud shouting from the head of the defile, which was already in view, and then a rapid chattering of guns. They heard the roaring of the hoofs of scores of horses before them. They saw the head of their own party rush away out of the defile at the full speed of their horses, their guns flashing repeatedly as they fired toward the right. And from the right, at the same time, there swept into view a veritable little army of horsemen, riding with the wildest determination, their guns blazing as they plunged along. One moiety of their number spurred off Harry Christopher and the foremost members of Christopher's gang. The rest swerved back and instantly choked all egress from the defile which had now become a perfect trap, blocked at either end with overwhelming numbers of the hard-fighting, hard-riding countrymen.

Well indeed had the men of Cranston County proved that they were worthy of all their reputation as upholders of the law! The very ground seemed to have put forth armed warriors in the way of the retreating bandits, before and behind.

There needed no commander at this juncture to tell Allan what he must do. Before him and behind came the enemy. On either hand arose a wall up which no horse, no matter what a goat-footed mountain climber, could have advanced for fifty yards. He threw himself out of the saddle and leaped up the rough slope. His companions on that wild retreat were already laboring in the same direction, with Hank Geer puffing and groaning in the rear. For strong walker as Hank was, his long bony legs were not meant for the labor of struggling and jumping up such a murderous incline as this. He was further impeded by the bulk and the weight of one of the sacks of the treasure, for he had been one among that original six into whose care loot had been entrusted.

All this was seen by Allan as he hurried up from the rear. What he lacked by a slow start he was making up for by the ease with which he climbed. It mattered nothing that he had no lifetime of training in mountaineering. The God-given strength and surety of his arms and hands was in his legs and feet also. Therefore, while his allies struggled on in advance, he could afford to turn his head and look back into the hollow. There the two tides of the pursuers met in the heart of the defile, met with yells of mingled disappointment and of triumph as they saw the prey had for the moment slipped out of reach but still remained so near—and on foot!

They abandoned their horses instantly. A mere handful remained behind with their cow-ponies; the others swarmed up the slope. A score of nimble-footed youths, each eager to surpass the other in the chase, leaped into the van and gained fast, fast upon poor Hank Geer, whose breath had already so far failed him that he dared not waste it in curses.

This was the situation as Allan overtook his lank companion. He said not a word, but from the shoulder of Geer he snatched the treasure sack. From his waist he dragged the heavy cartridge belt, leaving the naked gun alone in Hank's hand. There was a startled gasp from Geer as he realized what had been done for him. Then, redoubling his speed, he gained the top of the slope.

At least there would be no easy pursuit for the men of Cranston County. From the edge of the draw Jim Jones had opened fire, blazing away at the shadowy forms as they climbed and driving them instantly into cover from which they opened a return fire that swept the top of the cliff. Nothing could have lived there for an instant in the face of such a storm of lead, but nothing remained there to strive to maintain that position. The whole party was stumbling down the farther slope.

"Kid," said Geer, slapping the shoulder of his powerful companion as they ran on side by side, "that was a good turn. And Hank Geer never forgets a good turn."

"I blocked you in the pass," answered Allan. "It was only turn and turn about."

They were running down the surface of an undulating plateau which formed the uppermost crest of that sweep of

146

low hills. On either hand sharp-walled gullies stepped down into the narrow valleys beyond. And those valleys were crossed and recrossed by fences and lines of trees—a veritable mass of natural and artificial entanglements through which they would have to dodge their way.

"Which way?" gasped out Jim Jones in the lead.

"Straight on," said Sam Buttrick.

As he spoke, they dipped into a shallow, steep-walled hollow in the surface of the plateau. One bank shelved sharply back, its face masked with shrubbery. That natural shelter was espied by Jim. He leaped for it and dragged Geer after him. The others followed perforce, Sam Buttrick vowing that they had placed themselves in a trap like stupid rabbits, but there was no time for argument now. Behind them came the voices of the pursuers, who had already topped the rise and begun to race across the plateau.

CHAPTER 21

AL'S STUNT

Half a dozen jumped down into the very hollow at the edge of which the fugitives lay crouched. The others sped around on either side. But they all halted almost at once.

"I seen 'em about here," said one.

"What'd they do, then? Fade into thin air?" asked another. The heavy voice of an older man, already much spent with running, came up from the rear.

"They ducked down into the valley on one side or the other," he declared. "That's what they'd most nacherally do, ain't it? Look down the plateau? If they was still running that way, we could see 'em against the sky."

"Either that, or they've took to cover."

"What cover?"

"Rocks."

"Nothin' big enough to hide four men."

"There was six of 'em."

"Five, you fool!"

"Do something; we can't stay here all night while the skunks get clean away."

"Let one gent stay here," said he whose voice was deeper and older than the voices of the others. "Then we'll split up into gangs. Here's nigh fifty of us. Young, you take part. Shaughnessy, you take another. I'll take the boys that'll go with me. Langton can take another. Here's four gorges that run down, two on each side. Comb them places like they had diamonds in 'em! The gent that stays up here, if he sees anything, can give a holler and we'll hear him. On a still night like this, sounds travel pretty clear and pretty far."

"I'll stay," volunteered a voice. "Dog-gone me if I ain't tired of runnin'. I'll stay put."

"Good old Bill! Keep an eye open."

"You trust me, boys. I wasn't born yesterday."

There was a brief babbling of voices as the parties were made up. In another minute they were off to their work. Certainly the men of Cranston County were proving again that they were capable man hunters and organizers of man hunts on this night of nights!

The noise of the retreating footfalls died off; but still they could hear Bill, the sentinel, walking back and forth as he kept his post and whistled as he strolled about. One in so cheerful a frame of mind was certain to be vigilant. But he was now at such a distance that the four in hiding were enabled to whisper to one another, guarding their breath with the greatest care. Indeed, up to this point

148

they had hardly been able to enjoy deep breathing itself, let alone conversation. And for all the mighty depths of his lungs, Allan had felt himself stifled.

"One fine, sweet devil of a mess," was the first comment, and it came from Sam Buttrick. "It was the kid that done it. What kind of a hoss d'you ride, Vincent? An' how d'you ride it? Darn me if I don't wish that Geer had drilled you clean and——"

"Shut up," said Geer sullenly. "The kid ain't to blame. It was his hoss. Them Roman-nosed fools is always where you don't want 'em. But what's up to us to do?"

"Try to sneak off if we can," said Jim.

"With this gent Bill watchin'? Don't be a fool, Jim. If he was singing, we might do it, because a gent that sings partly closes his eyes. But a gent that whistles is seein' everything."

"What, then?"

"Somebody has got to get Bill."

"A gun would call up the whole gang on us."

"Something silent is better'n a gun—a knife, old son!"

"Who'll do it?"

"Me."

And Buttrick almost snarled with a savage anticipation of satisfaction as he swayed to his knees and hands to crawl out of his hiding place.

"He won't hear me no more'n a snake until I'm behind him—and then—I know where to put the ol' toad sticker. You can lay to that, old son!"

"For Heaven's sake," murmured Allan, turning sick. "Wait!"

"You got us into this. What you got to offer?"

"Let me get him."

"You? You'd make enough noise to wake up the birds!

"He didn't make none too much noise when he put you to sleep, Sam," broke in the grim voice of Hank Geer, who had evidently taken it upon himself to champion the youth whose clumsy riding had put them all in this terrible predicament.

There was a growl of beastly rage from Buttrick.

"It was a slip—it was a chance—you heard him say so himself."

"You never tried no second chance with your fists with him."

This from Geer, who now added as Buttrick snarled in his fury: "Go ahead, kid. It's your chance to do us a turn, and a big turn, too!"

There was nothing for it but for Allan to do as he had promised, although he realized that even the bearding of Johnston and Jardine had been a small danger compared with this adventure. For he had to attack an armed man studiously standing guard; and his own scruples made it impossible for him to use a deadly weapon, whereas the other would shoot with a practiced hand and shoot to kill at the first sign of so much as a shadow's stir.

He drew his belt close, for he was quivering with dread and excitement.

"Have you got a plan, Al?" asked the friendly voice of Jim.

"I have one," answered Allan, but there was not a vestige of an idea in his brain as he stole cautiously out of the shelter, putting back the branches of the shrubbery one by one with his hands so that there might not be even the brushing sound of the leaves against his clothes as he came out.

There was no need for that precaution, as it appeared, for when he gained the open and straightened to his knees to look over the edge of the hollow, he saw the enemy clearly outlined against the stars a full thirty yards away. Against the stars he saw the man of the posse, the same stars which, not long before, had seemed to him so beautiful as they looked down upon El Ridal and the lady of his heart who lived there. Here were the same bright clusters of them, for the moon which had drowned them earlier in the night had now clothed herself with a thick mass of cloud, of which only the outer filaments were a brilliant silver. Here was the same face of night, but with what a different heart he looked out upon it!

He thought of that, but only for a moment. He had not taken the first gliding movement in his approach before he began to be transformed. He could not use an upright gait. He had to drag off his boots and go upon toes, knees, and strong, sure hands, gliding as, in his boyhood, he had often watched the cat stalk a bird in the back yard.

He could understand, now, why the eyes of the stalking cat had become green with an ineffable and devilish joy, for the same joy was now in his heart as he looked across the rocks at Bill, his victim to be.

It was a hard thing to accomplish. Every moment the cautious sentinel was turning here and there, on the watch. In the hollows near by the sounds of the searchers were most plainly audible, floating up through the clear quiet air of the mountain night, now fast growing chill. Moreover, they might return in part at any time and make all his expedition fruitless—make it even impossible for him to regain that miserable shelter among the bushes in the hollow. Still worse, the rocks which scattered the surface of the plateau were, as one of the posse had said before, very small, not nearly big enough to shelter a grown man.

But he worked as the cat had worked in the back yard. Now he took a few gliding, animal paces forward upon all fours. Now, as the guard turned, he sank softly upon his face and his belly, watching with only one eye. So, for five eternally long minutes he glided ahead until the other was almost within his reach—a scant five or six paces away. But then, Bill deliberately turned upon his heel and walked to a new position—walked toward it passing within the length of a man's body from Allan.

The latter gave himself up, seeing the foe step directly toward him, and seeing the gun, too, naked in the hand of the latter. But luck, which favors the stealthy, was with him. The eyes of Bill were straining far away. He saw nothing of this misshapen shadow sprawled among the rocks at his very feet. But, as he passed, on, the strange shadow collected, bulged into the shape of a man rising to his knees, and then from silent, stockinged feet, the hunter sprang forward.

One hand with fingers like shrinking steel cables clutched the gun wrist of Bill, and just as the wasp's sting makes the spider numb, so that terrible grip turned the fingers of Bill limp and the gun dropped harmlessly at his feet. The crook of Allan's other elbow was at the same instant bent around the throat of his victim. They fell prostrate upon the ground.

All that he could think of was something out of his childhood. "Do you give up, Billl?"

There was a gurgling sound, and Allan released the throat-crushing grip of his arm.

"I give up!" gasped poor Bill. "But how——"

Voices came over the brow of the plateau and advanced straight toward them.

"Lie still," said Allan, through his teeth, as he felt a terrible fierceness sweep through him. "Lie still!" If they find us—if you make a move—I break your neck first. Then I'll tackle 'em."

He would have done it. There was no fear in him as he lay there, but all the passions of the devil were loosed in him at that moment, as all the passions of evil are loosed in the cat whose crafty, lucky spring has at last brought down the fluttering bird in its claws.

There were three voices in the party which approached.

"They're tryin' the valley on each side," said one. "If them four went down that way, they're done for. There's more searchers started up them valleys from each end. We've telephoned from the station to Hinchley, and that town has turned out a bunch to close in in this direction. We got 'em sure."

"Supposin' that they cut sidewise across the hills?"

"It don't make no difference. Only thing that they could of done was to cut straight back across country. We've drawed a circle beginning at the cut, yonder, where we blocked 'em off. We got the edges of that circle all lined with men, and the lines only got to move in closer to the center. The nearer they get to the center the surer they are of baggin' 'em. They're as good as ours."

"This'll teach man killin', murderin', robbin' swine to keep out of Cranston County!"

They drew nearer. One stumbled. He was so near that Allan could hear not only his exclamation, but the little indrawn breath of anger and of pain which preceded it. And then—they were past! He could turn his eyes and see them marching away across the little plateau in a line, talking busily, until they dipped into one of the gorges where the other hunters were busily at work.

CHAPTER 22

THE KID IS RIGHT

To his knees rose Allan, his mighty grip on the collar of his captive at the base of the throat where, with one powerful twist, he could throttle his victim. He looked around and made sure that there was no other man in sight.

"Now," said Allan, "you've had bad luck, Bill. You swear to keep still and make no noise?"

"You've got me," said the other. "I'm beat. I'll swear anything that you want."

"Get up and walk ahead of me—this way—that's right."

So he guided his man back to the hollow, carrying in his own hand the revolver which poor Bill had dropped. Bill was a middle-aged, stoutly built man with a pair of hanging side whiskers and a long, high-arched nose which gave his face, together with a glittering little pair of eyes, an air of the shrewdest penetration. At the hollow he gasped with amazement when the low voice of Allan called forth the hidden men from their place of concealment.

"And we was standin' right over you!" said Bill.

The first word for Allan was not praise for his accomplishment. It was the brutal snarl of Sam Buttrick.

"Why'd you bring him back to us? *I* don't want to see him. Make him safe and make him safe pronto, say I!"

There was no mistaking this butcher's meaning, and to make it all the clearer he drew his revolver, took it by the barrel and weighed the heavy butt as though prepared to dash out the brains of the captive on the spot. And poor Bill shrank back toward Allan.

The latter was sick at heart.

"Keep back, Sam," he warned the big man. "I've given Bill my word that he's safe with us so long as he treats us honestly."

"Your word?" sneered Buttrick. "What's the word of a kid like you among men?"

"You're out o' your head, Sam," broke in Geer. "But what can we do with this gent, Al?"

"Take him with us a way."

"To have him show us up?"

"Leave him here, then."

"We've got no time to gag him and tie him."

"Take him part way. And this is the way—back across the top of this hill and then down across the cut on the farther side."

"Do you mean it, Al?" asked Jim anxiously, while the two elder men merely stared.

"I'll explain while we go; I heard them say that they've drawn a circle around us. The best way is to turn straight back."

"It sounds queer to me," doubted Jim.

"He's nutty," said Buttrick. "He wants to run us all into jail and then turn State's evidence, or something, to save his own head. I know that kind!"

"We got to do something quick," said Geer, "An' I'm goin' to split the difference and start goin'."

With that he slung his treasure pack over his shoulder turned on his heel, and started off down the plateau at a long, slinking run which covered the ground with the greatest speed. Buttrick at once made off after him.

"Jim," pleaded Allan, "I tell you I heard them with my own ears; they said they'd drawn a complete circle around the whole range of hills in that direction."

"Looks like it's too big a job for them to have done that so quick."

"They've used the telephone, I tell you! The whole country's up and searching for us."

"No matter what the country's doin', Al, there go the gals that have rode with us to-night. Our place is with them."

And, with this unanswerable argument, he turned off to follow in their footsteps. There was nothing left for Allan to do except, with a groan, to order Bill to run ahead of him. In a trice they were streaking down the plateau and into the very teeth of danger, as Allan was certain beforehand.

For all the strength of Sam Buttrick's muscles, his weight told against him when it came to running. Even the solid form of Bill was lighter afoot, and they presently overtook Sam and Hank jogging on drearily, side by side. For a half hour they struggled on in this fashion. Nothing appeared before them. Nothing was heard on either side. They came to the end of the plateau and dipped among broken hill forms, interspersed with groves of trees and thickets. They had covered, perhaps, three miles in that time, and now Buttrick stopped and gasped; he could go no farther. He was exhausted, he declared, and would spend the rest of the night in hiding in the first covert. In the morning, which would come before long, one of them could keep a lookout. The others would rest until the dusk of the evening, and then they could all start forth again.

"We're putting the rope around our necks," said Allan. "They'll beat across this entire country, by that time."

"Does it look like they're beatin' this way?" asked Buttrick, and held up his hand to command silence.

In fact, there was neither sight nor sound to alarm them. There were other factors pleading on his side. It was pointed out that on the rocky plateau they would have left no trail which could well be followed. Furthermore it was well past midnight, and they were all, saving the inexhaustible Allan, well-nigh spent by the exertions of the day, which had begun early and had included so much hard riding and so much travel on foot.

"Besides," said Buttrick, "we got to understand right

here and now whether the old heads or the young uns do the commandin' on this here trip!"

To this even Jim responded that it would undoubtedly be best to do in all things what Geer and Buttrick should decide. That point was thus settled. In five minutes the party was curled up among beds of leaves in the heart of the first thicket before them, sleeping or trying to sleep, with the prisoner, Bill, securely fastened to Allan in case he should try to escape.

Indeed, within a few moments the others were asleep, saving Allan to whom sleep would not come, and Bill, whom constant terror haunted. He did not know what might lie in store for him on the morrow when he became an incumbrance upon the fugitives. They held a whispered little dialogue there in the dark thicket among the sleeping men. It was far from cheerful.

"We're lost, Bill," said Allan.

"They was fools to foller the gent you call Sam," said Bill. "Who is he?"

"Sam Buttrick."

It was a name, evidently, to conjure with. There was a frightened little gasp from Bill. Then he was silent for some time.

"Tell me one thing, young man," Bill said at length. "How did you happen to throw in with these gents?"

"That's a long story."

"It's a sad one," whispered Bill. "An' Heaven help you before you're done with 'em. You ain't their kind."

"What's done is done," said Allan gloomily.

"When you're all took," said Bill, "you can lay to it, son, that I'll have something to say for you. An' if you ain't got the blood of no man on your hands——"

"Why should you do so much?"

"You saved me from that butcher."

Some one of the other three stirred, groaned, and demanded silence and a chance to rest, so that all talking ended here, but it was a drearily long night for Allan. The hours dragged by and it seemed that day would never come.

Once, when the dawn began to creep up through the trees, making them tall, jet-black forms, and when the cold wind which rises before morning among the mountains was beginning to blow and search through Allan's clothes to his very heart, his captive ventured speech again.

"If you was to let me loose—like as if I'd got away during your sleep——"

But Allan shook his head. The right or the wrong of this particular matter he could hardly decide, but he felt that, having been hunted like beasts by this fellow among others, they had at least a right to render him helpless to betray them. As for Buttrick, he assured Bill that the butcher should not lay hands on him.

Morning, in the meantime, came fast. The sun rose, and when its radiance fell in cold, rosy patches through the trees, the sleeping trio were wakened by cold, by hunger, and by bitter thirst. They had not tasted water for twelve hours and more, and they had endured much physical fatigue in the meantime. Neither had they a morsel of food with them. Their breakfast consisted of a cigarette and belts drawn a few notches tighter.

Nothing could describe the gloomy savagery with which they regarded one another now. The sleep for which they had halted had not refreshed them. Their appetites, ravenous from work, anxiety, and the mountain air, became so many tortures, and the rest which they hoped for during the day now became manifestly impossible.

The first and bitterest need, of course, was water. Bill was questioned. He knew of no spring near by. In fact that whole district was unfamiliar to him, for he had ridden many miles from his home region with the posse.

"To kill—or get killed," snarled out Buttrick, his brutal eyes fastening upon the victim, and Bill turned pale, sallow yellow with fear.

Hank Geer, as being the most dexterous and cautious hunter, was commissioned to go out and locate water if possible. He was gone for an hour. He came back with a black face and sat down in silence. Instead of speaking, he merely rolled and lighted a cigarette, and smoked it in great drafts, inhaling the smoke so deeply that it nearly disappeared. It was a quarter of an hour before he spoke, and then it was to say, simply: "The kid was right."

"What kid?" growled out Buttrick, whose hatred for

Allan appeared to grow every instant with his own bodily fatigue.

"You know who I mean. Al was right. You was wrong. So was all the rest of us."

"Right?" echoed Buttrick, turning pale. "About what?"

"They're closin' in on us. They're all around us. Gents they've drawed a circle clean around us. You can toss a coin to see what we'll do!"

"They's only one thing to do," said Buttrick. "Bat this gent on the head and leave him here where he won't be no more trouble to us. Then the four of us bust through the line. A couple might get tagged. A couple might get through. There ain't no other hope."

CHAPTER 23

A TRUMP CARD

Four pairs of eyes turned fiercely upon Bill. He moistened his white lips and tried twice before he could speak.

"Gents," he said huskily at the last, "I sure see how you're fixed. What I say is, tie me tight. Use a gag that dog-gone near chokes me. What could I do then?"

"Wiggle out of the trees and show yourself."

"Tie me to a tree."

"Work the gag out of your mouth and yell."

"Not if you put it in tight enough. Nobody could do that."

"We can't take many chances," said Hank Greer thoughtfully. "I know the way Buttrick thinks. But maybe he's right this time."

He fixed his terrible, dreamy eyes, devoid of human emotion, upon the victim.

"There's four lives on that chance," said Sam eagerly. "Who'd do the work?"

"Me," said Sam.

"Gents," gasped out poor Bill, "I give you my word of honor that I'll not make no noise. I'll lie quiet. My word of honor that ain't never been busted."

Still they regarded him without a word, gloomily, fiercely, and he knew that his word to them was like a feather blowing on the wind. He turned desperately to Allan.

"Son," he begged, "would you sit by and see a man with four kids murdered?"

There was no answer from the latter for a moment, but he had determined in his slow way what he must do. It was to draw out his revolver without haste and rest it across his knee, pointing straight at Buttrick.

"Sam," he said at last, "it simply won't do. It may be right for the rest of you, but I can't stand it."

"Geer," said Buttrick at last, "the young skunk has me covered. You goin' to sit by and watch that? Are you goin' to murder me?"

The long, lean fingers of Geer were wrapped around his gun butt, but he did not speak. Action was close to his mind, but he had not yet quite determined.

"There's another way out," said Allan finally. "The three of you do as you please and stay where you please. I'll stay here with Bill."

The long fingers of Geer released his gun.

"You hear that, Sam?"

"I hear it. Then let's start. What's in his fool head I dunno. Maybe he figures that him and Bill could be hid where four would be seen. Maybe that's it. I say, let's start now—pronto."

Geer also rose to his feet. "Come on, Jim," he said.

"The three of us can make a way for the lucky one to get through—if we shoot straight!"

But Jim shook his head. "Me and Al," he said, "is partners in a way. It ain't my style to leave him behind."

That was all—very simply spoken, but with an unshakable determination behind it. Buttrick started to implore. For two to attempt to pierce the closing lines of the man hunters would have been insanity, obviously. But for three there remained a single chance. Was it not better than to calmly submit while the noose was being drawn about one's neck? It was all in vain. Hank Geer merely shrugged his shoulders and sat down, and Buttrick, with a final groan, submitted also.

"It's the kid," he declared solemnly. "He ain't brought nothin' but bad luck on us since he joined. He's our Jonah! Ain't it plain?"

Geer nodded. "He's got only one thing on his side," he said quietly. "He's square! An' while he's square, Jim is right. We got to stick by him."

It was an overwhelming majority, now, and even Buttrick could talk no more. At least they could cast about them for a better hiding place. First they scattered the leaves and buried the cigarette butts in the spot where they had camped. Then they started on their search, and as they started Bill, with shining eyes, clutched the hand of Allan.

"If my kids live to see me ag'in," he whispered, with his heart in his trembling voice, "they're goin' to learn to pray, and they're goin' to learn to put a new name in their prayers. Son, you're white—all white—clean through!"

They had no luck on their earnest quest. They went to the edge of the grove which sheltered them and saw a sweep of open ground leading back toward a plateau from which they had fled the night before. There was one small hillock in the vale like an island in the sea, crowned with a narrow circle of trees. And as he saw, an inspiration came to Jim.

"Where does gents always fail to look?" he said. "In the places that don't *seem* to have no chance of bein' the right ones. When I was a kid I always lost my hat on the hat rack. I could find it a pile quicker if it was under

160

the bed or stuck away in a corner. But if it was right under my eyes, I never had no luck. Would they ever think that we'd try to hide, all four of us, in a place like that over yonder? One look inside the circle of them trees would show us, if we was there. Nope, they'd never go yonder! Boys, ain't it a chance?"

They grew enthusiastic immediately. Even Sam Buttrick for the moment forgot his gloom and vowed that Jim was the good luck of the party, almost strong enough to offset their "Jonah."

So they went to the place at once and found it, in fact, ideally suited to shelter them from the casual view of any passerby. For, along with the circle of trees, there was a thick growth of shrubbery, so that they even had to break down a few of the bushes before they could make a place where they might sit down in a circle. Seated there they could see nothing of the outside plain; how impossible, then, would it be for them to be located unless a searcher actually walked within the circle of the trees?

Their spirits now rose to a high point, but at the command of Greer it was decided that they should not risk so much as a taint of cigarette smoke in the air. They began to wait, one of those endless times of suspense. Yet in actual minutes it was not long before the searchers appeared. And when they saw them as they peered out through their screen of shrubbery, they could agree at once that against such forces as these, any attempt to have rushed the lines would have been useless and instantly fatal. Over the sector which they could view themselves— and surely the rest of the circle must have been just as thickly manned—they could see twenty well-armed men advancing. All carried rifles. Many of them had revolvers also in their belts. And their bearing alone gave proof that they knew how to wield their weapons. They went like hunters of deer, with keen eyes playing over the country before them. These were the men of Cranston. One might have culled a great city to find such another twenty and culled it in vain for such work as this which lay at their hands. Even Hank Geer, that sad-faced fatalist, shrugged his shoulders and grew a little pale as he watched them.

They were on foot. By easier routes their horses were

brought on behind them. Seven horses came into view, led by one mounted man. He had avoided the plateau, apparently, and come on by a roundabout route, but in case of a sudden necessity, the horses would not be far behind the advancing line of the beaters.

Now the cheerful voices of those hunters seemed more terrible to Allan than any sounds he had ever heard. They called to one another that the work must be nearly at an end—to look sharp—to shoot straight—and the answers were always briskly alert. Hope made their fatigues seem nothing, just as despair weighed down the fugitives with leaden weights.

"Take those trees on the hill, there," called someone who appeared to be in command of that immediate section of the hunt.

Four revolvers were instantly drawn in the thicket. At least they would not sell their lives cheaply.

"There ain't no use. They couldn't try to hide there, all four of 'em," came the answer. And never were words spoken which gave greater joy to four men.

"Do what you're told to do," called the other. "We miss nothin' on this beat so long as I run the gang. Go on and look. It won't take long."

Peering eagerly through the bushes they could see two youths swing aside from the rest of the advancing line and step up the hillside to carry out the order. The end, then, had come!

"Bill!" said Hank Geer very softly.

The other started.

"Well?" he answered, quivering with his excitement.

"Step out in front of these here trees. Start talkin' to those two gents. Stop 'em from searchin' here, or else the first bullet I fire is into your back. Remember—I'm watchin' you hard. And—I don't miss no chances when I shoot. Remember that!"

And Bill, white of face, shaking, his bright little eyes intent with desperate thought, rose without a word and stumbled out of the thicket. He came out on the farther side just above the advancing pair, and he was greeted with a shout of surprise.

"Bill Tucker! Where you been, Bill?"

"You kids ain't got nothin' in your heads except a hope

162

to see them four crooks," responded Bill, with a voice somewhat unsteady. "If you'd been lookin' around you, you'd of seen me doin' more work than any. I been ahead of the line doin' a little prospectin' on my own account."

The other laughed. "Lookin' for that reward all for yourself, Bill?"

"Never mind me and the reward."

"What'd you of done if you seen all four of 'em?"

"I shoot straight enough an' fast enough, sons. Don't you worry none about me when it comes to a pinch. Old Bill can't talk as fast as some of you kids, maybe, but he can shoot just as fast and a dog-gone sight straighter." Then he continued, removing his hat and brushing his hair: "Whew, I wouldn't go through this here little thicket ag'in for ten dollars. Brush matted in close as a barbed wire tangle when the fence is busted down."

There was more laughter. "You're gettin' old, Bill. Ought to leave the real work to them that can do it."

"Them that can do nothin'. I don't need no pity, youngsters!"

"Don't get riled, Bill. Fool idea to hunt for four gents in a little rat trap like that, anyway."

"Fool, am I? Son, when you get to my age you'll know that little things can cover a whole lot—little things no bigger than a man's hat, say!"

"He's a trump card!" whispered Jim to Allan. "Who'd of thought that the old chap had that much sense in his head? He's steered them away."

"Come on, then," said the two. "Step on an' show us how fast you can keep step, Bill."

There was another tense moment in the thicket, but Bill answered very casually: "I dunno that I ain't done my share of the day's work already. I might set me down here an' have a rest. You kids trot along. I'll be after you when I've had a smoke, maybe. I'll be there when they tree the bear; you can lay on that!"

"All right, Bill. Never heard you talk so much before."

"I got reasons for talkin'," said Bill, "that you'll never know, son."

"What you mean by that?"

"Run along kids. I'm tired of your chatter."

They threw back a few jests at him, and Bill calmly sat

163

down under the nearest tree and began to roll a cigarette.

"Good boy!" called Hank Geer softly to their sentinel. "Stay where you are till you get a chance to come back to us when nobody else ain't lookin'."

Bill raised a hand for answer.

CHAPTER 24

MURDER NOT AN ADVENTURE

There was a general sigh of relief among the others in the thicket. Surely fire could not have come nearer without burning. But they had hardly escaped from one peril when another became apparent. He who rode with the horses now espied Bill, the smoking cigarette, and the coolness of the shade. He made instantly for the place with the horses tugging back on their leading ropes and then trotting obediently behind him.

"Hello, Bill!" he called as he came near. "Got room for company—hoss an' man?"

"Better keep up closer to the boys," said Bill without cordiality.

The other, however, was already in the act of dismounting.

"This here hunt is nigh ended," he said, "if they're

goin' to find the skunks to-day. Which I got my doubts. Things have been workin' too dog-gone smooth an' easy to suit me. They've narrowed down the ground until there ain't but mighty little left—hello, what's that?"

There was a chorus of shouts, ringing clearly across the open space. It came from that section of the thicket where the four had taken shelter during the night and the earlier morning and there could be no doubt as to its meaning. The searchers, in their careful beating, had discovered signs of the occupancy of that place. It would not be long, therefore, before they were beating their way back in the direction in which the four had retreated to their present shelter. In fact, when Sam Buttrick cautiously parted some of the shrubs just before him, he saw that a round dozen were already emerging from the other woods and approaching in the fatal direction. But Hank Geer had already risen and called out: "You there with the hosses!"

At that voice from behind, the horse keeper whirled as though touched with a bullet, and found himself staring into the muzzles of two revolvers, held as steady as rocks in the hands of formidable Hank Geer—Hank who never missed a chance when he shot.

"Stick them hands right up, son," said Geer.

He was obeyed; the guard stood shaking, round eyed, before them, helpless.

"Rustle out and get the horses, lad," said Hank, "while I cover my friend, yonder. We might be needin' hossflesh before the day is much older."

They were through the thicket like so many tigers. To such practiced eyes it was only the work of an instant to select the best mounts in the group. Into the saddles they flung themselves, while a wail of fury and astonishment showed that some of the hunters had already sighted them. They broke into a run, but they were far too slow Riding four and leading the remaining three animals, the bandits were off and streaking down the hillside, leaving the poor guard and Bill disarmed and helpless behind them. The rise of the hill protected them from rifle fire during their first rush. And before the hill was circled or climbed by the men of Cranston, the fugitives were dipping out of sight over the next hill beyond. Even so, out of pure fury and despair they tried a few random shots and one of these whistled unpleasantly close above the head of Allan. He regarded it not except with a sigh of relief, for, after the grim tension of the last few hours, such a small winged peril as a single bullet seemed nothing at all.

They rode hard, and yet with a great and growing hope as no pursuit developed at once behind them. As a matter of fact, they were not only well mounted, but they had robbed the hunters immediately behind them of the means of making speed. Other horses would be quickly gathered, of course, from more distant quarters of the circle, but before they could straighten out in pursuit, the fugitives would be well off to a running start. And a stern chase is proverbially a long one.

So it proved on that day.

They had a second advantage and a most vital one. In the hunt for them, nearly all the available men of the district had been drawn in to make the closing circle which was to entrap them and which had so nearly succeeded in so doing. Between them and the mountains were few horsemen indeed, and even the telephones would not be able to draw out any formidable posses to head them off.

Yet, though they thought of this advantage also, in good time, they continued to ride as hard as the horse-flesh beneath them permitted. For every mile took them closer to the mountains, and every mile closer to the mountains was a mile that much nearer to comparative safety—to a reunion with Harry Christopher, if the latter had succeeded in shaking off his own pursuers.

At the end of two hours every horse except the unusually fine animal which Jim had selected for his own use was staggering with weakness. Therefore all saving Jim changed to the fresher mounts they were leading and they pressed on again. And still there was no sign of the pursuit.

In fact, those who followed fast and hard had gone astray two miles on a false trail, and two miles in such a hunt was a fatal handicap. By noon the quartette were among the mountains, and in the golden time of the afternoon, when the air first was turning chill on the heights, when the blue of the shadows in the gulches turns dusky black, they came to the place of rendezvous—an old deserted shack at the mouth of what had once been a shaft of a mine. And behold, Harry Christopher and all of his men came out before them. In all that wild pursuit which the men of Cranston had undertaken, not one of that half of the band had been harmed. What had been the fortune of those led by Lefty Bill no one could as yet say.

Allan had expected that there would be some show of excitement when they came in, but the two sections greeted one another with perfectly casual words.

"We been writin' your epitaphs," observed Harry Christopher. "Have you got the money with you?"

It was handed over to him.

"How did things come with you?" asked Geer.

"Fine," said Christopher. "We give our hosses a little exercise, that was all. And I like to breathe my hossflesh good and plenty once in a while, you know. How was things with you?"

"We had a Jonah with us," said Sam Buttrick, staring darkly at Allan. "But we managed to pull through. There was two of us had old heads."

This self-praise drew forth no comments. The whole of Christopher's party, in fact, seemed buried in the most profound gloom. And the cause was not very deeply hidden. There had been one grave mistake made by Harry Christopher when he split his party into two divisions. Though he assigned the greater number to his own leadership, in the haste of the instant he had given to the party of Lefty Bill no less than four of the six men who carried the treasure sacks. Of the approximate million dollars in currency which must have been taken from the safe, two thirds now was held by a small party of nine men at whose head was one whose immense avarice was a watchword among all of his associates. That was Lefty Bill. And his daring and invention and persuasive powers being on a par with his lust for money, it was more than probable that he might get his followers to split the money equally among them and thereby secure shares more than twice as large as those which would ordinarily have come to them.

In the meantime, though there had been plenty of time for it, Lefty had not sent in a report of his whereabouts, neither had he come in with his whole party and their plunder. Matters began to look black, and every instant made them blacker.

Only to Allan these tidings were no great burden, but actually good news. And, when he and the others of the starving quartette had eaten their fill, he took Jim aside for a stroll in front of the shack.

"Do you see how it is, Jim?" he said to his friend. "They're a bad lot from the ground up. Didn't this trip show you that?"

"I've always knowed it," said Jim quietly. "They're out for themselves. They're simply crooks and me—I'm something else, Al, if I have to say it myself. You know why I throwed in with 'em to begin with. But even after I had to go in with 'em—or thought that I had to—there was something else that kept me. It looked sort of like having adventures. You understand?"

"Of course I do. But murder isn't an adventure, Jim. It looks to me simply like murder."

"I've never done it!"

"Suppose that some of those people had come into the thicket where we were hiding and fired at you. Would you have fired back?"

"Of course!"

"Suppose you had killed one of them. What would that have been?"

"Self-defense," said Jim promptly.

But when Allan shook his head, he saw that Jim was gravely thoughtful and that he remained so for many an hour thereafter.

CHAPTER 25

OUTLAWS AFTER OUTLAWS' GOLD

It was a gloomy party which rolled in its blankets that night, at last, but they had hardly fallen asleep when a rapid crackling of guns down the mountainside brought them to their feet again, reaching for weapons. Running to the front of the shack they could see a drama unfolding beneath them—a single horseman spurring a staggering animal up the slope while, behind him, three others rushed on, gaining at every stride. They had unlimbered their guns and were firing rapidly at the fugitive who, in turn, made no effort to return their bullets but bent low over the neck of his horse and urged the animal ahead.

"It's all that's left of Lefty's bunch," said Hank Geer, ever ready to look on the seamy side of things. "It's the last man of Lefty's party and that's the first of a posse. Boys, we got to hustle into the saddle again."

But Harry Christopher, instead of answering with words, took up a rifle and fired hastily, without taking aim. The single shot had a great effect, however wildly it may have flown. The three drew rein at once; a second shot made them wheel and gallop away while the rescued fugitive let his horse fall back to a jog trot coming up the steep slope. He gained the group in front of the shack and slid wearily from his saddle. It was Chick Martin, and he was indeed a member of the second half of Christopher's gang.

They surrounded him at once with rapid questions. But he brushed through them and went with sagging steps into the shack.

"I'm spent, boys," he said. "Gimme a cup of coffee. Or a slug of red-eye. Dog-gone me—I'm near done!"

He was spent indeed. He had slumped down against the wall, his legs sprawling on the floor, his head fallen on his breast, his breath coming in gasps. A flask was instantly placed in his hand, which trembled as it raised the bottle. He took such a drink as one exhausted and thirsty can take. Then he lowered the flask to the floor with a bump and continued to sit for a time with eyes closed, breathing deeply.

"What you got in the line of chuck?" he asked hoarsely, without opening his eyes.

They could see, then, as the fire was built up and the light from it flickered across the room that his face was pinched and haggard to an extreme. They brought him cold pone and raw bacon. He devoured it like a wolf, washed it down with more whisky, and then sat up like one transformed. Still a cigarette had to be rolled and lighted and a few breaths of smoke inhaled before he would speak. The others, in the meantime, waited in a circle, patient because they understood.

"It's Lew Ramsay," croaked Chick Martin.

That caused a stir and then a groan from the others, for Ramsay headed the meanest bunch of outlaws that ever roamed the hills.

"Tell it quick," said Harry Christopher, his face working. "Ramsay jumped Lefty and the rest of you and cleaned you up and grabbed the coin—is that it?"

"Ramsay met us comin' up through the pass," said Chick Martin, not to be hurried too much in the high points of his narrative. "He come by us and give us a good word. He could see by the way we was ridin' and the sweat on the hosses that we'd done something and

170

been ridin' to get away from what might happen later. He didn't say nothin', though.

"But that night, while we was camped, Lefty went out for a stroll all by himself after eatin'. You know that way he has of doin'. He goes out for a stroll and comes back hot-footin' it after a while.

" 'Jump them saddles onto the horses,' says he. 'I've seen a dozen or fifteen riders comin' through the hills.'

"We sure got up an' moved. We jumped them saddles onto them dog-gone tired hosses and we lit out fast as we could go. It wasn't fast enough, though. Ramsay's men was fresh and their hosses was fresh. He pretty near run us down, but then we got to the mouth of a cañon and started to ride up it."

Here there was a groan from Hank Geer. "It was blind!" he said.

"Nope," said Chick sadly, "it wasn't blind. But ridin' by night it looked blind to us. We seen the hills closin' together in front of us. We could see Ramsay's devils coming fast behind us. Then we seen an old shack that was standin' near the head of the cañon. Lefty Bill told us to head for it, and we done it. We got inside quick enough to bring Ramsay's gang up standing. They rode off in a circle around the shack and we started thankin' Heaven that we was safe.

"It wasn't long, though, before we seen that we wasn't safe at all. There was water in an old pump in that house, and we had enough water in our canteens to prime the dog-gone thing and just barely bring up the water. It was so choked with red dust that it looked like blood, and we had to take turns pumpin' for near half an hour before the water begun to run clear. After that it was like a spring; never tasted sweeter water in my life. Well, there was the water. But that was all. There wasn't no sign of food around that place."

"What about your packs?" snapped out Harry Christopher.

"Packs?" said the other angrily. "D'you think that we'd been out pleasure ridin' maybe? No, sir, we'd had that devil Ramsay behind us, and anybody that's ever rode with a tired hoss in front of Ramsay knows what ridin' means. We'd fed our horses the spurs till our boots was red. We'd throwed away everything that made a weight that we could spare. We even got rid of spare guns. We tossed off our blankets, our extra cartridges. Dog-gone me if Hammond didn't take off his saddle and ride along barebacked. Otherwise he sure would of been caught, because his old brown hoss was sure fagged. Anyway, we got to that shack I been talkin' about with nothin' but a loaded gun apiece, our hosses, and the coin. And the hosses wasn't ours very long. One of Ramsay's half-breeds sneaks up like a snake durin' the night and stampedes the hosses right under the nose of Champ Sullivan.

"We cussed the Champ so much for that that he got sure downhearted. That night we sat around wondering when we'd eat next, and when Ramsay's devils would rush the house. When the mornin' come we seen that Champ Sullivan wasn't no place around. We'd talked a little too much to him. Maybe he turned yaller, too. Him bein' such a great eater."

There was a universal snarl of rage from the others in the shack. There was no doubt of the fate of Champ if ever he should meet with one of these men.

"That meant," went on Chick, "that Ramsay knowed everything about us. It meant that Champ would tell him that we had half a million with us—an' no chuck! Of course we knew, after that, that Ramsay would stay by us like a wolf until he got that coin.

"We talked about tryin' to rush through 'em. But how could we rush when we didn't have no hosses?

"Nope, we was trapped, and the worst of it was that we could see, when the day come, that there wasn't no need for us to have settled down in that trap. Right plumb ahead of us the cañon narrowed down, but there wasn't no cliff there. There was a place where the wall broke, and we could see through that crack, you might say, that there was a way through the hills outside of the cañon. We seen that, and I'll say that it plumb made us sick. There we was done up in a knot, but if we'd kept right on ridin' we might of got into rough goin' where we could of dodged Ramsay and his murderin' crew, or else that end of the cañon was so dog-gone narrow that a couple of us could of crowded the pass full of lead and kept Ramsay back while the rest of us breathed our hosses.

"But we seen that we was cooped up and that we couldn't get out no way that we figured. All that we could do was to keep Ramsay's man-killers off as far as a rifle would carry in the day. In the night they might sneak up an' rush us. But they'd be pretty sure to wait a while for that until we was pretty weak from hunger and easier for them to handle.

"But there ain't any way of figurin' Ramsay. He does what you don't expect. However, there he was sittin' easy with three men for one that we had, and ready to jump us when he wanted to. And we had to get word through to you, Harry.

"Lefty got out a pack of cards. We drew for the jack of spades, and I got the unlucky card. I was to try to sneak through by myself tonight an' then make for you, because we knowed that you'd be up here, of course; so when the dark come, I sneaked out and rustled down the valley. I got along fine for a couple of hundred yards. Then I seen a gent ride right out from behind some rocks; he was ridin' the rounds of the cañon to watch for just that sort of a thing as I was tryin' to do. He seen me an' I seen him at the same time; we drawed at the same time; but I got in my slug a wink quicker'n him. He fanned the hat off'n my head, but I plumb centered him.

"I could hear 'em yell behind the rocks, but I was already in the saddle beneath an' ridin' hard for the mouth of the valley. They come like greyhounds after me, but I had a hoss that was a hoss beneath me. I shook 'em off, all except three, and them three had better hosses than mine. How I managed to stave 'em off till I got here, I dunno. I tried every trick an' hand beneath every step of the way. Anyway, here I am to tell you that there's half a million down yonder in Salisbury Cañon waitin' for you to come an' get it, Harry!"

With this concise statement of the case, he ended, and a little silence fell upon the group, each man thinking hard and fast, making every effort to evolve a plan for safety.

"There's one thing more," said Hank Geer. "Now that Ramsay knows you got the news and that you'll be comin' on the wing for him, he may try to make a dicker with them that are left in the shack alive. He may offer them their share of the coin if they'll surrender. The question is: What would they do in a case like that? Would they hold out when they got a good excuse to surrender?"

"They'd never trust themselves to a bunch of half-breeds like the gang that follers Ramsay," said someone from the back of the room.

"Ramsay," retorted Harry Christopher, "could make a man think that black was white. I know him an' his ways."

"We got as many men as Ramsay has," blurted out big Sam Buttrick. "Countin' in the boys that are in the shack, we got about as many men as Ramsay has. Why not go down and just fight it out with him?"

"You talk like a fool, Sam," said the leader with pronounced heat. "What good is it to have a massacre? Suppose we did beat him? We wouldn't beat him by more'n one or two men. And don't we all want to have our shares in the coin? Besides, if we rode down to force things, he could keep Lefty's party in the shack by throwin' three or four gents around the place with rifles. The whole rest of his men would be ready to mix up with us."

"Send in a message to Lefty," said Hank. "Try to slip somebody through the lines to tell Lefty when we're comin' and where we're comin'. Then at the same time that we bust in from the outside, he'll try to bust out from the inside. We'll catch Ramsay on both sides."

CHAPTER 26

TO SACRIFICE ALLAN

There was manifestly much good sense in this suggestion
of Hank's, and his chief nodded slowly. He believed in
taking good advice. He did not, however, believe in listening to the chatter of many men. He now asked Chick
Martin and Hank Geer to walk out with him so that they
could talk the whole matter over and come to some sort of
a decision. The three departed, leaving the others.

In an adjoining nest of rocks they built a fire and cow-
ered close over it, for the night was turning extremely
cold. With their hands extended over the flames, casting
great thick shadows over their faces, they drew up their
schemes.

First of all a plan of Salisbury Cañon, and the high
lands immediately around it was drawn up by Chick
Martin as carefully as he could draw and remember. It
was seen, then, that the narrow valley widened gradually
from its beginning to its mouth. In the upper portion it
was simply a shallow depression among sharply rolling
hills. Finally, in the cañon itself, the walls of the valley became steep cliffs which were quite impossible for a horse

to pass. It was toward the upper part of the cañon that the shack which was now the fortress of Lefty Bill stood. And obviously there were only two ways of approaching it. One was the more natural. It was to come up the valley from below, where there would be more room on either hand. The second was to travel around Salisbury's length and descend to the goal down the dry valley. Here they would be forced to enter through a much more narrow aperture where a few well-posted men would be able to hold them at bay, perhaps. On the other hand, their approach would be more apt to be expected from below, and there might be the advantage of surprise by swarming down through the narrower gulch.

"Which is just what that fox Ramsay would be likely to figure," said Harry Christopher. "Boys, we got to do something that has brain in it, here. Otherwise we're simply goin' to turn Salisbury Cañon into a butcher shop, and Ramsay's bunch will be the butchers. They know their ground. They're all good shots. They've done so many murders that they'd as soon shoot at a man as at a dog. And our boys in the shack there with Lefty Bill won't be much account. They'll make a noise with their guns, maybe, but gents that have gone without chuck for such a while ain't goin' to have steady hands."

This was all very obvious. But what was the brainy maneuver which could be accomplished? Harry Christopher was fumbling toward it.

"We got to make Ramsay and his gang think that we're sure to come in through one direction. Then we'll slip in the other way. We got to make him bunch his gang together, and then we'll come in from the other side."

"That sounds easy. How'll we do it?"

"With a false alarm."

"A what?"

"Send in a gent with a message that'll seem like it was meant for Lefty Bill but will really be meant for just Ramsay."

"Where'll you find a gent among the gang that'll be willing to put himself into Ramsay's hands?"

"Get one that'll run into Ramsay's hands—but *not* on purpose."

"What d'you mean, Harry?"

"Is Ramsay a fox?"

"Of course."

"If a fool was sent to get to Lefty Bill, would Ramsay get him before he ever reached to Lefty?"

"Sure. That's plain. It'll take a mighty smart man to break into the valley. Every night Ramsay'll have his gents out watchin'."

"Very well, then, I say that I have the very man for the purpose."

"What man, Harry?"

"Guess. A blockhead that don't know nothin'. A bull with his hands but a fool in the head."

"All Vincent!" cried Hank Geer.

"You're right."

"It'd mean that he'd be stopped with a bullet, Harry."

"What of that?"

"Only this: He's a dog-gone white kid, as square as they come. I seen him closer than the rest of you lately, and he's always played square and true to the rest of us. I've watched him through the thick of it."

"He near made the whole four of you get caught, Hank. Is that playin' square?"

"He had a hoss that he couldn't make run fast. That started things. But he got us out of one bad hole by takin' a growed-up regular Cranston County fightin' man with his bare hands."

"His hands are a great deal more useful than his head. I have said so before."

"I'd hate to see any harm come to him."

"Hank, don't be a fool. Is he worth half a million to you?"

Hank, chewing his nether lip, was silent.

"Besides," said Harry Christopher sneeringly, "he'll die with no pain. The gents that ride with Ramsay shoot mighty straight, Hank; here's our chance to win back the whole slough of that coin!"

Twice the thin lips of Hank parted to speak in behalf of the youth; and twice the words failed to come. For, after all, money was money and a fool was sure to die soon, at any rate.

There by the fire on a scrap of paper the leader wrote his message to Lefty Bill. It read:

177

·DEAR LEFTY: I'm sending in a message to you by Al Vincent, because I intend to come to give you a hand right away. Vincent will get to you about dusk. I'm pretty sure that he'll win through to you because he's as clever a fellow as I know. This will let you know that I intend to come right up through the valley, from the mouth, because I think that Ramsay won't expect us from that direction. I'll have extra horses with me. The minute you see the sun stick up over the mountains, bust loose and start for the mouth of the cañon. I'll be ridin' as hard as I can, and all my boys behind me. We'll meet you more'n halfway, and when we meet you, we'll have horses for you to jump onto. We'll be in and out ag'in before Ramsay and his bunch of man-killers know what we're about. All depends on you making a quick start. The minute you see the edge of the sun showing, come hell-bent for the mouth of the cañon.

Give our best wishes to the boys. I'm sending in some chuck by Al. It'll be enough to give you one square meal, at least. Then pull your belts tight and get ready to work fast in the morning. I'd try it at night, but a lot of things can go wrong at night, and, besides, the dark is the time when that gang of Ramsay's will begin to keep the sharpest lookout. As soon as the morning light begins to get bright, they'll be thinking about hitting the hay.   HARRY.

This composition he read aloud to his companions and their applause was most heartfelt. If there had been some doubts and some remorse in the mind of Hank Geer, he forgot them now. The beauty and the simplicity of the scheme appealed to him like delicious music full of surprises, constantly revealing new charms. For, as he saw it, this letter, captured on the person of poor Allan, would undoubtedly induce Ramsay to concentrate his forces of ruffians around the lower end of the cañon, and from the upper mouth of the ravine the rescuers could strike quickly in to the shack, gather the fasting friends whom they found there, and so sweep away again, cutting to pieces whatever guards might be on duty and avoiding a battle with the bulk of Ramsay's forces until all of Christopher's men where joined together. Indeed, it was very doubtful if even Ramsay would persist in schemes of robbing the robbers if he had once received such a repulse as this would be!

And then the two halves of the gang would be united. The plunder could then be shared, and all of this would be accomplished, if matters went well, at the risk of a few chance bullets and, at the most, the certain death of young Allan. Such a death was an unfortunate sacrifice, but prices must be paid for all good things. And with this reflection, all the remorse died away in the mind of Hank Geer.

There remained to persuade the gull to undertake the journey, and this Harry Christopher took upon his own shoulders. He made no attempt to talk to Allan that night. He waited until a night's sleep had rubbed the weariness out of the brain of his recruit. But after the breakfast coffee, as the rest of the party sunned itself before the shack and yawned at the breathless distances among the mountains, he took Allan to one side and opened the affair to him.

"Al," he said, "I have been watching you since you joined us and everything that I've seen has been right. There's some things that you don't know. But you're picking up quick. What you've got most of all is a good head on your shoulders. You take time, you think things out, and you're cool. And that's why you're the only gent in the gang that I can come to at a time like this. I got to get a message to Lefty Bill. Will you take it?"

Had Allan been asked to accept sudden death, such a question could hardly have been more welcome, but Christopher went on as though he did not expect an immediate answer and as though he had paid no attention to the pale face of his youthful companion.

"It'll be a harder job than the one that Chick got away with. Ramsay will be on the lookout as sharp as a cat, now. That's why I have to send my best man. And take it by and large, you're the man I mean, Al. What d'you think of it?"

"I haven't had a chance to think," said Allan.

"Take your time. I don't want you to jump at this. I want you to take it easy, partner, and figure this out carefully. You understand? It's a big chance. I need a

179

man with a big heart to try it. But there's six poor devils dyin' in that cañon. Along with the message, there'd be some chuck for 'em."

He had struck skillfully upon the right chord, and he swallowed a smile as he saw Allan straighten and draw in a deeper breath.

"After all," said Allan quietly, "I've given you my word that I'd do as you want me to do. If you choose me, I suppose that I have to go. When shall I start?"

The leader reached out his hand and clasped that of Allan. "Son," he said, "you got the makings of great things in you. You're goin' to win through with this here game. I feel it in my bones. An' when you've finished it, you an' me are goin' to be a pile thicker than we've been up to this time. I've been holdin' off, Al; sort of studyin' you, but I liked you right from the first, y'understand?"

There was no reply except a murmur from Allan. He turned away to find Jim Jones, for he was in sore need of council. And as he went, Christopher summoned Geer with a gesture.

"Keep the straight facts dark from Jim," he said. "If he finds out that it's a plant, he'll be plumb wild."

CHAPTER 27

SLOW AL ENTERS THE RACE

The plan which was suggested by the leader was simply that Allan should reconnoiter the mouth of the valley and, if it proved to be only remissly guarded, slip through with his horse and proceed at full speed straight up the cañon toward the shack. If he had fortune, it might be that he would not be seen until he was close to the shack, and then he could trust to the speed of his horse and to the darkness of the night to shield him from the fire of Ramsay's fighters.

If he found, however, that the entrance to the cañon was closely guarded, then he should not attempt the impossible but, giving up the effort to penetrate by that direction, he was to ride around to the side of the valley and climb down the precipitous wall of rock on the north of the shack, abandoning his horse and the precious provisions. For, after all, the message he carried was to be considered far more in importance than the mere food he might bring to the besieged. Having reached the foot of the wall, he was to attempt to slip through the line of the besiegers and reach the shack, and this was the scheme

which was most favored by Jim Jones, as he anxiously
went over the possibilities with his friend. In the first
place he had striven ardently to dissuade Allan from the
attempt, but the latter was adamant. He could never be
forward in the crimes while he was among them. But here
was an opportunity to serve without violating the law, and
he determined to do his best in the desperate matter.

There was nothing that could be done for him by Jim
except to equip him with the best possible advice. And
that advice was to treat the men of Ramsay as though
they were wild beasts, for Ramsay himself was little more
than a predatory animal, and he had gathered around
him a crew of desperadoes of his own ilk—outcasts from
every society but their own, half-breeds and white men
who had forgotten everything saving the brute in their
natures.

"Remember that," said Jim. "Because the trouble with
you, Al, is that you figure on every gent being as decent
under the skin as you are yourself! But if you get into a
mix with Ramsay's men, shoot!"

That was the parting injunction after which Allan started
on the long trail across the mountains with the lofty head
of Salisbury Peak to guide him in the distance. By mid-
afternoon he was within striking distance of the mouth
of the cañon, but there he made a camp, let his horse
graze, and rested until the dusk began, partly because he
must have the night to cover him when he made his
attempt, and partly because both he and his horse should
be fresh when the time came for the effort.

It was well after sunset when he started on again, and
the red had faded to a faint stain along the horizon, and
the stars were beginning to wink in the black upper arch
of the sky before he came to the mouth of Salisbury
Cañon. It was like a gate to a ruined city. The wide,
flat entrance was like a great avenue whose paving had
been worn away by centuries; on either hand were huge
towers of red stone, curiously sculptured by the wind; and
after these sheer walls stretched away like ramparts with
broken battlements. What lay within those gates he could
not make out beyond a thick pool of the evening gloom
broken by the shrill, wavering yelp of a coyote far away
in the cañon.

He had been told to reconnoiter that entrance before he attempted to pass through it, but just how he could maneuver he could not tell. And there was no scheme in his laboring brain to tell him what might be done. So, shrugging his shoulders, he rode slowly forward, very slowly. Coming in such a casual manner, it would be hard if he were recognized as an enemy. And, brutes though they might be, the men of Ramsay could hardly shoot him down before they had recognized him as one of the men of Harry Christopher.

He had passed within the outer line between the two natural turrets when he was hailed. He looked to the right and made out very clearly the long, faintly glimmering barrel of a rifle which peered out at him from among a cluster of rocks. That sight made his whole body quiver with the thundering of his heart. He checked a foolish impulse to spur his horse and dash on through the gap. Instead, he brought his mount to a halt and waited for an instant until he could speak with some control.

"Hello!" called Allan. "What's up?"

"What're you?" growled out the other.

"Tom Smith," said Allan, "from the Circle Z Bar Ranch."

He had seen some of the cattle with that brand on them wandering through the hills and Jim had explained the brand to him. For all he knew, this sentinel might know all about the Circle Z Bar outfit. If he did, there would be a rifle bullet through his body in short order.

"What're you doin' up here, Tom Smith?" asked the watcher behind the rifle.

"We missed some cows. I started out to find what I could. Thought that I'd camp in Salisbury Cañon tonight. It's too far to ride back to the ranch, and my horse is tired."

"He looks tolerable rested to me."

For something had stirred in the shadows, and Allan's horse began to dance. He bit his lip and quieted the animal with a crushing pressure of his knees and a strong pull on the reins. He wished, for the moment, that he had not been given such a picked horse for the trip.

"He's a nervous fool," said Allan with some heat. "He can prance a long time after he's played out."

"I know them kind," said the other more amiably. "I had a dog-gone red-eyed Roman-nosed fool once that used to act like he was on fire to go till you give him the reins and the spur, and then he backed up and done most of his travelin' at a walk. But what made you pick out Salisbury Cañon for a place to camp in?"

"There's an old shack up the cañon where I can get water, and I have enough chuck with me to cook supper and breakfast."

"Since when did old Jeff start in sendin' the boys out from the Circle Z Bar with chow in the saddle bag?"

"It's a habit of my own. Jeff doesn't do it."

"You got a long eye for chances, then. I got to say that!"

"A man never can tell what may happen. One may ride into a cañon, for instance, and be held up with a rifle and a man behind the rifle. What's the trouble, partner?"

The other chuckled. "I'm here to tell folks that there ain't no good campin' in Salisbury these days."

"Something wrong in the cañon?"

"I'll tell a man! Mighty queer thing, too. There's a sort of a fever that catches gents in Salisbury Cañon if they ask too many questions. I've knowed some that never got over it." He enjoyed the obliquity of his own wit so greatly that he laughed aloud.

"Well," said Allan with the utmost good nature, "I'm not going to try to get in if your gun says no."

"It sure does! I see that fightin' ain't your middle name, Tom Smith."

"I carry a gun for the look of it. That's all."

The hidden man snorted; perhaps in amusement, perhaps in contempt.

"How's old Carey up to the ranch?" asked he.

"Fairly well," said Allan.

"That's so? I thought that the doctor had given him up."

"Doctors makes mistakes," said Allan.

"They sure do. A doc give me up for a lunger, once. Look at me now!"

He rose, a shadow among shadows—tall, wide shouldered, a giant among men.

"You *are* big," said Allan mildly.

He added, fumbling at his pockets: "I've dropped my Bull Durham. Got the makings, partner?"

The other hesitated. Plainly he did not wish to take any chances, but the good nature which had taken possession of him on account of the easy manners of Allan seemed to persuade him that there could be no danger here. He tucked the rifle under his right arm, with the muzzle still pointed at Allan and his finger on the trigger. Then he advanced with the "makings" held out before him.

When Allan came near enough to take them, he made out a face as formidable as the body of the stranger, a broad face, set off with a short, curling beard. And little, bright, agile eyes played over Allan and over his horse.

In the meantime, it was the first cigarette which Allan had ever attempted to roll, and after he had torn out the fluttering little filament of brown paper and sifted the tobacco into it as he had seen the cow-punchers often do, he went slowly on with the rolling. He had only seconds in which to act, now. In another moment his slowness would awaken the suspicions of the guard. And the rifle was still leveled squarely at him from under the arm of the big man.

"Your hoss ain't sweated up much," said the sentinel.

"I stopped a ways back while I was wondering whether I'd ride in or camp out. That gave him a chance to cool off," said Allan.

"But they ain't much sweat *dried* on him, neither. How come that?"

"These buckskins don't sweat a great deal—any of them!"

"That's true. When they begin to sweat they're apt to be ready to drop. What's the matter with your pill?"

"I tore the paper," said Allan. And he allowed the makings to flutter to the ground.

"Well," said the other, "darned if you ain't unhandy! I ain't tore a paper in the makin' since I was a kid!"

"You haven't?"

"I'm tellin' you, no!"

"The trouble is in my hand," said Allan. "Look at this."

He held out his right hand toward the other and at the same time he loosened his foot in the stirrup on the farther side of his horse.

"What's wrong with the hand?" asked the sentinel.

"Don't seem nothin' queer about it to me. What's wrong with it?"

"Nerves," said Allan, and since that hand was now only inches from the face of the other, he thrust it suddenly forward, drove the fingers through that short, curling beard of black, and buried them in the thick muscular throat beneath.

The other dropped the rifle and, gasping, reached up his right hand and tore away the tearing grip of Allan. But the latter was already lurching out of the saddle and as he fell he struck with a swinging left fist. It landed squarely upon the mouth of the stranger and smashed to nothing the cry which was beginning to form on the lips of the watcher. The force of the blow drove him staggering back. And then Allan was at him like a tiger, sparing no atom of his strength.

There might be, there probably were, other watchers near the mouth of the cañon. They must not hear this struggle. Neither must the big man have an opportunity to cry out.

He cast his fist into the face of the big fellow again. It was like striking a rock, and now, with a snarl, the latter tore a revolver from the holster at his hip. Under the swinging gun Allan dove. His shoulder bit against the hip of the stranger and both went down among the rocks. Then he felt the other's body relax suddenly as though he had fallen into a sleep.

He got to his knees, panting.

The big man lay with closed eyes and crimson running from a gash in his head where the sharp edge of a rock had torn a furrow. Was he dead?

Allan had no time to stay to make sure, but, sick with horror, he swung back into the saddle and started through the entrance gate at a gallop. Once on the inside, he saw the glistening sands stretched far before him in the starlight. The black faces of the cliffs walled in Salisbury Cañon on either side. All between them was plainly visible, and he knew, now, that there would be no obscurity on this night sufficient to shelter him. If only he could slip through the enemy unobserved—

That thought had hardly formed before a thick, heavy

voice boomed behind him, and then the air was split by the ringing explosions of a rifle, fired rapidly.

CHAPTER 28

TO THE STARVING

Through that clear mountain air the noises of the gun must pass from one end of Salisbury Cañon to the other, with a thousand echoes clearly speaking back from the tall faces of the cliffs. There was no hope that he could escape unobserved, but at least he would not be foolish enough to remain in the center of the narrow little valley. He swung sharply to the right and brought his horse back to a jog. For he knew that a fast-moving object is far more easily caught by the eye of the watchful than the motionless or the slowly moving. Under the very shadow of the cliff he continued, and had hardly reached that position when he saw a flight of five horsemen spurring at full speed straight for the mouth of the cañon. They swept past not a hundred yards away, furiously bent on their goal.

That was the charge which he would have met had he not changed his course. They had not far to go, however, before there met them from the starlit gleam a shouting, raging, raving form on a great horse. Allan, glancing back, could see the figure dimly and hear the distant thunder of his voice. He saw, too, that the whole group instantly turned. In another instant, with a wild chorus of yells, they headed straight toward him. Even the screening shadows beneath the cliff had not been able to shield him from their hawk eyes. He loosed the reins, punished the buckskin with the spurs, and raced ahead.

It was a chosen horse, that buckskin, famous among the men of Harry Christopher. And it had been recently rested so that it could give of its best to Allan in this time of need. But though he urged it forward, the yelling behind him continued to gain, as though the strength of their fighting fury added power to the animals which they bestrode.

There was another purpose served by that clamor of theirs, however. It would serve as a warning to the men who waited up the cañon, and who must already have been alarmed by the firing of the sentinel's gun. Yes, even as the thought entered Allan's mind he saw them come before him—a man here and another there—two more in the distance, stretched out in a thin, powerful line to sweep him back from the vicinity of the shack.

He saw that, and he looked back and watched the pursuers gaining. He decided, logically, that his case was hopeless, and then he went suddenly berserker. Another being poured into his body as it had come on the night when he hunted the watcher on the plateau after the robbery. Out of his lips came a cry that tore his throat and which yet gave him a thrill of the most exquisite pleasure.

The horse beneath him started, as though that cry meant more to it than quirt or digging spurs. It flashed ahead with redoubled speed, and the voices behind jerked away and grew smaller.

The four horsemen in front now converged, reining back their horses as they saw that they could focus on the point toward which he was driving. He saw them clearly, clearly in the starlight and even caught the glimmer of the weapons in their hands.

He swung the buckskin to one side. He turned again, and now he whipped the good horse straight at the enemy.

They sat their horses in a loose semicircle, emptying

their revolvers. His own gun was out. No one could take careful aim when a horse was racing at such a speed. But he fired as he had been taught to fire—a mere gesture, pointing with the forefinger while the middle finger drew the trigger. He fired; the four still sat their horses unharmed. He chose the central form just ahead of him and fired again, while the horse, as the gun spoke close to its head, snorted with fear and ran faster than ever.

That central man no longer sat still in the saddle. He had cast out his arms wildly, as though he were attempting to run through darkness and feel his way. Then he toppled to the side and poured out of the saddle like a fluid thing. There he lay flat on the ground, while his horse reared, wheeled, and shot off into the gloom.

Three men sat before him in a loose semicircle, in the midst of which there was now a gap. They sat calmly, taking good aim, firing fast. Then something like a clenched fist struck Allan on the side of the head, and swayed him far across the saddle. It was like a fist blow, but it was also like the running of a red-hot point of steel across his scalp. Something warm began to run down his face, and he knew that a glancing bullet had struck him. Life had been spared him by a fraction of an inch!

He fired again; there were still three before him. He fired again; still three guns were spitting fire out of the darkness and a knife edge now slashed him across the right shoulder. There was a twitch and his hat was off; there was another jerk at his coat, where it bellied out at his side in the wind of his galloping. He fired again. Only two men sat their horses, and between the two, on the tips of the horns of the semicircle, he galloped the buckskin.

Allan saw, on either hand, how their guns flashed up and then hung in midair, suspended like charmed things. They had found one another exactly in line with the fugitive, and they dared not fire for that instant. However, one stride more, and, as he shot past them, their guns spat. He felt the good gelding stagger beneath him, but still the gallant horse kept on, and just in front, a scant three hundred yards away, was the shack where he would gain shelter and to which he would bring food for the famished!

He rode with a tight rein. Jim had told him that that was the manner to hold up a stumbling horse, and the buckskin was beginning to falter and to fail. But still, though it staggered, it kept valiantly on, and every stride meant yards and yards neared to the shack.

From before him he heard a wild carnival of yelling—shrieking voices which he could hardly recognize as human. Why did they not fire to drive off the pursuers? Simply because they feared to kill him who brought them rescue, perhaps.

The saddlebag with its thirty pounds of provisions he loosed and tossed over his left arm. In case the good horse dropped, he would himself attempt to carry the thing on foot. A hundred yards was wiped away. Two hundred remained, and then the buckskin tossed up its head and fell with a human groan. Allan pitched into thinnest air and landed with a shock that tossed flame points of red across his mind.

It was only for an instant. Then he pushed himself slowly up on his hands. He was no longer pursued. The instant horse and man had fallen rifles were chattering from the shack, and that humming flight of lead drove back the men of Ramsay. The rifles were still barking, but when Allan raised his arm the firing ceased—a wail of unhuman joy went shrilling up from the squat little hut while three of the garrison leaped out to his help. He needed no aid to rise and run in, with his precious burden over his arm. He cast one backward glance where the gallant buckskin lay dead. Chance alone had determined that the horse must die instead of the man, and here on his head, his shoulder, his side, were the hot needle stings which told him how near death had come to him.

If they could not carry him in, at least those lean-bellied, hollow-eyed, starving men surrounded him, beat his back, shouted, and danced with their joy. They swept him within doors.

"I have brought word from Christopher—" he began.

Let it have been word from heaven, they would not have paid attention to him. Their eyes were on the fat canvas bag which hung over his arm, and their nostrils, keen with famine, seemed to have scented the bacon which was in it. After that, the half-starved men, wild with their fast of days, swept him into a corner with his tidings untold, and they fell to work at preparing the food. A fire roared in a trice, the bacon was sliced, the flour was stirred with salt and baking powder to make pone, and the exquisite aroma of coffee was floating in the air. They danced and they sang as they worked. They smote one another on the back, yelled and laughed like madmen. Half mad, indeed, they were.

Allan, in his corner, tended to himself. A bit of cracked mirror served him to dress the wound along his head. It was the merest scratch saving for a place near the back of the head where the flying bullet had bitten into the bone and delivered the blow which had so nearly stunned him. When the blood was now washed away, and a rag tied around the place, he became comfortable enough. The scratch on the shoulder was literally no more. It had caked the sleeve of his shirt with crimson. Otherwise it was nothing. He had various small bruises from the fall from the horse and particularly a swelling on the top of his head. But what are small things to one who has seen the very face of death and yet escaped to tell the story?

In the meantime, the food had been half cooked and the the meal began, but it seemed to Allan that if these men were all off guard, now was the very time for so enterprising a ruffian as Ramsay to try a rushing attack, for surely he must know that food had been brought to the starving, and that they would forget danger in order to eat. So he took up a rifle and posted himself at the door, which swung half ajar. Behind him were the warm odors of the cookery, the joyous voices of the men. Before him was the quiet of the night and the soft gleaming of the stars.

Who could have connected such a landscape with tragedy? Yonder something stirred in the shrubbery—perhaps that very prowling coyote which he had heard singing up the cañon earlier in the evening. Another shadow stirred among shadows. And Allan brought the gun to his shoulder just as a human form crept out and began to move stealthily toward the shack. He took aim with unsteady hands, for all his nerves were twitching with excitement. He had been right, after all, in reading the mind of the bandit leader. Here they came, two, three,

191

and four of them. Perhaps others were stealing up from other directions. If he paused to call for help, they might be at the shack in a rush. So he steadied the weapon as well as he could, and then pulled the trigger.

He knew even as he fired that he had missed his target. But he had the satisfaction of seeing the four leap to their feet with a shout and fade into the shrubbery, which crashed about them as they leaped to safety. Those same yells were echoed from three other quarters of the compass, and he could hear the noise of rapid retreat. The whole gang of Ramsay's men must have been drawn up to make a desperate effort, but feeling themselves discovered, they had no desire to charge into the face of a gun fire delivered by practiced hands.

CHAPTER 29

DANGEROUS DECISION

The meal was interrupted; there was a rush for the doors and windows, weapons in hand. But they had time only to put in two or three random shots at disappearing figures. Then they came back more soberly to finish their eating.

"If those skunks had rushed in when they heard the kid's gun," said "Denver Charlie," scowling, "they'd of

had us fine and easy. Lefty, for a general you ain't commandin' this here army none too well."

All eyes focused with a reproof upon Lefty Bill—all
saving those of sturdy Tom Morris, who, since the part he
had played in the hold-up of the train, had a right to be
considered at all times.

"There ain't any general except our empty stomachs,
right now," he declared. "Keep off of Lefty. He's done
good enough. Here's the rest of us that should of give
it a thought. But none of us had the idea. It took a kid—
a tenderfoot!" And he turned with a sort of admiring
affection to Allan.

"Al," he said, "dog-gone me if I ain't glad to say that
you've surprised the whole of us. You keep us from
starvin' one minute. You keep us from havin's our throats
cut by the half-breeds the next! Son, put it there!"

He shook hands with Allan most solemnly, and the
others followed his example. It was not a casual thing,
such as Allan had seen performed every day of his life
while he was in the bank. This was done grimly, carefully,
gripping the hand hard and looking long and deeply into
his eyes. They murmured at the same time such things as:
"Kid, you ain't the worst I ever met," or "Old-timer,
you've done noble." But there was the air of a religious
rite behind their roughnesses of voice and of word. They
meant a great deal above and beyond what they expressed,
and he could not help understanding that he had now been
admitted into a select fellowship, a brotherhood of gentry
who would stand by him to the bitterest of ends, give
him the last water in their canteens, stay by his side till
the last cartridge was fired, stand at his back in the face
of a world of enemies. He felt all of this, and he was
deeply and warmly grateful for it.

He felt a little like one who receives great praise for a
small deed. No doubt they thought it was quite wonderful,
but as he looked back to the passage of the gates of Salisbury Cañon and the ride up the valley and the passage of
the line of watchers at the end of that ride, it seemed
that he had been favored by ignorance and luck. There
had been nothing remarkable in what he had achieved.

So, when he had received their thanks and seen them
open their hearts to him, he did not therefore enter into

the discussion which followed like one has a right to express himself and to be listened to. He sat back in a corner and let the others thrash out the message which he had brought to them from their absent chief. And, for his silence, he was more highly regarded by the others than ever for the heroism of his services to them. For, above all, be he good or bad, a Westerner loves modesty in his companions.

That message was now first read silently to himself by Lefty Bill. Next he read it aloud to his companions, and they listened to it dubiously. When the reading was ended, they sat about silently. Someone had to begin the discussion. Who would it be?

Sturdy Tom Morris spoke up at last. "Looks to me," he said, "like Harry was sick. That there don't sound like his line of talk most usually sounds."

"He don't aim to take no chances like that, usually," said Denver Charlie in whole-hearted agreement. "Start out at daybreak—when Ramsay's dogs can see to shoot straight—and they sure can shoot by daylight, no matter how many times they might miss at night!"

Here he nodded at Allan, as though the latter might congratulate himself that he had not attempted his feat of reckless courage during the shining of the sun. And Allan, shuddering, nodded his head in return. Those bullets which had touched him and a score of others whose humming was yet in his ear would not have missed striking home had there been anything less treacherous than starlight when they were fired.

"Start out at daylight," continued Tom Morris, "and start trampin' down the whole dog-gone cañon. Start *walkin'!* Mind you that! Suppose that Harry and his boys didn't arrive in time? We'd get shot up fine before we'd gone half a mile!"

The others nodded—except Lefty Bill. He had waited until the other side expressed itself. Then he said quietly: "Charlie, you've got quite a little coin stowed away in a bank some place. I've heard you say that you had."

"What's that got to do with it? Sure. I ain't been a fool and blowed everything."

"You've put away something, too, Tom, ain't you?" went on Bill.

"I been a little lucky, I guess."

"Well, boys, did you have a cent when you joined up with Harry Christopher?"

He waited for that shot to find its target. Then he continued: "Neither did I have a red cent when Harry picked me up. I'd done a few good turns, but they never come to nothin' in the long run. I'd make a hundred here and another few hundred there. But when I joined up with Harry I started in makin' money faster'n I could spend it. So did the rest of us. He's brought in the coin. We might think that we could do just as well by ourselves. That's because we forget what Harry's turned up since we joined."

"If we've made something, how much has Harry made?" put in Charlie, adding hastily: "Mind you, I ain't sayin' nothin' ag'in Harry. He's a card, of course."

"He buys the news that we turn into money," said Bill promptly. "It's right that he should get his share of the loot, ain't it?"

There was no answer to this.

"How'd we ever have got on the track of this coin that we got with us now?" added Bill.

There was a pause, after which Tom Morris said: "I don't see why the chief didn't have us all meet up at one place. If we hadn't been split in two, we could of handled Ramsay easy enough."

"Suppose that the Cranston gents had stuck to our trail, where would we of been?" answered Lefty Bill. "And if we'd all rode together, you can lay to it that we'd of left a track behind us that they'd of followed."

Here was another answer which could not very well be controverted. "The long and short of it is," went on Lefty, "that we're stuck in a bad hole and we want to blame somebody for it. How would Harry of knowed that we'd bump into Ramsay? He figured on things so that we'd be able to beat out the gents that followed us up from Cranston County. And he figured it right. We got away clean. You got to admit that. He simply couldn't know that Ramsay would pop up in between."

Neither Charlie nor Tom could speak a word in answer to this. It was too apparently just to be controverted. And having made his opening, Lefty went on with his argument.

"This here walk down the cañon in the mornin' looks risky. It *is* risky. Any fool could see that. But ain't we in a risky position right now, and every minute we stay here, ain't it going to be riskier? We would of given a bad nickel for our lives an hour ago. Along comes the kid and brings us in chuck. We got our stomachs full and now we feel mighty fine. But how much of the chuck is left? In another day we'll be starvin' again. And Ramsay and his swine can live on the rabbits they shoot, if they ain't got nothin' better.

"Boys, maybe the chief wants us to try this game just because it *is* risky. Anyway, let's not think no more about it now. I'm for doin' what he wants us to do. If it don't work, then we can take our chance and die, with our guns talkin' for us. If it does work, we'll all think that Harry is the greatest gent that ever come along. Go sleep on it. I'll wake you up in time in the morning for us to have another talk about things before sunup. We'd better bury the coin here in the shack and then come back for it when we've joined up with Christopher."

So it was done. Tom Morris had his turn at standing guard that night. The others, and Allan among them, rolled up in their blankets and were soon asleep. To Allan it was a long time. Several times the ache and the fever in his wounds wakened him. And he was glad when, at last, the deep, weary voice of Tom Morris called: "Gents, roll out. We got half an hour till sunup. Roll out. We got no time for sleepin' now!"

They sat up yawning. Then, in a trice, remembering all that lay before them on this day of days, they stood up and looked to their weapons. They stood about in a circle, as grim a set of fighting men as ever stood in silence and debated a matter of battle. Then Lefty Bill put the question to them in a fashion which he had first carefully considered by himself.

"Gents," he said, "are we goin' to stay here sittin' while Harry and the rest come into the valley? Are we goin' to sit here and let Ramsay shoot 'em all down an' then come back here and finish us? Or are we goin' to turn out like gents that live up to their word, and are we goin' to march down there an' join our mates?"

It would have been hard to return a denial to such a

proposition. Three voices spoke in assent. The silence of
the others showed that they had submitted.

CHAPTER 30

ON THE TRAIL OF ALLAN

A long time had passed since that first clash between
Walter Jardine and Elias Johnston and Allan, and how
far the reputation of those gallants had sunk in their two
encounters with Allan and Jim Jones would have been
hard to estimate. This much was certain, that if Johnston
had run for sheriff before the first clash, he could have
unanimously been elected, and if he had run since the
second time he encountered him who was known as Al
Vincent, he could hardly have polled a single vote.

The result of that second clash had been that a coldness
grew up between the two companions. No matter that
Elias had proven a true prophet and that "Al Vincent"
had indeed returned to El Ridal. What counted was that
the outlaw had come and gone again. From that point
onward, Walter Jardine refused to listen to his friend's
counsel. And he insisted that they take the trail at once.

They heard, shortly, afterward, of the train robbery,
and since they were reasonably certain that Allan was a

member of Christopher's gang, they started at once in that direction and rode steadily for Cranston. There they arrived to find that the whole county was buzzing with the tale of what the robbers had done. And, particularly, they heard one man blamed and blamed again. It was poor Bill Tucker, who had been taken prisoner by the four outlaws and who had been used by them as a tool. Not that many men could tell themselves that they would have done differently under the compulsion of leveled revolvers, but there had to be some scapegoat, and Bill was the only possible one.

The Cranston posses had returned from the mountains where they had ridden their horses lame in a furious endeavor to find the trails of the missing outlaws. The whole county was black with gloom. For it was said that, having been once the prey of criminals, crime would spring up again as it had done before. To Bill Tucker, accordingly, the pair of warriors went, and they found him sunk in the profoundest gloom. It was broken by the adroitness of Elias Johnston.

"Partner," he said, "all we want to know is: was there a gent in that gang that went by the name of Al Vincent?" And at this, the face of Tucker lighted strangely.

"If there hadn't been," he said, "I'd be rotting by this time out in the woods. It was him that took me and it was him that kept the others from murderin' me when they wanted to, half a dozen times. Al Vincent is sure with 'em. But why a gent as white as him should herd with them mavericks I can't make out. Can you?"

"He's goin' to leave 'em pretty soon," said Elias Johnston with a profound meaning. "He's goin' to leave 'em as soon as we can persuade him to quit. That's why we're on the trail—just to meet up with Al Vincent. All we wanted to find out was if he was with 'em. Thanks a lot!"

And he and Jardine rode off on the trail to the mountains.

They had no definite plan, except to reach the upper mountains. There the outlaws must have taken refuge. There they would divide the loot, no doubt, and remain quietly for some time until the countryside had settled down and the posses ceased to comb the hills for them. They camped among the peaks on the shoulder of a moun-

198

tain the first night, and it was well past midnight when a horse neighed in the valley and the neighing brought them bolt upright in their blankets. The cold moon was high in the heavens, well past the full, now, but still shedding that bright light which only those who have seen the moon in the mountains know of. And, in the hollow beneath them, they saw a troop of men riding in single file along a difficult trail, leading with them a number of horses.

They flattened themselves instantly upon the ground and, having reduced their size, they stared again, until the troop was out of sight around the corner of the mountain. Then Jardine spoke.

"Elie," he said, "did it look to you like you'd ever seen the hoss that that first gent was riding?"

"I didn't recognize no hoss."

"Well, old son, I'd bet a thousand to one that that's Harry Christopher's nag. And if I'm right, them was Christopher's men."

Johnston drew a great breath. "Then Vincent is with 'em!"

"Maybe. But what would the empty saddles mean?"

"I can see through that. It simply means that when they was dividin' the stuff they got from the train, they got to arguin'. There was guns pulled. Them that shot quickest and straightest lived. Them that shot too dog-gone slow didn't live. They was left to die in the moonshine. And here's the rest of 'em goin' along takin' the hosses of them that dropped. Could anything be easier than that?"

It seemed a reasonable explanation, though Jardine pointed out that the rule of Harry Christopher was so exact that it was unlikely that any of his gang would rebel at the division of the spoils which he had ordered.

"That would be right enough most times," answered Johnston, "but they never had so much loot before. Near a million dollars was took, the papers say."

"Divide that in two. Papers always multiply, dog-gone 'em. When I met up with 'Bad Sim' Harper, the papers come out and said that I shot him five times before he died. Which was all a lie. I hit him once in the leg, and then I shot him through the heart as he was fallin'. You'd of thought, to read that paper, that I didn't know how to

199

use a gun—havin' to shoot a man five times before I finished him!"

Johnston smiled at this outburst of temper, for there was ever a great deal of the child in Jardine. But, in a trice, they had decided that these must indeed be Christopher's gang, and that they must follow, not for the sake of coming to sword's point with the whole crew, but in the hope that they might be able to encounter Allan lingering behind the rest, or at least to spot him among the crew when the sun rose.

Accordingly, they saddled swiftly and hurried their horses down to the trail. It is rare to find a group which can make as much speed as the individual. And though the horsemen in front were urging their mounts, it was easy for the two who followed to remain in touch. They rode carefully far to the rear. As a rule, they did not even have to keep in distant sight of the others, but as the trail wound and twisted sharply through the mountains, they could follow the strangers by the noise which the armed hoofs of the cavalcade made against the rocks, reflected back from the hillsides in many far-traveling echoes.

So they journeyed on until the gray of the dawn came and then the moon grew pale as a tuft of cloud while the eastern light increased. They had been descending from the upper level for some time, and now they began to climb, and twisted rapidly up the side of a steep slope.

"D'you know these parts?" said Jardine to Johnston. "Or where the devil they can be heading for? Is there anything to be reached up here?"

"That's Salisbury Mountain, and here's Salisbury Cañon down below us. If we was to ride a hundred yards to the left, you could see it easy. What they're aimin' at, I dunno. The right trail, if they want to go in this direction, is right up Salisbury Cañon, where there's one as round and smooth and as easy as a road. Old-timer, they got something up their sleeves!"

They continued now for some time straight ahead, and then turned to the left and descended into sharp-sided stumbling hills. But, before they went down in the rear of the party, the two could see the cañon stretched beneath them, long and narrow as a square-walled trough.

And they could see down its length, all revealed in the limpid purity of the morning air, the spotted shrubbery, the circling nests of rocks, the old shack, staggering to one side like a falling man—and above the shack a slender wisp of smoke rising from the chimney. They saw this and wondered at it. It was strange that such a ruin should be inhabited. And in the desolate and the cold beauty of that morning light they wondered who could have chosen to stay there.

"It's some tramp that blowed in the cañon and stopped there for the night. Most like he'll touch a match to the old shack and warm his hands at the fire when he goes this mornin'."

With that, they passed on down from the hill and so came into the narrow ravine which led up from the head of the cañon. There the abruptly rolling hills shut out their view of the cañon and at the same time they saw a rosier radiance fall upon the other side of the ravine.

It came from the newly rising sun which, beginning as a small disk above the eastern hill, slowly floated up until it showed a broad face, intolerably bright, at which they blinked and then turned their heads away.

And, a moment later, the far-off rattle of guns began from the heart of the cañon.

CHAPTER 31

"DO YOU SURRENDER?"

They had gathered inside the shack, the handful of fighting men who were to undertake the wildest of wild adventures on this day. They began looking to small matters of their equipment. They drew their revolvers and examined them carefully to make sure that that delicate and terrible mechanism worked smoothly in their familiar hands. They took up their rifles and went over them in the same fashion. Such preparations required few minutes. For, like men whose profession is war against other men, they never lay down at night without first going carefully over their weapons. This was only the last nervous survey before going into action.

They hitched their belts a notch or two above the accustomed point. They look dubiously down to their high-heeled, narrow-toed, long-spurred boots, so admirable for riding and so wholly inappropriate for the work afoot which they would now have to perform. Last of all, they settled their hats upon their heads and each man looked earnestly about him upon his neighbors. Here were the men with whom they had fought through many and many an adventure before. Here were men whom they might have thought, the day before, that they knew. But when this great final test came, how many would fall short of the testing?

Such, at least, were the emotions of Allan as he stared on those sun-blackened faces, marked with hard labor, with great vices, with a hundred debauches, but stamped equally with that great redeeming virtue of heroism. Would they all die together before the sun was an hour old? Or would some, perhaps, reach their companions charging swiftly up the cañon with snapping guns and a swirling dust cloud above them?

At last, Lefty drew the front door open, and there to the east the red rim of the rising sun showed above the mountain.

"There, gents," said he, pointing, "is our order to start. Boys, I'm goin' out first. I figger that the rest of you'll come close behind and stay close behind all the way."

And he stepped out into the morning air with his head high and with every muscle tensed to meet, perhaps, the tearing impact of a bullet fired by some alert watcher.

But there was no gunfire. Not a sound was heard, and nothing living moved before their eyes. The gravel and the sand crunched beneath their feet. The first desperation and terror left them. They began to walk more freely, with the hearts beating to a steadier rhythm and the color returning to their sallow, thin cheeks. They covered a hundred yards and gained a little eminence a few yards in height above the rest of the valley floor. There was nothing to be seen! Still nothing moved, but the rocks, here and there, stared back at them, and surrounded them with a gloomy meaning.

"Gents," said Denver Charlie, "it looks to me like maybe we was going to have a chance—"

Something thudded against the body of Denver. He wheeled and pitched on his face with his fingers digging into the sand. His long legs writhed together, and he was still, while the ringing report of the rifle beat against their ears. They were seen indeed!

"Go back!" shouted Tom Morris. "Christopher ain't here. Go back, boys, before we're all slaughtered."

A singing volley whirled around them to give weight to

his words, and the party sagged back to flee, all saving Lefty Bill. For, like a true standard bearer in the time of danger, his heart was true to his chief in this crisis. He leaped ahead and waved his hat.

"It's as hot work goin' back as goin' forward," he cried. "Come on, boys!"

And he raced ahead, a gallant, stodgy little figure with his spurs flashing and clanking as he ran. And behind him the others started. The whole of the little party plunged ahead through the sand, crying aloud to one another, each man to raise his own spirits more than to encourage his comrades. But in half a dozen steps another man was down. For those were practiced hands which fired on either side of them, and also straight in front. There men were lying at their ease with their rifles couched, and their bodies protected by natural entrenchments. There was nothing to shake their hands saving the knowledge that they were shooting to destroy human beings, and to those marksmen a human life was nothing.

Still, it was obviously true that it was as dangerous to recoil as to go ahead. Another dropped, the third to fall in that deadly moment as the battle began, and still they had not been able to do so much as return a single shot. Lefty Bill, leaping with fury, raced still in the lead, heading squarely at the little cluster of rocks straight ahead from which two guns were barking. Then another figure came up beside him, swinging a rifle as though it were made of painted, hollowed wood. It was Allan, running like a deer, and shouting like a madman, for the spirit of the fight was in him. Yonder were enemies no more to be protected or respected than the wildest Indian who ever painted their faces and whooped on a war trail, hungry for blood.

Already that charge was ruined. But still they pressed ahead, mad for vengeance. It was Allan who reached the circle of rocks first. Behind him came Lefty and Tom Morris, gasping and blowing, their teeth set for the work which now lay at their hands. As for Allan, he leaped high above the circling rocks. That leap saved him. The bullet which had been aimed for his heart whirred past his leg, and he descended on him who had fired the shot. One blow of the rifle butt; and when he looked up, Morris had finished the second man.

Here, at last, was some revenge. They flattened themselves in the entrenchment while the swift bullets spattered against the outer faces of the stones. They were, for the moment, fairly safe. But now, through the crevices, the bullets were finding a way. Tom Morris winced and gasped. A flesh wound, but it showed them that their case was indeed desperate.

Three of the enemy threw themselves on horses and rushed to a more commanding point which would overlook the circle where the others lay. In vain Morris and Lefty pumped bullets after them. The move had been too sudden, the race was too brief, the distance too great for them to become accurate in their shooting.

"We're only half paid for," said Lefty savagely. "And look! They're makin' sure of the boys that have dropped."

In fact, those savages were pumping bullets at those of the party who had fallen on the way.

A diversion, however, was coming. There was a steady rushing of hoofs from the head of the valley, and then—here they came, a splendid sight in the slant morning sun, their horses gleaming, the brims of their hats blown back by the rushing wind of their gallop. Here was Harry Christopher, a revolver caught in either hand, firing as he rode, and firing straight. For, out of a nest of rocks, they saw a man leap high into the air with a death cry. There was Harry Christopher, fighting like a gallant knight, and with him all his men, and with his men, the led horses.

Two men toppled from their saddles, but that splendid charge trampled through the rock nest with guns thundering, and swept on toward the next point, where Ramsay's fellows lay entrenched. Here the enemy was in force. The roar of his guns, as the repeaters were fired until the barrels grew too hot for handling, made a continuous noise like the falling of masses of water. Three empty saddles now, but they reached the rock nest, and there they whirled for an instant in a terrible hand-to-hand encounter.

There remained one point of vantage left to Ramsay. From that rock cluster suddenly a tall, thin man jumped into view, tossed off his hat, and his long hair blew in the wind. Allan heard his yell of defiance.

"Ramsay—gone crazy—fightin' is like booze to him," panted Tom Morris. "That devil! He ain't a man!"

Lefty was shouting: "Come on, boys! We'll join in from this side. That's the last of 'em."

And there they were racing across the sand. Tom Morris stopped, wheeled, and tumbled head over heels, dead. But the others still raced on; and from the farther side they saw Harry Christopher pushing home the charge to the last ounce of his energy.

Then the rock nest was reached, and before Allan he saw a swirl of bodies, battle-maddened faces rising to meet him and to meet the thinned group of horsemen. He saw teeth from which the lips were grinned back. He saw glittering, red-stained eyes. He saw the flash and the shimmer of steel. The stinging powder smoke was in his nostril. And in his heart was a raging fury. There was no fear. There was no room for fear. There was no room for thought or for compassion.

What he did he could not tell. He knew that he struck with the gun and that the butt splintered to bits on some yielding thing. He knew that he smote with the naked gun barrel, and that the steel bent like untempered iron in the terrible fury of his stroke. He cast that bent weapon away. He reached with his bare hands, and something crushed in his grip.

Then, through the swirling blackness of the battle madness, a voice pierced to his heart and to his mind; the voice of Jim, groaning.

Allan stood up, disentangling himself from a limp weight. And no other man stood in the death pen beside him. He looked wildly about him and something like a voice cried in him that this was the work of God, using the enemies of man to destroy one another.

There lay Jim, propped against a rock, his hands fallen limply at his sides, his head rolled back, and his eyes fixed upon Allan not in pain, not in appeal, but in a very horror of fear.

He reached out his hand and spoke. Behold, he did not know the iron tone of his own voice, or its husky depth. He had been changed in body and in soul, and after that day would he ever be the same? Even Jim shrank from him—his tried and well-proven companion, Jim! And he fell on his knees, beside Jim.

"Jim," he said, "are you badly hurt?"

Jim shuddered and raised a weak hand as if to push him back.

"What's wrong?" cried Allan.

"I seen you at work—I seen you, Al. What are you? A devil?"

All of that thought Allan brushed from him. "No matter about the rest," he said as a pitiful groan spoke near by. "There's no good man among 'em all except you, Jim. Where are you hurt?"

"I'm done," said Jim. "I'm finished. If I'd had a chance to live another little while, I might of had a chance to show folks that I ain't so bad. But now I'm finished."

"Where?"

"It hit me some place here in the side. They don't get well when they get punctured there. I know that. I've seen it before." He stopped and began to cough weakly. Then when he could speak again, he gasped out: "Who's won?"

"Nobody. They're all gone."

A wan smile came over the face of Jim. "Then you're near a million to the good, old man. What'll you do with it?"

"Give it back to those to whom it belongs."

Jim started. "After we've worked like this and died like this for it?"

"It's dirt," said Allan with a sudden solemn conviction. "I used to think people who had it were great folks. But I see that what they have is only dirt and nothing else. Good old Jim, keep your head up. You're not dead yet, and with God's help, we'll bring you through."

Far up the cañon he heard the pattering hoofs of horses. He looked up and saw two riders approaching at a swift gallop.

"Perhaps they're coming now," he cried eagerly. "If they're honest, we'll pull you through, Jim. If they're more of Ramsay's men——"

He reached down for his rifle to finish the thought. But, the next moment, he tossed the gun down again with a strange cry.

"Honest men, Jim; and you're saved."

For he had recognized Jardine and Johnston. And those worthies had the strange spectacle of their long-hunted man waving his hands to them and shouting to them to hurry.

They dismounted gingerly as they came up, still covering him with their guns.

"Do you surrender, Al Vincent?" they demanded.

"Save Jim," he said, "and I'll follow you to jail!"

CHAPTER 32

A FIRST-CLASS FOOL

How they saved Jim Jones the newspapers told. The three worked to bring the wounded to the shack and give them what treatment they could. Nine men were living, but helpless. The rest were dead, and Christopher and Ramsay were among them.

Then Johnston rode ten hours to the nearest village, gave the news, and rushed back again with help—and plenty of it. Luck had placed a newspaper correspondent in that town. He had come out to get a cattle story. But he forgot about cattle when he heard the tale. He was with that first rush of men, and it was he who gave the world the strange story of Salisbury Cañon. He told of the place, and of the dead men, and how they were buried, and of the epitaphs which were cut in stone above their graves, and of how he found Walter Jardine playing nurse to nine starving invalids helped only by a paroled prisoner. He heard, too, how that prisoner had surrendered himself for the sake of an injured comrade, and had thrown away the chance of winning three quarters of a million in cash for himself—three quarter of a million which he might have had by throwing himself on a horse and galloping away.

There was so much story here that the reporter worked himself into a fever. Every moment red-hot copy was flowing into his hands. Even when the buckboards carried the prisoners out of the valley, fresh copy came from their lips with every word they uttered. From the village, every day, he issued copious reports. A New York editor had gone delirious with joy. For five whole days he had a scoop. And he ordered his correspondent to spare nothing, to leave out no adjectives, to say everything he saw and heard and felt. The correspondent obeyed. And that was how Vincent Allan became a national figure.

His photograph went East as fast as express trains could rush it. It appeared in many poses in Sunday supplements and picture sections. Sentimental lady writers went forth to interview him and to retell his story. He acquired many adjectives before his name. He was called "The desperado, Vincent." He was termed bandit, gunman, caveman, aboriginal man killer.

And, in the midst of all this, the manager of a branch bank in which he had worked saw the picture, recognized it, and gave the reporters what they turned into a four-column story of the youth of this Western hero.

Altogether, it was a perfect newspaper story. It had a sensational side. It had a sentimental side. For Jim Jones had confided that the only reason Vincent Allan had joined Christopher was because of their friendship. This was the final touch, and the most was made of it.

The name of Vincent Allan became table talk. On account of him business men got up earlier to get their newspapers at the front door. And in the meantime? Poor Vincent Allan sat in a cell in the little town of El Ridal and heard the people of the town cheering their new sheriff, Elias Johnston.

He bore his honors mildly. He even told them that what he and Jardine had done had been nothing, that Vincent Allan had merely surrendered of his own free will. But this was termed modesty and not truth. They made a hero out of Johnston and Jardine in spite of the facts of the case. They made a villain hero out of Vincent in the same manner and for the same reasons.

"When we get a few more like him hung," ran public opinion, "that mighty and subtle triumph, 'the West,' will begin to be a decent and a safe place for law-abiding folks to live in."

In the meantime, newspapers had been brought to Allan. He had an opportunity to see himself as others saw him, and he used to say to Sheriff Johnston: "Is it all true, Walt? Am I all of this?"

Then came the trial. It was spectacular partly because it came after so much that had gone before and partly because it was so brief. The State claimed that this man had been a party to the killing of the guard on the train. At least, it could be proved that he was present. As for those who fell in the cañon, their lives were all long since forfeited and their killing did not matter.

Allan simply said that he believed he was guilty enough to die, that the matter confused and troubled him, and that the newspapers alone were enough to convince him that he was deeply in the wrong all through. And the young lawyer whom the judge appointed to see that justice was done to the prisoner, hardly knew what to say. He ended by saying nothing except to advise his client to plead guilty, and that was exactly what Allan did.

The jury stayed out for ten minutes for the sake of decency, and then came back to give their verdict, after which Allan stood before the judge with a man on either side and received a sentence to be hanged by the neck until he was dead. But all the time that the judge was speaking, the words meant no more to him than the tolling of a bell. What his mind was really busy with was a sparrow which was hopping about gayly on the sill of a window which was open, letting the hot wind stir through the room. And he saw the broad, hot square which the sun dropped upon the floor. And he saw the well-oiled hair of the clerk, shining like polished wood as the man bent over his broad book, and he saw the court reporter's flying pencil, and he saw wrinkles stand out and disappear and stand out again upon the forehead of the kind-faced judge who was saying these terrible words.

Then he turned, and there were the faces of the audience, stricken with horror and with interest. They had packed in every one who could enter. Others were jammed in the doorway. The death silence had ended, now, and little whispers were beginning. He heard some of them as he passed down the aisle.

"He don't look so very bad, Tom. D'you think so?"

"Don't be foolish, Betty. It ain't what they look like on the outside, but it's what they are on the inside that counts."

"Look at him! Ain't turned a hair. Nacherally bad blood in that young gent, and you can take it from me."

"Dog-gone me if he ain't as cool as a cucumber. I'd hate to meet up with a fellow like that on a dark night. Cut your throat and think nothing of it. Look at them eyes. Nothin' in 'em. A brute."

He listened to these things very calmly, and when each one spoke, he turned his quiet eyes for a deliberate instant upon the speaker, according to his old habit. But what he was feeling was that they knew only a few surface truths about him. Under that surface there was much, much more. He could hardly explain it himself. But he felt as though he had been through a dream, and that, if the chance came to him, he could step back into the bank which he had left and sit down on the high stool as though nothing had happened. They could not tell this. Yet he knew that there was no malice in his heart against them.

He had simply gone mad and become a destroyer for a moment. If any one had told him that he had really done nothing vitally wrong, he would have been the most astonished man in the world, and the most disbelieving. If any one had told him as a matter of fact that his every action had been based only upon a greater devotion to another than a devotion to himself, he would have thought that they spoke out of pity.

And he did not want pity. He wanted only to face the penalty and pay the price. The world said that he was very bad; he was much too simple to ever dream of denying the world's verdict. What he wished most of all was to have the business over with, pay that debt, and pass to the endless silence after having seen only one thing—and that was the face of Frances.

There she was in the corner of the courtroom, wonderfully pale, with great still eyes fixed upon him. She had a look, somehow, as though some one had been beating her and as though the ache of the pain were still in her flesh and in her heart. Why she should have come there he could not tell. At least it must mean that Jim was better. He paused in the aisle opposite her and he asked her with his lips: "Jim?"

"Better!" said the pale lips of Frances.

And then what a smile came on her face. Another man would have seen pity and tenderness and the whole expression of a great, warm heart in that smile, but Allan, as he went on, was only saying to himself: "Having Jim get well will make her mighty happy. How she loves him!"

In the jail Elias Johnston sat down in the cell beside him. "Al," he said, "why didn't you make a fight of it?"

"Why," said Allan, "you could see that people knew I deserved what I have got."

"D'you know something?" said Johnston.

"What?"

"I think you'd be ashamed to take the present of your life from the governor if you knowed that the majority was agin' you. But wait till to-morrow. The governor will have time to telegraph."

But the governor did not telegraph. In due time a letter arrived. It informed the sheriff that the governor had perused the letter of that official with the most intense interest. But, having reviewed all the facts of the case, he could not but feel that the sentence was justified and that he did not see any way in which he could reverse the opinion of so excellent a judge and citizen as Herbert Thomas in order to set at liberty a man slayer. The sentence would stand.

The sheriff balled the letter into a small knot and hurled it through the window.

"He's reviewed the facts!" groaned the sheriff. "He's reviewed 'em in a newspaper, and he's let it go at that!"

Then he forced himself in to tell Vincent Allan. But all that Allan would say was: "You see? You're too good-natured, Elias, to see that the others are right."

They took Allan to the penitentiary to wait for his execution. But before he left, Frances came to him, and Johnston broke sundry scores of rules in order that she might go into the cell of the prisoner.

"Do you know what has happened?" she asked.

"Something good about Jim?" he answered, studying her shining face.

"He's pardoned—freely pardoned for everything. The law has no claim on him now!"

"God bless old Jim. I knew that things would turn out well with him."

"But you, Al! Oh, the governor is a blind man."

"Not blind, Frank. He simply sees the truth about me. I deserve what's coming."

"But what have you done, except to help Jim and to help me?"

He shook his head and smiled down at her.

"Al, you make me mad!" she cried, stamping. "As if you knew something mysterious about yourself that was wicked and terrible. Al, don't you see that what they ought to do is to—to——"

"What, Frank?"

"Put a crown on your head and a pair of wings on your shoulders. You're—you're simply too good for the world, that's what!"

He smiled at this jest and then murmured: "Frank, you're so angry with me that you have tears in your eyes. I'll call myself as good as you wish, if it'll make you any happier."

"Oh," said she, "what can be done with you?"

"Nothing except what they intend to do."

She caught him by both shoulders and looked him squarely in the face, while great tears rose brightly in her eyes and then ran over.

"In the name of Heaven, Frank, what's wrong?"

"Can't you see?"

"That you're troubled, Frank. I wish there were something that I could do——"

"You? Something that you could do? You could do everything?"

"What!"

She turned from him and blindly found the sheriff's arm. And he led her into the outer office and bodily threw out two men who were waiting there to see him. Then he put her in a chair.

"Sit right still and have a cry," said Johnston. "It'll do you good!"

"Was there ever such a man?" sobbed Frances Jones.

"There never was," agreed the scowling sheriff.

"I—I hate him!" said Frances.

"So do I," said Johnston.

"I wish I'd never seen him!"

"So do I," said the sheriff.

"He'll never understand!"

"Never," agreed the sheriff.

Here the tears came in such floods that she rocked herself back and forth in her chair. It was a long time, and two of the sheriff's capacious handerkerchiefs had been soaked before she was able to speak at last.

"What shall I do?" she said huskily.

"God knows!" said the sheriff.

She stood up and before the mirror she touched at her hat to put it straight and at her face to remove the tear stains. Then, at the door, she rested her forehead against her arm and her arm against the wall.

"Will you try to tell him?" she said brokenly.

"I'll do my best," said the sheriff humbly.

After she had left he went back to Allan. "Al," he said somberly, "you're a first-class fool."

Allan grew judicious and then nodded. "I suppose I am," said he.

"Is that what makes you look sort of sad, right now?" continued the new-made man of the law.

"No," admitted the prisoner. "It was quite another matter. It was quite another person, in fact."

At this the sheriff suddenly sighed. "She's got the

looks," he said. "And she's got the heart. Dog-gone me if she ain't a fine woman!"

Allan smiled faintly. It was such a small way of expressing a great truth, he thought!

"She asked me to tell you something that you was too wooden-headed to understand when she was here."

"Ah?"

"She loves you, Al!"

It brought Allan stiffly to his feet, staring. He stood with a tranced face as though light had fallen upon him from heaven.

Then the light went out as suddenly as it had come. He sank down again on the cot.

"What's wrong?" asked the sheriff curiously.

"Why," said the prisoner, "it's like her, isn't it? She wanted to make me happy. And so she asked you to tell me that. Well, it *did* make me happy for a moment. Until I understood."

"Understood what?"

"That they're only so many words. But I care all the more for her because she even thought of having you tell me that lie."

"Lie?" said the sheriff.

He stared wildly around him. Then, with a groan, he rushed from the cell and returned to his office. He could be heard for a long time afterward stamping up and down the floor, and muttering all the while.

CHAPTER 33

COMPLETELY REFORMED

"A young lady——," began the secretary.

"About five feet five?" said the governor.

"Yes," said the secretary.

"Blond, curly hair?"

"Yes, sir."

"Fine blue eyes?"

"Quite so, sir."

"Pretty as the devil?"

"Prettier than that, even!"

"I know what she wants. She wants to see me about young Vincent Allan."

"Ah!" sighed the secretary. "I suppose——"

"Exactly. The law has to take its course. There is a time—I'll not go through it all again! Besides, the people have expressed their opinion."

"Certainly, sir. I'll tell her that you cannot see her."

"She's probably from a newspaper," said the governor. "Put it gently. You never can tell——"

The secretary left in deepest thought. How one with

such power to please a girl with such a face could overlook his opportunities he could not understand. But the ways of the great were often beyond and above his ken. He went back to Frances Jones and told her, gloomily, with his glance on the floor, that the governor was deeply engaged and regretted that he could not see her.

There was a sigh. He could not help looking up, and the sad eyes took hold on him again.

"There's no way?" she murmured.

"I'm very sorry. I'm afraid not."

"I only have two days left."

"I understand."

All at once she stamped and tossed her head. "There has to be a way!" she said, and slipped from the room.

He was so alarmed that he followed her to the door and saw her going out to the street. Then he went back to sit with his hands folded, dreaming dreams of blue eyes and trembling smiles; and now and again heaved a long, mournful sigh.

As for Frances, she had turned at the door and walked straight back again and up the hall to the door which bore the dignified sign: "Private." The knob of that door she turned and stepped briskly inside. The governor looked up, saw her, and groaned.

"My dear young lady——" he began.

"It ain't going to do," she said. "You've got to talk to me."

He noted the "ain't" with great relief. Certainly she had not come from a newspaper. And with that, he became firm.

"I am really too busy to talk with you," he said.

"You were not too busy to have your heels on the desk and your eyes out the window," said she.

The governor flushed. "Young lady——" said he.

She shrugged her shoulders. "It's life and death," she said. "You got to listen."

"I'm very sorry," said he, "but my time belongs to the State, my dear girl, and not to individuals."

"That sounds nice. I dunno what it quite means," said she, and with that she turned the key in the big lock and sent the bolt snapping home. The governor leaped from his chair.

"What? What?" he breathed. "Give me the key."

She slipped past him to the window. "I'll throw it out if I have to," she said.

"This is an abuse of the rights of woman," he declared.

"Sir," said Frances, "I only want five minutes."

"Five damnations!" said the governor under his breath. Then he drew out his watch and placed it on the desk.

"You may have five minutes," he said. "Do anything you wish to, except cry. Do you understand?"

"They's only one man in the world that's ever made me cry," said she.

"And who is that?" he asked, interested in spite of himself by this personal touch. "Your father and his switch?"

"Vincent Allan."

"Ah?" said the governor. "He has made you suffer, then? I thought that you came for another reason. But surely you must know that he is about to suffer the full penalty for all his crimes!"

"He's never committed a crime."

The governor groaned. "I knew it would be this," he said. "He's killed half a dozen men. But pass that by. He has virtues, you'll say. He can ride a horse and he dances well, eh?"

"I've come to tell you the whole truth about him. He joined Harry Christopher because my brother, Jim Jones was with Christopher."

"You are Jim's sister, then?"

"Yes."

"Well, well! I'm glad that it was in my power to help Jim. After all, you see that justice is merciful when it can be."

"If Jim was taken ten times over," she said firmly, "you could put all his goodness into Al and there'd still be so much room that it would rattle."

"Not exactly a sisterly speech."

"I ain't here to be sisterly. I'm here to talk facts. I say that what Al done was to join Christopher because of Jim. He busted the law first to save Jim from prison. You know that."

"I remember," said the governor, his mind going back rather dimly over the record of the criminal.

"Then he rode with Christopher, and he was there when the train was held up. What he did was just to line up one carload of passengers while Jim went through them."

"I can't withdraw my pardon of your brother even if you wish me to."

"I say that Al didn't shoot the guard. Tom Morris did, and ten men could swear to it, if they'd been asked to talk. Afterward, there's nothing against Al. He saved Bill Tucker from being murdered. That was all."

"This man Tucker," said the governor, "has been writing letters—it seems an oddly confused case. But—justice must take her course. We must have examples, even if they are cruel ones."

"Those are the facts. Do they sound wrong?"

"Justice——" began the governor.

She dropped on her knees in front of him.

"Oh, sir," she said, "if you could see poor Al! He's as simple as a boy. Because people have been calling him a bad man, he's begun to believe it. He won't even believe —he won't even believe—that I love him!"

The governor scratched his chin. He was beginning to grow nervous, for, after all, the eyes were exceedingly big and exceedingly blue. And there was not a tear in them, only a desperate eagerness. Besides, he was not altogether politician. He was a man with core of the heart of a man. Also, he had a child of his own.

So, presently, he leaned and took Frances beneath the arms and raised her and led her to the window, and let the light shine into her eyes.

"Why, my dear," said the governor, "I believe that there may have been a mistake."

And the girl sobbed suddenly: "Thank God that you are a good man—like Al—like Al. He would be like this!"

"It will cost me thirty thousand votes," said the governor.

"It will make you happy," said she.

"And, after all," said the governor, "that is the main

thing. However, I wish that my son could meet——" He coughed. "Everything you wish shall be done!" said he.

The papers raged for three weeks. The editorial writers exhausted the vials of their sarcasm. But the governor had still two years to reign, and several things happened in the case of Vincent Allan before the two years ended.

In the first year he married. In the second year he became a father. In the same year, as a deputy sheriff under one Elias Johnston, he went on the trail which ended in the capture of "Twister" Joe Matthews. That was a story all in itself.

At any rate, public opinion began to change very fast, and when the governor ran again, his campaign managers could point to a prospering little ranch among the mountains near El Ridal, and call their political star a prophet.

The ridiculous part of it was that while everyone believed that Vincent Allan had completely reformed, they were just as convinced that he had at one time been a very bad man. He himself, of course, believed it more firmly than ever. And he, like the others, waited in a daily dread lest the evil nature should break out and reassert itself. That fear gave a certain grave sorrow and dignity to his face and to his manner.

There were only two people who understood and did not go in some awe of the gentle, kindly fellow. One was the sheriff, Elias Johnston, who had paid with a broken right hand for one of the things he knew about Allan. The other was Allan's wife. These two refused to be overawed. And when he sometimes talked seriously of his sins and prayed that they would not reappear in their child, Johnston and Frances would look at one another and smile behind their hands.

But they never could convince Allan that he had not been a dissolute and abandoned character. When they strove to argue with him, he would smile sadly and say nothing in reply, as though he knew that they were merely trying to make him happy, and that they were not speaking their true convictions at all.

Indeed, he would never quite believe that Frances loved him because he was so very much beneath her in his own estimation; he simply felt that she had married him from pity.

But, after all, if there were a shadow on their home, it was only enough to make the real happiness seem more delightful and more golden bright.